"A clever whodunit, this fast-paced novel will have you flipping the pages in anticipation—a savvy mix of glamour and suspense."

—*The Arizona Republic*

"A nice mix of glamour, mommy lit, and mystery . . . It's a good thing Kaplan has a sequel in the works."

—*Library Journal*

"Stylish and playful . . . *The Devil Wears Prada* for the interior-design crowd."

—*Booklist*

"A mystery filled with gossip, glamour and Gucci."

—*Parade*

"With her trademark combination of savvy wit . . . and classic sleuthing, Kaplan delivers a mystery that will keep you guessing long after your own pedicure has dried."

—*Asbury Park Press* (New Jersey)

"Deliciously dishy! A fun and fast-paced read you won't want to end."

— Meg Cabot, #1 *New York Times* bestselling author

"An appealing heroine, breathtaking pace, and gilded lives suddenly tarnished make Janice Kaplan's *Looks to Die For* a spectacular mystery debut. Intelligent, beautifully crafted, and riveting."

—Carolyn Hart, author of *Dare to Die*

These titles are also available as eBooks

A Job to Kill For

A Lacy Fields Mystery

JANICE KAPLAN

A Touchstone Book
Published by Simon & Schuster
New York   London   Toronto   Sydney

TOUCHSTONE
A Division of Simon & Schuster, Inc.
1230 Avenue of the Americas
New York, NY 10020

First Touchstone trade paperback edition August 2009

TOUCHSTONE and colophon are registered
trademarks of Simon & Schuster, Inc.

For information about special discounts for bulk purchases,
please contact Simon & Schuster Special Sales at
1-866-506-1949 or business@simonandschuster.com.

The Simon & Schuster Speakers Bureau can bring authors to your
live event. For more information or to book an event contact the
Simon & Schuster Speakers Bureau at 1-866-248-3049 or
visit our website at www.simonspeakers.com.

Designed by Laura McBride

Manufactured in the United States of America

1   3   5   7   9   10   8   6   4   2

Library of Congress Cataloging-in-Publication Data

Kaplan, Janice.
A job to kill for : a Lacy Fields mystery / Janice Kaplan.
p. cm.
"A Touchstone book."
1. Interior decorators—Fiction. 2. Los Angeles (Calif.)—Fiction.
I. Title.
PS3561.A5593J63 2009
813'.54—dc22   2009021174

ISBN 978-1-4165-3213-2
ISBN 978-1-4165-3214-9 (pbk)
ISBN 978-1-4165-7965-4 (ebook)

To Ron, *amor vincit omnia.*
Love conquers all.

Chapter One

——— • ———

If I'd known Cassie Crawford would die, I might not have joked about wanting to kill her.

I'd been at her brand new three-million-dollar penthouse overlooking Los Angeles for almost an hour this morning, making sure all the details were perfect. Fresh calla lilies in the Steuben vase. Stainless steel Italian cappuccino machine properly filled with organic, shade-grown Sumatran ground beans. Electronic shades opened at the right angle to let in the light but not the UV rays. At 12:17, Cassie strode in, wearing a sheer white blouse, white jeans, and strappy gold high-heeled sandals, looking even blonder and slimmer than the last time I'd seen her. Our appointment stood at noon, but given the commission she was paying, seventeen minutes late counted as on-time performance.

"Is everything done?" Cassie asked anxiously. Apparently we weren't going to bother with *Hello, How are you,* or even *Nice to see you again.* Cassie took off her Chanel sunglasses but didn't even glance up at the hand-made Swarovski crystal chandelier that sparkled overhead, sending gleams of sunlight flickering across the foyer.

"Done," I replied simply.

"Thank God," Cassie said. She made a quick movement of hand against chest, and I thought at first she was crossing herself. But instead she religiously adjusted the seven-carat diamond pendant hanging just above her cleavage. As she patted it into place, the necklace clinked against her wedding band, so heavy with sapphires and diamonds that Cassie risked carpal-tunnel syndrome every time she lifted a well-manicured finger. Of course, now that she'd married Roger Crawford, she never needed to lift a finger again.

Without another word, Cassie pivoted on the four-inch heels of her Jimmy Choos and headed to the bedroom. I followed, traipsing comfortably if not quite as elegantly in my Lilly Pulitzer pink flats. If the ability to stride seamlessly on stilettos was required before you married a billionaire, I'd obviously never be so blessed.

Or maybe cursed. Despite the perfect outward appearance, Cassie seemed to be in a controlled panic as she checked out the penthouse for the first time. Her eyes were bloodshot, and she raced around the room snapping her head like a Perdue chicken. She opened and closed the storage drawers I'd cleverly tucked behind floor-to-ceiling lacquered doors, then moved quickly on.

"Do you think Roger will like the bed?" she asked, sitting tentatively on the edge of the fifteen-thousand-dollar Hypnos mattress I'd had flown in from London.

"It's the same one Queen Elizabeth sleeps on," I said, as if that settled it. Though who knew where Prince Philip slept.

"And the sheets?" Cassie asked, running her fingers over the linens that were so soft they made 600-thread-count sateen seem like sandpaper. "Frette?"

"Definitely not," I said firmly. "Frette is so last year. They're now used in some"—I lowered my voice—"hotels."

Cassie looked briefly uncertain, but then nodded. At age twenty-eight (according to the gossip columns), she couldn't know everything. I couldn't either—but being older meant I knew how to sound like I did.

She sighed. "Well, I'm counting on you to get everything right. Isn't it funny? Until I married Roger, I lived in a furnished sublet in Studio City. This is the first place I've ever decorated myself."

She'd decorated this place herself? "You did a nice job," I said encouragingly. I'd been in the business long enough to know that the person signing the check got to take credit for the success. Cassie had turned up as a new client not long ago, calling me out of the blue and asking if I could furnish the just-bought penthouse from top to bottom while she and Roger cavorted on a three-week trip to Hong Kong and Tokyo.

"It'll be tricky with such a quick turnaround," I'd said.

"Price isn't a problem," she'd insisted.

With any luck, the combination of Cassie's bank account and my eye for style would land both of us in *Architectural Digest*. However difficult she turned out to be, I'd cope.

Cassie and I had met twice about the design, but when I tried to show her samples and discuss the virtues of Carrera counters versus granite, her eyes glazed over.

"Whatever you think Roger will like. That's the only thing that matters."

"You should like it, too," I'd said.

"Roger has to be happy," Cassie said firmly. "Pleasing him is my only job at the moment." Apparently, the calendar had flicked back to 1950 when I wasn't looking.

I'd never met Roger Crawford and Cassie happened to be his new (or at least newest) wife. But when it came to decorating, I didn't really need her advice on how to keep him satisfied. I just turned the penthouse into a marble-and-brass version of jewel-strewn Cassie: something to help him feel sexy and young, and make it clear to anyone around just how successful he must be.

I knew Roger would admire the result. But now Cassie continued dashing around with an anxious expression. She came to a dead halt in the dining room, glancing at the gleaming onyx table and the chairs covered with zebra skin.

"The fabric's fake," I assured her. "A combination of silk, cashmere, and linen. Probably more expensive than importing the real thing from Africa, but ecologically better. Everything else in the room is so minimalist, I thought we could have some fun."

"Fun," Cassie said grimly.

She marched into the second bedroom suite and began opening and closing drawers. She peeked into every possible nook or cranny, as if hunting for lost keys.

"Are you looking for something in particular?" I asked as she walked out of the walk-in closet. I'd lined two of the walls with mirrors, and Cassie's image reflected over and over, repeated forever. Her eyes flitted worriedly, but not a single line popped out on her forehead. Either she was genetically incapable of furrowing her brow, or she'd already had her first Botox injections.

"I don't know, something just doesn't feel right."

"Doesn't feel right?" To my eye, the place looked darn-near perfect, but my client had to be satisfied. If she wanted a Prince poster instead of the Picasso, I'd dash out to find it a fabulous frame. "Maybe you don't like the pale green color on the wall," I said, trying to be helpful. "To me, it feels peaceful, but if you want something brighter, we could repaint it in daffodil. Or magnolia."

"No, it's not that. I can't really explain it." She shook her head. "Something's got me spooked. Isn't it weird? I feel like a little kid at Halloween going into a haunted house."

"No ghosts here," I said.

Cassie gave a rueful laugh. "I'm Roger's third wife. Trust me, there are ghosts everywhere."

From what I'd read about him, Roger Crawford had variously owned a ranch in Montana, a waterfront casa in Costa Rica, a townhouse across from Buckingham Palace, and a sprawling estate in Beverly Hills. I didn't know which of those had gone to previous wives and which were now "home" to Cassie.

"The penthouse is brand new," I reminded her. "All yours and ghost free. You and Roger start fresh here."

Cassie gave a little frown, then darted off. I followed her into the kitchen, where she gazed blankly at the six-burner Viking stove. She opened the door of the oven warily, as if nervous that the Pillsbury doughboy might pop out.

"Combination heat, with electric and convection currents," I explained. "The temperature stays even, so it's ideal for baking."

Cassie nodded, but from the empty expression on her face, I realized she didn't plan to be whipping up big batches of Bundt cakes. Probably the only "baking" she'd do was at the Sunless Tanning Salon in Beverly Hills.

She sauntered over to the kitchen pantry, where the smooth-glide shelves rolled out effortlessly. Since she'd asked me to take care of everything, I'd stocked the pantry with life's necessities—from Hawaiian macadamia nuts to Macallan single-malt scotch.

"Champagne and chocolate truffles on the bottom shelf," I said. "From my experience, that's the solution for any marital spat."

Cassie looked stricken. She'd been married less than a year, so maybe she couldn't imagine a marital spat. Or maybe my friend Molly Archer was right when she told me Cassie's marriage had veered into trouble.

As the head of Molly Archer Casting and able to influence most of the media hotshots in Hollywood, my old college pal stayed tuned in to everyone. She'd called me to report that Cassie and Roger had been seen arguing at the chic Japanese restaurant Koi a few nights earlier. After Cassie stormed out, Roger went over to the celebrity-packed Skybar, where he drowned his troubles in a martini—and later left, several sources reported, with "an amorous but unidentified redhead."

"You realize what that means," Molly had said ominously.

"He's lusting after the ghost of Lucille Ball?"

"I like to think Lucy's happily married in heaven."

"Isn't Roger?"

"Darling, this isn't about passion. It's about the prenup." Molly had paused meaningfully. "Young Cassie gets a million bucks if she and Roger split anytime in the first year. After that, the payoff jumps to ten million."

"He's a billionaire. That's not exactly a kick in the wallet."

"He's a businessman," Molly corrected me. "He calculates his investments carefully."

Now looking at Cassie, I wondered if her panic about the penthouse could be connected to the expiring prenup. Maybe she figured that if she decorated right, she could buy herself another year and a bigger payoff. No wonder she seemed nervous. Much harder to decide whether the antique rug should be Tabriz or Turkish with nine million bucks on the line.

Turning away from me, Cassie opened the Sub-Zero refrigerator and unexpectedly gave a broad smile.

"Kirin green tea!" she said. "I didn't see this before. How did you know?"

I peeked inside the refrigerator where three green bottles with Japanese letters on them stood neatly lined up.

"It's always been my favorite," she said. "A little bitter, but much better than anything you can get in America." She grabbed one of the bottles, cracked open the cap, and took a long swig. She gave a little shake of her head, then drank some more.

"Did you have this imported from Tokyo?" she asked. "I can't believe it. You're really the best, Lacy."

When I didn't answer, Cassie gave a tentative smile.

"I've loved this stuff since I went to Kyoto during spring break in college. This trip, I drank it all the time in Tokyo." She took another long sip, then smiled at me, relief written all over her face. "Roger told you to get it, right?" Her smile got even wider. "He's such a sweetheart, after all. He wanted to surprise me!"

She finished drinking, then put the bottle on the counter-top. I had a lot of questions I wanted to ask—including why any college kid would take spring break in Kyoto instead of Cancún—but instead, I stared at the tea. I believe in giving credit where credit was due. But in this case, I didn't know where it was due.

I picked the bottle up, puzzled, then put it back down.

"Oh, I just remembered something," Cassie said. "The Rothko in the study."

She hurried down the hallway into the room that had rapidly become my favorite. I'd had the floor in Roger's study bleached and cured to a pale maple, and tinted the angular bookshelves that lined three of the walls exactly two shades darker. A stunning brass-and-glass desk stood in the middle of the huge expanse, and the floor beneath it was accented with a checked-tile inlay. I'd provided rolling ladders so Roger could climb up to reach a book at the top of the towering shelves. Instead of the standard wooden library ladders, these were made of sinewy steel. The room felt familiar—but still fresh and modern. I liked giving a new twist to an erstwhile style.

Cassie paused and looked appreciatively at the books. I even had the feeling she'd read her share of them. But then she turned to the simple two-toned painting that would probably bring in twenty million bucks at auction at Sotheby's. "I think there's something wrong with the frame," she said.

The Rothko had been in one of Roger's other houses and I'd had it brought in. I'd used the most reputable art-trucking firm I knew. They'd never damaged anything before, and come to think of it, I'd inspected the picture carefully when it arrived. But sure enough, the lower-right-hand corner of the frame was freshly broken off.

"No damage to the picture," I said, studying the orange and red color fields.

"Can you get it fi-fi-fixed?" asked Cassie, suddenly panting slightly. I looked over. Her forehead was sweating and she clutched her stomach. Something more than art-lover's distress had struck her.

"Are you okay?" I asked her.

She was almost doubled over now, and when she opened her mouth to speak, she seemed to be gasping for words.

"I—I have to . . ." Her eyes rolled toward the top of her head, and she seemed to be choking. But she grabbed for the ladder by the bookshelf and put a foot on the first rung. Swaying heavily, she started to pull herself up.

"Be careful," I said from across the room.

"Up—up," she said, gasping. "Have to g-g-get it." Her voice was raspy, and her face was suddenly whiter than a geisha's. She kept climbing, and I saw a spittle of drool dripping from the side of her mouth.

"Cassie," I said anxiously. "I think you're sick. You'd better come down."

"Delta," she said. She stumbled on one of the rungs and barely managed to catch herself. She kicked off her shoes and the Jimmy Choos flew down, landing with a thump on the ground.

"Come down, Cassie." Worried, I took a step forward. "If you need a book, I'll get it."

Cassie shook her head. The penthouse ceilings soared twenty feet high, and Cassie had to be eight feet off the ground now. Suddenly she gave a shout of pain and turning, clutched at her throat with both hands. Nothing connected her to the ladder except her pedicured toes. Her head bobbed, and then she plunged forward, her arms spread wide, as if she planned to soar across the room like an angel.

But Cassie was no angel. She wasn't even the Flying Nun.

She landed with a sickening thud, head first, on the polished floor.

"Cassie!" I screamed, rushing over.

I fell to my knees next to her. A huge gash had opened in the back of her head. Cassie gave a little moan and then turned silent.

I watched in horror as the wound began spurting, covering the floor in blood, the deep red color of a Rothko.

Chapter Two

—— • ——

Even as the blood gushed, I knew I had to stay cool. Last time I saw a spurter like this I panicked, which hadn't helped anyone. Running in our backyard, my then-two-year-old daughter Ashley had crashed into an Adirondack chair (did toddler-proofing require rubber furniture?) and split her forehead. I'd rushed her hysterically to the hospital where my husband, Dan, the best, kindest, and handsomest plastic surgeon in LA, met us at the emergency room. While I sobbed that he couldn't let our baby die, Dr. Dan stopped the bleeding and pointed out that Ashley didn't even need a stitch.

All that happened years ago, but I always remembered what Dan told me that day.

One: Head wounds bleed profusely, even when they're innocuous.

Two: People don't die as easily as you think.

Three: I love you.

Number three didn't happen to be relevant right now, but hearing Dan in my head did calm me down.

I tried to assess the situation.

Cassie's head wound was bleeding profusely—but given rule number one, the injury could be innocuous.

On the other hand, if people don't die that easily, why was Cassie not breathing?

I made a fast call to 911, then dropped the phone. CPR. I'd taken a class back when I was pregnant the first time, wanting to be prepared for all emergencies. Could I remember anything? I pushed Cassie's jaw forward to open the airway, then put my lips against hers and breathed twice. I sat back, put my palms against her chest, and pumped fifteen times.

No response.

I kept going. Breathe twice, pump fifteen times. Breathe twice, pump fifteen times.

Cassie sputtered.

Thank God.

Her chest was moving up and down, just slightly. I had to do something about the head gash. I rushed to the bathroom, grabbed a pale yellow Hermès towel, and charged back, pressing it against the wound to stanch the bleeding. In a moment the towel was bright red. I got another and held them both tightly against her head.

"Cassie, what happened?" I whispered.

Her lips were chalky, her eyes still closed.

I heard someone pounding on the front door and rushed to the foyer, flinging open the door. Two EMTs in short-sleeved blue uniforms stood at the ready, holding their emergency medical equipment.

"She's barely breathing!" I screamed. "You've got to do something! She could die!"

"Where is she?" asked the taller of the two, who couldn't have been old enough to buy a beer. His elbows stuck gawkily from under his sleeves, and he had a rash of acne across his forehead, but he charged in, not hesitating for a second, and followed as I raced back to the study.

"Tell me what happened," he said.

Choking out a few details, I dropped to my knees next to Cassie. The lanky young EMT pushed me aside and quickly evaluated the patient.

"No pulse. No breath," he called out, starting to press on her chest, with the CPR maneuver I'd already tried. "Prepare to intubate her. Start an IV."

The second EMT—shorter than his partner, but with the broad chest of someone who spends a lot of time at the gym—put a hand under my elbow. "You need to move aside," he said, practically lifting me up. Then he grabbed for his radio and I heard him calling for backup.

The next few minutes passed in a confusion of blood, equipment, needles, and tubes. I stood to the side, reeling in horror.

"No response," said one of them.

"Give her some epi," insisted the other. "We've got to get this heart started."

The backups started arriving, two by two. A pair of policemen came in, and then two LA firemen. A second pair of EMTs dashed in, and then another couple of cops—the emergency-response version of Noah's ark. People called out suggestions and radios spluttered with static and barked instructions.

"Let's get her to the hospital," someone said. "We're not saving her here."

In seconds, Cassie was on a stretcher, being whisked out the door. I rushed after, negotiating with the EMTs about which hospital they'd go to. We exchanged a few sharp words, but then they nodded and were gone. Far below, I heard loud sirens blaring—and then silence.

I went back to the living room, sunk into a chair, and dropped my head to my knees. The buttery leather cuddled around me, but I didn't feel any comfort.

"You okay, ma'am?"

I sat up and looked straight into the concerned face of a

cop. She was slim, with clear skin, bright blue eyes, and straight brown hair pulled into a ponytail. The stiff uniform masked her shape, but she'd cinched her belt tightly around her waist and her gun just accentuated the gentle curve of her hips. I had to figure her for a real cop, but she might as well have wandered off a primetime set at CBS.

"I'm okay, but I don't know about Cassie. It happened so fast," I said.

"Are you a relative?"

"No, I'm Lacy Fields. A friend, I guess. Her decorator." I shook my head, trying to clear the confusion. "But her husband. We should call her husband. Roger."

The cop—whose nametag identified her as Officer Erica McSweeney—pulled out a clunky phone that doubled as a walkie-talkie. "What's the husband's phone number?"

"No idea," I admitted. "Maybe I can find it on Cassie's cell." I stood up shakily, headed back to the foyer, and grabbed Cassie's bag from where she'd casually abandoned it on the gold-flecked eighteenth-century table. At another time, I would have paused to admire how the bold shades of the leather-and-alligator Louis Vuitton purse played gracefully against the mellow-colored antique. Now I just grabbed the bag (which, according to *Vogue*, cost fourteen thousand bucks and had a four-month waiting list) and rummaged inside, finding a slim silver phone tucked inside a perfectly sized felt pocket. With Officer McSweeney peering over my shoulder, I scrolled down, found an entry for ROGER—CELL, and hit the button.

Three rings. Four. Just as I started to hang up, I heard Roger's voice.

"Cassie, hello," he said. The caller ID must have flashed on his screen, and I noticed a slight chill in his voice.

"It's not Cassie. It's Lacy Fields."

No reply, but I could hear noise in the background and a waiter saying, "May I get you another glass of wine?"

"Lacy Fields, the decorator. I'm at your apartment, and Cassie . . ."

"I know who you are, Lacy," Roger said, his voice unexpectedly warmer. "In fact, I'm having lunch at The Grill, and you'll never guess who's with me."

He repeated my name to someone, and suddenly I heard gales of female laughter. Roger chuckled, said something sweet to his companion, and handed the phone over.

"Lacy, you caught me having a drink with my darling Roger," said a familiar voice. It took me only a second to place it.

"Molly, is that you?" I asked. Molly Archer, my best friend since college, my Tri Delta sorority sister.

"Yes, darling, of course it's me."

As fresh-faced kids just out of Ohio State, we'd moved to LA together, and while I got married and had babies, Molly built one of the most powerful casting agencies in Hollywood. She had recently made *Variety*'s list of the town's most powerful people—well below Jerry Bruckheimer, but several spots above Paris Hilton's hairdresser.

Next to me, Officer McSweeney shifted uncomfortably, anxious to do her job.

"Molly, tell Roger something happened to Cassie," I said firmly to my friend. "Something awful. She's just been taken to the hospital."

"Oh my God." The flirtatious tone drained from Molly's voice, and I heard her repeat the ghastly news to Roger. He got back on the line, and I handed the phone to the concerned cop.

"Officer McSweeney here. LAPD. Am I speaking to Cassie Crawford's husband?" she asked, as if worried that I'd mistakenly dialed Cassie's chef, chauffeur, or masseuse. Roger must have said yes, because she reported that Cassie had suffered a medical emergency and the ambulance had taken her to Cedars Medical Center.

"EMT usually goes to LA General, but your friend insisted on Cedars," McSweeney said, looking at me. Cedars was the best hospital in town—the place where my husband, Dan, had been a plastic surgeon for most of his career.

From my position five feet away, I could hear Roger firing questions at McSweeney. How had this happened? How serious was it? Would she be okay? His loud voice sounded scared.

"She stopped breathing from unknown causes," said Mc-Sweeney, avoiding any specifics. "You should get over to the hospital right away."

"I'm on my way," Roger said.

When she hung up, I shakily shoved some papers and fabric samples back into my own Coach tote—not as classy as Cassie's, but functional—and got ready to leave.

McSweeney casually put herself between me and the door.

"Um, Ms. Fields, if you wouldn't mind, I could use your help. You're the only one who might have a clue what happened."

I should have felt a thump of hesitation. Almost a year ago, Dan had been charged with murder for a death he had nothing to do with. We'd found the real killer, and all had returned to normal. But I didn't want to go through anything like that again.

On the other hand, nobody had mentioned foul play here. And I had nothing to hide.

"Can I ask you a few questions?" McSweeney asked.

I nodded and sat down on a black Breuer side chair. She put a small digital tape recorder on the table between us. "If you wouldn't mind, just give me a chronology of events. Everything you saw."

I didn't mind at all. I spoke carefully, struggling to make sense of what had happened. But it didn't make any sense. I had just gotten to the part where Cassie climbed the ladder when McSweeney's walkie-talkie burst into activity. She apologized and began talking. In the rush of static and excited voices, I finally realized that it wouldn't have mattered if the ambulance had gone to LA General, Cedars, or the moon. The victim had no heartbeat. The doctors in the ER had valiantly tried to resuscitate her, but it was too late. Cassie Crawford was dead.

If the police had mobilized quickly when Cassie fell, now they rushed in like bargain hunters at a Gucci sample sale. In what seemed like minutes, so many uniformed cops and plainclothes detectives swarmed in that they probably had a quorum for a union vote.

I had barely absorbed the news about my latest—and late—client when white-coated forensics experts appeared and began dusting for evidence. I sat numbly as my decorator's dream transformed into a *CSI* showcase. I finally thought to call Jack Rosenfeld, family friend and lawyer. His secretary said he had run out of the office, but when she heard my trembling tone, she connected me to his cell phone.

"Cassie's dead?" Jack asked, stunned, after I'd quickly outlined the situation for him. "Cassie Crawford, Roger's wife?"

"It's too unbelievable," I said, my voice breaking. "One minute she was showing me a damaged picture frame, and the next minute she was dead."

"You were the only one with her."

"Right."

"Listen to me, Lacy," Jack said sternly. "I'll get there as soon as I can. But be careful about saying anything until I arrive."

"You want me silent?"

Jack sighed. "I've learned not to ask for the impossible."

"Well, it's too late, anyway. I've told them what happened, and they asked me to stay and sign a statement. I'll just stick with the truth. I didn't do anything wrong."

"That's what Martha Stewart said before she went to jail."

Given the current stock price, jail had turned out to be a

good thing. Before I could mention that, I heard a loud *thwack* in the background.

"Are you playing tennis?" I asked. Not really a surprise. Jack played hard in a court of law, but he generally preferred a court with a net.

"I'll shower and come right over."

"Don't worry. Play well," I said, nobly.

"No, I'll quit right now," Jack insisted. "My opponent happens to be the LA district attorney. If I default, he moves up the ladder. He'll love that. And from what you're telling me, I'd better keep him happy."

Default a set? Jack must be seriously worried. The tennis ladder at the Beverly Hills Racquet Club aroused more competitive instincts than *America's Next Top Model*. The winner got a magnum of champagne, and the sixty-buck bottle of bubbly seemed to mean more to most of the men at the club than their seven-figure salaries. Now Jack would give up a victory to come be my advocate—and I hadn't even known I needed one.

We hung up, and a thought about Cassie's last minutes suddenly struck me. I headed back to the library to investigate, but yellow crime-scene tape had been strung across the doorway and two burly cops stood staring at the blood-spattered floor.

Unexpectedly, I heard the melodic notes of Beethoven's Piano Trio in B flat, also known as the *Archduke* trio. The frenzied activity in the apartment came to a sudden halt as everyone looked around.

"What's that?" asked one of the cops.

"The doorbell," I said, slightly abashed. I prided myself on being the decorator who thought of everything. Setting the right mood mattered, and I'd decided that a simple *ding-dong* would never do for the Crawfords. So I'd had the ringer programmed with something a little classier.

In the foyer, the front door stood slightly ajar. With all the cops coming in and out, nobody had actually closed it. When the Beethoven sounded again—wrong music for the current mood—I followed Officer McSweeney to the front, where she swung open the door.

"Can you believe it?" said the man on the other side, loudly. "I never even got keys to my own apartment. Cassie had them."

With that, Roger Crawford strode into the penthouse he'd paid for but apparently never seen. A few worry lines streaked across his brow, but otherwise he seemed like a man in control. His perfectly tailored, blue-striped Brioni suit didn't have a wrinkle, nor did his crisp white shirt. The French cuffs at his wrist sparkled with engraved gold cufflinks and were just the right length not to cover the Patek Philippe watch. In the areas money couldn't buy, he was less impressive: slightly balding and barely average height. He got his stature from his success, not his size.

The woman who came in a moment after him, however, took my breath away.

"Molly, what are you doing here?" I hissed to my barely recognizable longtime best friend.

"Roger needs me," she said nobly. "He's devastated. I couldn't abandon him at a time like this."

"Cassie's dead," I said bluntly.

Molly nodded. "We raced to the hospital, but it was too late. Roger wanted to come over here. He's shocked. We're both shocked."

Something about that *we* sounded a little too cozy to me. And everything about Molly had me reeling. Instead of the practical Prada pantsuit she always wore to work, she'd wrapped herself into a neck-plunging Diane von Furstenberg dress that swung sexily as she walked. She'd traded her much-loved Tod's flats for strappy stiletto sandals that showed off an unexpect-

edly perfect pedicure. Most stunning, Molly's trademark mass
of thick dark curls had disappeared and shiny, stick-straight red
hair now framed her pretty face.

"What did you do to yourself?" I asked, too distracted by
her transformation to stick to more serious subjects.

Molly coyly tucked a glowing strand of hair behind her ear.
"Fabulous, right? Japanese-process hair-straightening. Seven
hours, but worth every minute."

A plainclothes cop came over, planting himself a little too
close to Molly. "Ma'am, I'm Detective Burrows. If you'll come
with me for a moment, I'd like to ask you a few questions," he
said.

Molly looked briefly shaken, probably more at being called
ma'am than at the thought of talking to a cop.

I put a hand on Molly's arm.

"She needs to come with me to the ladies' room first," I
said, anxiously digging my fingernails into her soft skin.

Molly looked puzzled. "Why is that?"

"Tampax problem," I said.

Detective Burrows stepped aside stiffly, too embarrassed
(or confused) to follow us. I practically dragged Molly into the
guest powder room, quickly locking the door.

"Tampax problem?" she asked, with a little giggle. "Have
you forgotten how to use them?"

"I had to think of something to say," I said brusquely. I took
my hand off her arm and sat down on the red brocade bench
I'd imported from Paris to grace the far side of the makeup
table. No guest of the Crawfords should have to stand to put
on lip gloss.

Molly took a bottle of Annick Goutal perfume from the
countertop (I'd accessorized every inch of the place) and started
to dab a drop behind her ear. I grabbed the bottle from her and
slammed it back into place.

"What's going on?" I asked angrily. "Roger's wife is dead.

The police are swarming. And you flounce in here like some femme-fatale floozy. Are you crazy?"

"Roger's a friend," Molly said mildly.

"I had no idea you even knew him."

She raised a well-tweezed eyebrow. "How do you think you got the assignment to decorate this place? I mentioned you to Roger and he told Cassie."

I started to stand up, then plopped back down, my knees shaking too hard to hold me.

"You never said anything."

Molly sat down next to me. "I would have," she said putting a comforting hand on my shoulder, "but we haven't seen each other much lately. I've been wild at work. You've got those three gorgeous kids keeping you busy. It's happened before. We always catch up eventually."

True enough. My daughter, Ashley, and her new best friend, Tara, talked together all day at school, gossiped via cell phone in the afternoon, and IM'd all night. But friendship changed between fourteen and forty.

I looked at my redheaded pal.

"Are you and Roger involved?" I asked.

"It's complicated," she whispered, even though nobody could hear. "Involved, but not how you think. We'll talk about it later."

I nodded. "We will. But get this—cops don't deal with complicated. They deal with suspects. Here's how I see it. Roger's the husband, so he's tops on their list already. I happened to be the last one to see Cassie alive, so put me at number two. Now if you're involved with him *and* me, you're right up there at number three."

"Roger wouldn't kill Cassie," Molly said, a look of horror crossing her face. "Neither would you. Or me. Anyway, who says someone killed her? The doctors told Roger the cause of death was unknown."

Now I did manage to stand up. "Maybe it's unknown to them right now," I said. "But trust me. By tomorrow, everyone in LA is going to know that Cassie Crawford was murdered."

"She couldn't have been murdered. It doesn't make sense."

"Murder never makes sense."

"What are you going to do?"

Well, that seemed a fair question. I peered in the mirror and swiped on some Kiehl's lip balm. What was I going to do? In the midst of all this madness, I had to keep my priorities straight.

"I'm going to Jimmy's swim meet," I said calmly. "If I leave this minute, I can get there before the medley relay."

"You're joking."

"Why would I be joking? Cassie will still be dead tomorrow. But today is the only chance for the Pacific Palisades Porpoises to win the six-and-under league championship."

I tucked the Kiehl's back in my bag, kissed Molly on her perfumed cheek, and left the bathroom. As I swept out of the penthouse, I smiled at the cop now positioned by the front door. Right now, I wouldn't worry about anything except whether or not Jimmy had finally learned how to do a racing dive instead of a belly flop.

Chapter Three

———— • ————

I got to the pool and grabbed a spot in the stands just as eight little boys in red-and-blue team swimsuits scrambled onto the starting blocks at the other end. I waved, hoping one of the would-be Michael Phelpses would wave back. Nobody did, so I leaned forward and squinted. The kid in lane 4 had dark curly hair, and the one in lane 8 towered above the others. The rest were sandy-haired six-year-olds with skinny legs, tanned tummies, and big round Speedo goggles that obscured their features. "Which is Jimmy?"

Ashley, my fifteen-year-old daughter, slipped onto the bench next to me. I hadn't known she was coming to watch her little brother swim, but I kept my surprise in check.

"Got me," I said. "They all look alike at fifty meters, don't they?"

"You don't recognize your own *son?*" she asked, contempt dripping from her voice. She'd stopped being my sweet baby girl a long time ago.

"Help me out," I said mildly. Arguing with Ashley was never the way to go.

Ashley, who looked suspiciously blonder than usual, crossed her arms over her too-tight T-shirt. With a scowl, she leaned back—a good trick on a backless bench.

"I don't even want to be here," she moaned. "Grant made me. I mean, he's supposed to drive me home from school. That's the deal, right? Since when does he get to tell me I have to make a stop along the way?"

I turned around to see Grant sitting behind us.

"Hi, Mom," Grant said cheerfully.

"Hi, sweetie. Jimmy will be thrilled you're here," I said.

"You've dragged that little kid to so many of my tennis matches, I figure I could make his big swim meet," Grant said.

Now I smiled. Where did I get a seventeen-year-old like Grant? Handsome, smart, and good-hearted, he'd never bothered with teenage rebellion.

Ashley, however, filled the James Dean quotient for both of them.

The starting gun blasted off, and the six-year-olds splashed into the water.

"Go Jimmy!" I yelled as the flailing freestylers approached our end of the pool. Hearing his name, Jimmy popped his head up and grinned at us before doing a flip turn.

"Nice work," said Ashley snidely. "You probably added three seconds to his time."

I kept cheering loudly and Jimmy kept kicking—and a minute later, he touched the finish line in second place.

"Hooray for Jimmy!" I screamed.

Still grinning, my youngest son climbed out of the water and shook hands with the tall boy in lane 8—who'd won by half the length of the pool.

"That big kid doesn't look like he's six to me," said Grant, who'd jumped down to join us. "Think he was red-shirted? Maybe the coach didn't let him turn seven."

"That's stupid," said Ashley. "Red-shirting only works if it's by grade."

"A joke," said Grant, patting her on the cheek. "Lighten up, huh?"

At the other end of the pool, a race official—actually a mom in white short shorts and a blouse tied at her midriff—handed Jimmy his red second-place ribbon. He turned and waved it madly to show us while we jumped up and down and applauded. It wasn't exactly his first awards ceremony. Every race at every meet ended with a blue ribbon for first place, red for second, yellow for third, and green for everything else. Heaven forbid anyone leaves without feeling like a winner. Jimmy had so many ribbons that his bedroom looked like the Macy's gift-wrap desk.

"Can we go now?" Ashley asked.

"Jimmy's in at least two more races," I said.

"Don't make me stay!" Ashley howled. Then she quickly added, "I mean, I have *homework* to do. Algebra. Quadralatic equations."

"Quadratic," I said automatically. With pronunciation like that, the only person who'd hire her would be George Bush.

"Quadralatic. Quadratic. *Whatever*," she said, rolling the word like a would-be Valley Girl.

I suspected Ashley had more interest in working on her manicure than her math, but if I mentioned that, she'd wail that I didn't trust her. At which point, I'd guiltily 1) beg forgiveness, 2) offer to help with her homework, and 3) promise a mani-pedi the minute she was done. Sometimes better to take things at face value.

"I'm sure Jimmy wouldn't want to come between you and *x*-squared plus *y*-squared," I said.

Sticking around for the whole meet really was beyond the call. With backstroke, breaststroke, butterfly, and freestyle (not to mention individual medley and medley relay) for every age at every distance, a swim meet could last longer than most Hollywood marriages.

I turned around to check out Grant's plans, but he was talking on his cell phone, his brow wrinkled in concern. Catching my eye, he took the phone away from his ear and looked at me quizzically.

"Mom, I'm talking to Ryan. He says his dad's looking for you."

For a moment, I froze. In our circle in LA, two degrees of separation was about as far as anybody got.

For example: Me–Ryan–Ryan's dad.

Grant and Ryan had been close buddies since about second grade, and our families had become friends, too. Last year, the boys had been doubles partners on the school tennis team. Ryan got all his racket skills from his dad—attorney Jack Rosenfeld.

I'd run out of the Crawfords' so fast that I forgot that Jack was on his way.

"Tell Ryan everything's okay," I said, pulling out my cell phone to call Jack directly.

Grant relayed the message, but then he listened to Ryan for a minute, and his face darkened.

"Mom, it's not okay," Grant said, turning back to me. "Ryan says some woman got murdered. You were at her apartment. Mr. Rosenfeld went over to get you out of hot water."

"We don't know the woman was murdered," I said, ignoring the comment about my being in hot water. At least it wasn't boiling.

"Murdered?" asked Ashley, her eyes getting wide and her voice rising. "Who was murdered? Oh my God, who was murdered *now*?"

"It doesn't matter," I muttered.

"A woman got murdered and it doesn't *matter*?" asked Ashley, practically screeching.

We all stared at one another.

"Mom, are you in the middle of a murder again?" Grant asked bluntly.

"I just happened to be in the wrong place at the wrong time," I said. "Or maybe the right place. I tried to save her."

"Are you a suspect?" asked Grant.

"Of course not."

Ashley started moaning. "I can't handle another killer in the family," she said, groaning.

I wanted to remind her that we had no killers, criminals, or crooks in the family. Her father had been totally cleared of all charges months ago. But who could speak reason to a teenager? Give Ashley an hour with Spinoza, and the entire Rationalist theory would go out the window.

Grant handed me his cell phone. "Ryan just conferenced in his dad. Talk to him."

I took Grant's RAZR and heard Jack Rosenfeld's booming voice.

"Lacy, are you there? It's Jack. I just left the Crawfords'. I tried calling you half a dozen times. I was getting worried."

I glanced at my own Motorola and realized I'd unwittingly set the ringer on mute. If only these hi-tech toys had buttons you could actually see.

"Sorry, Jack, I should have called. I raced out to Jimmy's swim meet."

"Frankly it's just as well you got out when you did," Jack said ominously. "Roger started strutting around demanding action, and the police went into panic mode. You and I need to talk."

I opened my mouth and then closed it again. Ashley and Grant stood staring at me. Ryan might still be listening on the line. From the corner of my eye, I saw Jimmy running toward us with his ribbon. (Didn't anybody tell kids not to run on slippery surfaces anymore?)

"Where should we meet?" I asked Jack, hoping Jimmy

would understand if I missed his medley for a murder. "Your office?"

"Actually, I'm heading over to Beverly Hills to pick up something for Gina. Today's our anniversary." He cleared his throat. "Uh, want to meet me? I could use some advice on necklaces. Gina loves your taste."

I gave a little smile. Fair swap. Jack needed something pretty to put around his wife's neck. And I apparently needed someone to save mine.

"Be there shortly," I said.

Traffic moved slowly on Santa Monica Boulevard, so I turned north onto Sunset Boulevard and drove west. What happened to the famed LA smog when you needed it? The sunny blue sky blazed so brightly that even my oversized Chanel sunglasses couldn't keep out the glare. I sped easily along Sunset and turned south on Rodeo Drive, getting caught only briefly at the intersection of Santa Monica Boulevard. My roundabout route might have added extra miles, but it saved at least ten minutes. Nice to be smarter than my GPS.

I ignored the municipal parking lot on the corner and cruised along, pulling up next to a small sign for valet parking. I opened the door of the Lexus, leaving the key in the ignition. A handsome young actor type in khaki pants and a pink polo shirt rushed up. His arms were so muscular he could probably appear in Matthew McConaughey's next film, but for now, he handed me a parking stub.

"Just leave it right here," he crooned. "I'll take care of everything."

I smiled gratefully. Having grown up in Wisconsin, I've kept my Midwest frugality in most matters. I don't indulge in facelifts, Ferraris, or foie gras. But valet parking is something else. Nothing is better than stepping out of a store and having your car magically materialize. The rap on LA is that people come here from all over America in search of a dream. For me, that dream includes never having to parallel park.

I crossed the wide, sunny boulevard of Rodeo Drive, brushing past a tall woman wearing crystal spike heels, a black sequined miniskirt, and a V-neck angora sweater that barely contained her size D fake breasts. A round, bald man—a foot shorter and three decades older—had his arm around her. He might have bought her for the day, though the diamonds dripping from her neck and ears suggested a bigger investment.

Passing Bijan, said to be the most expensive store in America, I peered through the window. An obviously bored salesman smiled at me. Big surprise that a place where socks are ninety bucks isn't packed day and night. I had a sudden urge to go in, but a bold sign confirmed shopping by appointment only. Still, I had a feeling that if I rang with fifteen thou to spend on a suit, he'd let me in.

Continuing down the street, I spotted the jewelry store David Orgell. A discreet Harry Winston–type place, it hit the big time years ago when Michael Jackson would come by to shop and the store would close to give him full attention. Now, if Jackson dropped in, the owners would probably summon security.

I went inside and paused to get my bearings. Cases with sparkling jewels on one side, distinctive silver and tableware on the other. An attractive young woman asked my name, nodded slightly, and said, "The gentleman is expecting you."

As she led me to the back, I played with my wedding ring, and she gave a little smile.

"Don't worry," she whispered. "We're very tactful."

I laughed. "Jack's not buying the jewelry for me, if that's what you think. I'm not his mistress. I'm his client."

She raised an eyebrow, but—tactfully—said nothing more.

When he saw me, Jack gave me a hug.

"I intend to lecture you later," he said. "Right now, help me pick." He had two black velvet trays in front of him, each holding a necklace.

"Oooh, how beautiful," I said, gazing at an oversized choker that interwove clusters of crystals, colored gems, and gold wire. "That's gorgeous. So creative."

Jack looked relieved. "So I'll go with that one?"

"No." I shook my head. "Creative is good for kindergarten kids in clay class. Dance troupes on Doheny. But for an anniversary . . ." I looked at the other tray, where an oval-cut emerald hung on a gold chain, surrounded by baguette diamonds. "Got to go with class."

Behind the counter, the store manager, a slim man named Ali, held up the necklace, catching a ray of sunshine from the window. Light-filled bursts of green and gold suddenly exploded all around us.

Jack looked at me, and I gave a tiny nod. Ali caught the exchange and smiled.

"Excellent choice," he said. "I'll go have it wrapped."

After Ali stepped away, Jack shook his head. "I trust you, Lacy. But twenty's supposed to be the big anniversary. If I get Gina the emerald for nineteen, what happens next year?"

"Check with Indiana Jones," I joked. "He found some nice baubles inside that tomb, didn't he?"

Jack smiled and I looked down into the glass case. A bracelet with gleaming diamonds shaped into dozens of delicate flowers caught my eye. What exquisite workmanship. Delicate, different, and well designed. Just what I liked.

"Lovely," said Jack, following my gaze. "Want to try it on?"

"Well, I've had a tough day so I deserve a splurge," I said. "But I'll hold off on the diamonds. Maybe a mocha Frappuccino at Starbucks."

"Big spender," said Jack.

We smiled at each other, and then he turned serious.

"Okay, Lacy. Matter at hand. I got the full story about Cassie Crawford from the cops. What do you know that they don't?"

"A lot," I said briskly.

Jack looked around, but the store was mostly empty. An attractive Asian couple studying antique tea sets stood too far away to hear us—and we weren't as interesting as nineteenth-century pewter, anyway.

"Something doesn't add up," I said, speaking softly and quickly. "She knew about a chipped frame on the Rothko in the study before we got anywhere near the room."

Jack wrinkled his brow. "I'm not following."

"Cassie said she hadn't been to the apartment since they bought it. The Rothko arrived two days ago. Unless she had a private ghost whisperer, she'd been there since."

Jack took in my news, but seemed unimpressed. "It's her place. No crime in stopping by."

"Right. So why was it such a secret?"

"Maybe she wanted to check out what you'd been buying."

"I asked her half a dozen times to come over with me. She had no interest. Zilch."

"She could have been cheating on her rich husband," said Jack, "but I don't really see that. Drug orgies or wild parties?"

"Who knows," I said. "But here's the other thing. Somebody put a few bottles of Kirin iced tea in the refrigerator. Cassie gave me the credit and made a big deal that Roger must have tipped me off how much she liked it. She drank one down in one chug."

Jack sighed. "Now I'm fully confused. You think she snuck into the apartment and put Kirin in the fridge?"

I shook my head. "Bigger problem. She didn't put the tea there. Somebody else did. I'm pretty sure the tea was poisoned."

Jack jerked back, catching himself on the big glass jewelry case.

"It didn't hit me right away," I said, continuing, "but when I replayed the day in my head, I realized everything about her changed right after she drank the bottle."

"Did you tell that to the police?"

"No."

Jack looked at me. "We'll have to, so they can test it."

I pinched my lips together. "When they find out it was poisoned, who gets blamed?"

Jack took a moment thinking about it. He got my drift.

"Murder needs opportunity and motive," Jack said carefully. "You had the opportunity, but that's it."

"I don't know if Roger had motive," I said, "but when he showed up, he rang the bell. The cops had left the door open, but he didn't just come in. I had the sense he wanted everybody to hear that he didn't have keys."

"Let's get some facts before we speculate," said Jack, suddenly every inch the lawyer.

Ali came back with an elegantly wrapped package and discreetly took Jack's American Express card.

"Gina's going to be thrilled," I said as we waited for the transaction to be finished.

Good old Jack. I looked longingly again at the bracelet inside the case. If I mentioned it to Dan, he'd probably tell me to buy it. But nah. Given my allergies, the diamond daisies would probably make me sneeze.

Chapter Four

— • —

My cell phone started pulsing at 6 A.M., announcing an incoming message, but it didn't wake me. I'd already spent an hour culling through fabric samples for a client who wanted ginger-colored upholstery. She'd previously rejected sixteen different silk swatches, and so far this morning I'd come up with fourteen more possibilities. But I didn't like a single one. Whether the labels said ginger, carrot, or tangerine, the fabrics looked orange. Good enough to eat, but all wrong for dining room chairs. Unless you expected to spill a lot.

After scanning the message, I texted back and then went downstairs to the kitchen. Twenty minutes later, I opened the back door for Molly. She stumbled in and collapsed on the couch.

"Are you okay?" I asked, tugging at the belt of my soft cotton Hanro robe.

Molly had on the same neckline-plunging dress she'd worn the day before, but her makeup was streaked, her lipstick bitten off, and her perfect Japanese-straightened hair in a tangle.

"Cassie died of arsenic poisoning," Molly said, without bothering with any niceties. "They found it in her urine and traced it to a bottle of tea in her refrigerator."

"Arsenic," I said slowly. Well, that seemed simple. Not long ago, the Russians had poisoned a former spy with rare polonium, but here in LA, we didn't fuss that much. No need to go to elaborate lengths when you could find arsenic in everything from pressed wood to pesticides.

"Don't pretend you didn't know," said Molly. "The cop who questioned me all night said you tipped them off. You thought that since I'm so close to Roger and probably want him all to myself that I might be responsible for Cassie's death."

I swung around so fast that I almost smacked Molly in the face. "Not true!" I said. My voice rang out unexpectedly loud and high-pitched—and I immediately worried that I'd woken the kids, still sleeping upstairs. On the other hand, my scream couldn't be any more jarring than the Jay-Z CD that Ashley blared every morning on her Bose radio.

"That's not true," I repeated, more calmly this time. "I never said you might be responsible."

"It's precisely true," said Molly. "At least true that the cop said it."

She stared at me, and I took a deep breath.

"He's lying," I blurted. "I mean, not about the first part, the tipping them off, because I did tell Jack that I thought Cassie had been poisoned, and he reported it. But I never, ever, I mean never, ever, *ever,* said a word about you. For God's sake, Molly, why would I do that? Even if I thought it could be true I wouldn't say it, and it couldn't be true so I couldn't say it without . . ."

Molly held up her hand to get me to stop babbling.

"Okay." She looked miserable. "I didn't really believe the cop. I just wanted to hear a denial directly from you."

I sat down next to her.

"A cop was interviewing you all night?"

"Seemed like it. Then Roger found out and sent one of his lawyers to rescue me."

"I didn't even know about you and Roger," I said softly.

"Nothing to know," Molly said stoically. "We're friends. Just like those *Friends* you can watch every night on three different channels. Our Central Perk just happens to be The Grill in Beverly Hills. Better coffee."

"Those *Friends* all ended up lovers, as I recall. Not to mention that at least one set got married."

"Roger's already married," Molly said.

"*Was* married," I said emphatically.

Molly looked at me, and our eyes locked for a long moment. Her expression changed—as if the point had finally sunk in.

"So I'm a prime suspect," she said slowly. She stood up and went over to the counter in the center of the kitchen, leaning her elbows against the slab of Giallo Antico granite I'd imported from a little town in northern Italy. Frankly, I'd have done better buying one of the cheap synthetic rip-offs available at any strip mall. The Umbrian original had gorgeous color and an intricate pattern, but it turned out to be way too porous to be practical. Some runny cooked carrots had caused a stain, and the counter still smelled of garlic a week after I'd made pesto sauce. I could have been twice as happy for a tenth the price.

"Let me get this," said Molly, walking around the granite island and patting it every few feet, as if she were playing Duck Duck Goose. "Rich man's wife dies unexpectedly. So first suspect is the devoted friend and pining spinster, who must have knocked her off to get said rich man for herself. Is that how it goes?"

"It's hard to cast you as the pining spinster."

"I'm over forty, darling. That's not just pine—it's petrified wood."

Molly leaned against one of the ultrasleek kitchen stools that looked like elongated, inverted mushrooms. Modern and amusing, but frankly, another mistake. Other than a beetle, who wants to sit on a mushroom?

"Maybe Cassie wasn't poisoned on purpose," Molly ventured. "Remember all those problems with products from China? Could be the same with Japanese imports. Easy enough to figure the Tokyo factory got mixed up and put in arsenic instead of sugar."

"Unsweetened tea," I said mildly. "And besides, somebody placed those bottles in the refrigerator."

Molly closed her eyes briefly. "I'm so exhausted I can't think anymore," she said. "Actually, I don't *want* to think anymore. I'm going to catch a couple of hours' sleep and get to my office. Just pretend last night didn't happen."

"Want to crash here?" I asked. "Nobody will bother you. The guest bedroom has a new handmade quilt and goose-down pillows."

"I'm allergic to down. The only pillows I can stand are cheap foam." She rolled her eyes. "See? No way I'd need a billionaire to keep me happy. I'm more Ramada Inn than Four Seasons."

Just then Grant sauntered into the kitchen, wearing new Banana Republic jeans and a button-down shirt. He had on Top-Siders instead of Nikes and looked a little neater than usual for school.

"Aunt Molly!" he said, seeing her. "What are you doing here so early?"

"Having breakfast," she said, perking up enough to give him a little hug. "Best places to eat before noon in LA are Roscoe's Chicken and Waffles or your mom's kitchen."

Grant grinned. "Mom hasn't figured out that nobody but us sits down to breakfast anymore. You know her theory: Life's problems can be solved over cereal."

"Or made better with a bagel," said Molly.

"She's a danger to Dunkin' Donuts," joked Grant.

"A menace to McDonald's," parried Molly, and they both laughed.

I rolled my eyes. They could make fun of me, but I firmly believed that family meals were the key to civilization. I had breakfast with the kids most mornings and insisted on family dinners at least a few times a week. I suspected that lively conversation at the kitchen table could add more SAT points than any Princeton Review course.

Grant popped a piece of whole wheat into the toaster. "Can I make you some toast, Aunt Molly?" he asked.

"No thanks. By the way, you don't have to call me 'Aunt' anymore. That was cute when you were little, but you're definitely all grown up." She looked fondly at my six-foot-tall son.

"Oh, come on, Molly, you're the only aunt I've got. Even if you're a fake one," Grant joked.

"He's right. You're family," I said, going over and putting my arm around her. "Sorority-sister blood is thicker than water."

"Did I hear something about blood?" Ashley asked, flouncing into the kitchen. She had on a pink ruffled mini-dress (vintage sixties), purple leggings (forgettable eighties), and bright red Pumas (what decade would be willing to claim those?).

"Blood as in bloodlines. I've apparently been adopted into yours," said Molly. Then, taking in Ashley from head to toe, she added, "Your outfit is fabulous, darling. So retro you're postmodern."

Ashley did a little pirouette. "I guess I got my style from you," she said, her voice dripping sarcasm. "Very retro that you're hooking up with a married man, Molly. But postmodern that he's a billionaire."

The room fell as silent as if we'd been hit by a nuclear blast.

"What are you talking about?" I asked finally.

Ashley smiled smugly, pleased that her bombshell had landed. "I got up early to finish my history paper, and as soon as I turned on my computer, I heard everything," she said. "Check it out, Molly. GossipGrrls.com says you and Roger have been sneaking around together. They put it at two-to-one that you killed Cassie. YouTube has a video of you and Roger dancing at some fancy party last week. Lousy footage, probably from a cell phone. But still."

"Geez, Ash, is that how you write a history paper?" asked Grant. "From GossipGrrls? When your teacher said to write about the storming of Paris, she didn't mean Hilton."

"Thank you, brilliant brother," said Ashley snarkily. She stomped over to the refrigerator and took out a plain yogurt. "Oh, by the way, CNN says the police are calling Molly 'a person of interest.'"

The kitchen got suddenly quiet.

"Molly *is* interesting," Grant said loyally.

"I don't think they're referring to her profile on eHarmony," Ashley said with a snort.

Molly struggled to her feet. "I have to get to my office," she said shakily. "I'm doing a screen test this afternoon with a young actress for an indie flick. Daniel Craig's coming in to work with her. James Bond."

"Ooh, I love him," Ashley said, briefly impressed. "Tara and I saw *Casino Royale* three times. Best part was that scene in the shower where he kisses the girl's fingers. Sooo sexy."

"Daniel's got everything," Molly agreed, recovering slightly. "Those blue eyes that bore right through you. Face so craggy it should be on Mount Rushmore. Never lets down his guard. He's so cold it's hot."

Ashley dipped her spoon into the yogurt and slowly swirled it around. "No way he shows up at Molly Archer Casting this afternoon. No way."

"Why not?" Molly asked. Her normally porcelain skin seemed flushed and blotchy and a little tic fluttered under her left eye.

"Oh, for goodness' sake, Molly, don't you get it?" asked Ashley, sounding a little too much like a character from *Mean Girls*. "You're poison in Hollywood now. Whether you poisoned that girl or not, you're poison."

I spent much of the morning furious that my daughter had been catty, crude, and rude.

And much of the afternoon fuming because she'd also been right.

Just before noon, Daniel Craig's agent contacted Molly to say 007 couldn't do the screen test.

"When should we reschedule?" Molly asked.

"Maybe never," the agent said bluntly. "He has an aversion to arsenic."

Molly called me and reported the news. "James Bond is afraid of me," she said despairingly. "He can outlast torture and terrorists, but I'm too dangerous."

"Bring back Sean Connery,'" I said. "He'd be willing to die another day."

"Sean Connery wasn't *Die Another Day*. That was Pierce Brosnan."

"Fine. My point is that most people in Hollywood aren't totally judgmental. They're willing to live and let live. Or Live and Let Die."

"Roger Moore."

"Who lost his Licence To Kill, I believe."

"Not him. Timothy Dalton."

"You remember everything. You're still the best casting agent around."

"Right now it doesn't matter. I haven't heard 'yes' in so long I might as well be Dr. No."

"For heaven's sake, pull yourself together. Daniel Craig may be the world's sexiest spy, but he's just one client."

"If only it were just him. My phone hasn't stopped ringing this morning, and none of it good news. Producers are flipping me off faster than burgers on the Fourth of July. Studio heads are acting like I have bird flu. ABC pulled the plug on a pilot I'd already started casting."

"ABC's owned by Disney," I said. "They're a Mickey Mouse organization, so of course they're acting daffy. The hint of scandal scares them. When Rupert Murdoch cancels, I'll worry."

The next day, Rupert Murdoch cancelled a contract for Molly to cast a FOX sitcom. I was officially worried.

"Forget cops and courts—I've been convicted on the Web," Molly said.

She decided to close her office for a few days, hoping the rumors would recede. But instead the situation got worse. On day four, Officer Erica McSweeney rang my doorbell at ten o'clock at night.

"May I talk with you for a few minutes?" she asked with a friendly smile. "I'd like to update you on the Cassie Crawford situation. After hours, so off the record."

I hesitated briefly. Did I want to let in a cop? Upstairs, Jimmy was sleeping, Ashley sulking, and Grant studying. Dan had gone back to the hospital for an emergency, which in his plastic surgery practice could mean anything from a horrible accident to an actress with a zit.

Jack Rosenfeld had warned me not to talk, but Officer McSweeney seemed more friend than foe. I opened the door and she sauntered in, looking even more striking than the first time we'd met. Her glossy brown hair swung freely at her shoulders, and her face glistened with shimmery eye shadow and shiny lip gloss. She still had on her standard-issue police uniform, but given that it was after hours, she'd opened the top button, revealing an antique gold locket on a chain.

"Pretty necklace," I said, leaning in to look.

She fiddled with the clasp and snapped it open. "My mom," she said, displaying the woman's picture inside. "She died two years ago."

"I'm so sorry."

"It's been hard," she admitted, closing the locket. "I miss her."

I touched her elbow sympathetically. "I lost my own mom to breast cancer right after I got married. I know how you feel. You never get over it."

"Your dad?"

"Never really had one." It was too complicated to explain and didn't even matter anymore. "But you know what? You go ahead and build your own family. That's why my husband and kids are so important to me. I'd sacrifice anything for family and friends. Nothing matters more."

"For sure." We looked at each other, an unexpected understanding passing between us. Then Officer McSweeney regained her official composure and stepped back toward the door. Something was up.

"Actually, I have a colleague in the car who wants to talk to you," she said. "Mind if he joins us?"

Too late now. I nodded, annoyed at my own naïveté. Did I really think the lady cop had come by for an evening of pity-party girl talk?

Stepping briefly outside, she beckoned in the direction of the black Chevy parked in the driveway. A fireplug of a man jumped out and hustled up the flagstone path, almost knocking over one of the bamboo-shaded lamps that subtly lit the way. He didn't wear a uniform, but his outfit screeched cop—a non-descript navy suit, wrinkled blue shirt, and well-worn brown shoes. He came in, wiping his feet on the Persian rug in the foyer, apparently confusing a hand-tied antique Sarouk with a Kohl's welcome mat.

I pursed my lips and didn't say anything. Annoyed or not, I'd be a proper hostess.

I led them through the living room, past the library, and into the new room Dan and I had added on to the back of the house. I felt a tingle of pleasure all over again at the gracious room. The glass walls dissolved any distinction between indoors and outdoors, and a semicircular atrium swept up into the night sky. Jutting from one end was a greenhouse, twenty feet long by ten feet wide, a place for relaxing and enjoying nature.

Or for talking to cops.

"What an amazing spot," said Officer McSweeney, looking around appreciatively. She squinted into the darkness, catching sight of the dimly lit greenhouse. "Will you show me your flowers later?"

"There's not much to see yet," I said modestly. "This is the first time I've started with seeds indoors. Right now the pots are mostly varieties of roses and orchids. But I do have one beautiful pale yellow *Oncidium*."

"La-di-dah," muttered the man, speaking for the first time. "Who do you think you are, Nero frigging Wolfe?"

"Pardon me?"

"Nero frigging Wolfe," he repeated, a little louder. "Fictional detective. Grew orchids in the top floor of his townhouse. That who you're trying to be?"

"I'm not trying to be anybody except Lacy Fields," I said, taken aback. "I have enough roles, thank you. Wife, mother, interior decorator. I don't need to be a detective to grow orchids."

"Well, I *am* a detective, ma'am. Detective Brian Wilson." He glared at me, as if daring me to make a joke. When I didn't say a word, he added, "Yup, same name as the lead singer of the Beach Boys."

He'd probably spent his whole life being teased. Everything about Detective Wilson suggested beach ball, not Beach Boy.

He was short and stout, with a ruddy face and an almost completely bald head. Give him a little kick and he'd probably roll smoothly across the floor.

"I believe you wanted to give me an update, Officer McSweeney?" I said courteously, turning away from her rude partner.

She exchanged a look with Detective Wilson. The department had let her stay on the case, partnered with a detective. Probably a big break for her.

"A few things about the Cassie Crawford case," McSweeney said, her voice as gentle as his was gruff. "We confirmed that she died from arsenic in the bottled tea. Without your tip, it might have taken us a long time to get to that conclusion. So thank you. Very perceptive."

"A little too perceptive," said Detective Wilson, moving closer and planting himself a few inches in front of me. "Even Nero friggin' Wolfe would have taken a while to figure that one out. So I'm guessing you knew about the tea before you saw Cassie drink it. Which makes me wonder how you knew. And why you tipped us off."

Since we were almost eyeball to eyeball, I took a step back, trying to get him out of my personal space.

"I appreciate your updates," I said pleasantly. "But if you have questions, I'd like to have my lawyer present."

"Oh, that's not necessary," said McSweeney.

"Nah, not necessary," echoed Detective Beach Ball. "Why lawyer up? We don't think you did it."

One entry for the good news column.

"I never knew about that Kirin tea until I saw it in the refrigerator," I said. "After Cassie got sick and, um, died, I just put two and two together. And got to four."

"Yeah, the obvious answer," said Detective Wilson. He picked at the cuticle on his thumbnail. "The other obvious answer is your friend Molly. She likes this rich guy Roger, but she doesn't like that he's married. You give her access to the penthouse, she brings in the tea."

"We're not saying you knew her plan," said Officer McSweeney quickly.

"But once you realize what happened, you feel guilty," continued Wilson. "Death's never as simple as it seems, right? You don't want to be charged as an accessory. So you help us along by mentioning the bottles in the refrigerator."

I stood frozen for a moment. At least I knew the police theory now. Molly brought in the Kirin to kill Cassie. I knew about it, or at least had guessed. Now I could either turn in Molly or face charges of my own.

"Interesting speculation, but I decorate on my own. Molly never came with me to the penthouse."

Detective Wilson seemed to be waiting for that. "So you wouldn't know anything about the fingerprints," he said.

"No, I wouldn't."

"Remember all that powder being shaken around the penthouse? Wasn't to take care of babies' bottoms. CSI identified three sets of fingerprints on the refrigerator: Cassie's, yours, and Molly's. We know you were there. We know Cassie was there. But Molly? She didn't say a word about an earlier visit. Makes you suspicious, doesn't it? Even of your own friend?"

I ambled over to the door of the greenhouse.

"Officer McSweeney, would you like to see my flowers?" I asked.

She looked surprised. "We should finish talking first."

"We're finished," I said calmly. "As for the flowers, I'm told there are at least twenty-five thousand species of orchids. I have a very beautiful *Phalaenopsis* with purple and white stripes on delicate petals that's my favorite right now. But who knows what else is out there? I'd hate to jump to a conclusion. I'm sure you understand. It's the same with what you do."

The cops looked at me blankly. Okay, I'd spell it out.

"Flowers are like suspects," I said. "Don't pluck the first one you see."

Detective Wilson snorted. "Flowers and suspects? Sure thing. They both stink."

The next day, Molly drove with me to Cassie Crawford's memorial service. The funeral had been private—this clearly wasn't.

"Is it a memorial service or the Academy Awards?" Molly asked, as I tried to maneuver the Lexus through the lengthy stretch of black limousines double-parked in front of the church. It seemed like half of Hollywood had come out either to remember Cassie or suck up to Roger.

Inside the church, throngs of LA power players milled around, their concerned expressions offset by Armani suits and Zegna ties. With the town's executive suites emptied, any deals that got done today would involve a handshake in the back pew. Molly and I both wore tailored black dresses, but I noticed a fleet of suits in navy and enough in dark chocolate to significantly raise HDL levels. Apparently gloomy didn't sell in LA, even for funerals.

Roger stood near the front as colleagues and friends huddled around him, offering sympathy, hugs, and pats on the back.

"Do you want to extend your condolences?" I asked Molly.

"Not in public," she said. "Later."

Molly and I drifted toward the back of the church, away from Roger and his crowd. Here everyone was quieter—in both spirit and jewelry. I guessed that the row of young women who seemed genuinely devastated had been Cassie's college friends and the men wearing khakis rather than Canalis were her pre-Roger pals. I got only a glimpse of Cassie's family as they walked in—an attractive, dignified couple flanking another daughter, who looked strikingly like Cassie. Unlike Roger, the three of them spoke to nobody but one another, their grief palpable across the church.

We slid into seats and picked up the white-ribboned book-lets waiting at each place, an unusual cross between *Playbill* and prayer book. Cassie Crawford had lived a short life, but she'd earned a long service. Six people were speaking "in memory" and five "in tribute"; there would be four "prayerful remem-brances," three "poems and writings," and two "musical salutes." Either Roger had dedicated himself to creating the perfect program or some LA party planner had a niche market in me-morial services.

"Check out the second musical tribute," Molly whispered. She leaned over and pointed to the name on the program.

"Paul McCartney?" I asked. "The Beatle? Singing an origi-nal song?"

"Roger knows him," Molly said with a hint of pride.

"I bet Roger paid him, too," I said. Not that Paul needed the money. Even after the divorce.

Molly pursed her lips, but she didn't reply because the first chords of the organ sounded. Mendelssohn's Fugue in A Minor. Roger had definitely gotten advice.

The next hour and a half provided a crash course in Cassie's life. From the various speakers, I learned that she'd grown up in Orange County, the younger of two pretty sisters, attended UCLA, and had a brief first job in television. She returned to UCLA to work in the development office, raising big bucks from already big donors. A dean who spoke explained that Cassie met Roger on the job and convinced him to give five million dollars toward a library. "But Roger didn't need any convincing to give her a Harry Winston engagement ring," the dean said with a little chuckle.

Paul McCartney's song had been rewritten especially for the occasion. It wasn't exactly "Candle in the Wind," but it brought plenty of people to tears.

Despite everything being said, nobody could address the one subject that really mattered: who killed Cassie. I kept looking around the church, convinced somebody here had the answer—as well as the motive and means. Assuming Cassie had visited the newly decorated penthouse before our meeting, she probably hadn't gone alone. Somebody had come along who knew her well. And a good bet said that person also knew her taste for iced tea.

In the little time I'd known her, Cassie had struck me as egotistical, entitled—and scared to death. I'd thought her biggest fear involved keeping her husband happy. Maybe it was keeping herself alive.

I noticed several people glancing over at Molly, and others staring at her while whispering to friends. A haze of suspicion seemed to have gathered around her like dust around a comet. I clenched my fists. Since college, Molly had been a real friend whenever I needed her. My kids considered her their aunt. I might not be Nancy Drew, but I had a little experience now in solving mysteries. A haze of suspicion? Time for Lacy Fields to help clear the air.

Chapter Five

—— • ——

At 9:30 the next morning, I got to the FOX lot on Pico Boulevard and found my way to a silver trailer marked Genius Productions. I had a 10 A.M. appointment with the head genius, Andy Daniels. I'd arranged the meeting after the memorial service when Molly suggested it. She didn't know Andy well, but she'd done casting on some of his hugely popular reality shows.

"Reality shows get cast?" I'd asked Molly, surprised. "Doesn't sound very real."

"And the Easter Bunny brings painted eggs," she'd said, rolling her eyes.

Now I strolled over to the front desk, where a pretty young assistant sat applying Lip Plumpers Lip Gloss to her already shiny and full red lips. She rubbed a tiny dot of gloss into each cheek (the secret of an all-over glow! Who knew?), then snapped her little mirror shut. She tossed back her thick hair (could I ask what conditioner she used?) then flashed her BriteSmile white teeth.

"You must be Lacy Fields. I made the appointment for you," she said eagerly, as if the call had bonded us for life. Maybe we'd become Facebook friends.

"Right, thanks," I smiled tentatively. "I got here early."

"What a shame. You shouldn't have done that. Andy is always late." She peeked at the watch on her wrist, the face almost hidden by the puffy pink leather band. "Oooh, way early."

"Should I walk around and come back?" I asked. I wouldn't mind wandering around the FOX lot and peeking into one of the soundstages. A lot of the TV shows were shot right here. Maybe I'd get a glimpse of Kelsey Grammer. Or Homer Simpson.

The assistant, whose name card said Dawn Rose, tucked her hair behind her ear. "It's hard to know when Andy will arrive. He likes to have breakfast at home with his wife. Then he has to drive all the way in."

"Where does he live?" I asked.

"Thousand Oaks."

"Thousand Oaks?" The swanky horse country outside LA offered elegantly gated communities, but the commute would be at least an hour. Two, if traffic turned bad.

"Why don't you schedule his first appointment later in the morning then?" I asked, trying not to get grumpy.

"Doesn't work. Sometimes after Andy gets in, he has one meeting and then heads home for lunch."

I believed in family mealtimes, but this sounded ridiculous.

"He must be a fussy eater," I said, though who would go bumper-to-bumper on the freeway for a turkey sandwich? Even if Andy were a vegan, he could bring his broccoli with him.

"Andy likes to have lunch with his wife," Dawn Rose said, trying to hide her grin.

"Tell me about the wife," I said, curious now. "Did she win *American Idol*? The Powerball lottery? First prize in Miss Universe?"

Dawn Rose nodded toward a framed picture of a pleasantly

smiling woman in her early thirties who seemed to be average height, average weight, average looks.

"If you figure it out, let me know," she said with a shrug. "Meanwhile, you can wait in his office. Play with anything you want."

I stepped into Andy Daniels's huge suite and my mouth fell open. I hadn't seen this many diversions since I took the kids to Six Flags Magic Mountain and Jimmy threw up on the Canyon Blaster. A foosball game filled one corner of the room and a basketball hoop hung from the ceiling on the other side. In between stood an Xbox 360 with half a dozen video-game boxes scattered around it, a flat-screen TV, pinball machine, jukebox, miniature pool table, Nintendo Wii, and a half-filled Scrabble board.

I sat down on a slightly ratty sofa—shabby but not chic—and glanced at the disheveled stack of magazines on the Lucite cube coffee table. If this decorating style caught on, I'd be out of a job. An hour later, I'd gone through a week's worth of *Variety*, four *Hollywood Reporters*, three issues of *Maxim*, and a very old *Playboy*. I got up, took a quick look at the pinball machine, and wandered over to a ledge cluttered with a dozen or two bobble-head dolls.

"You found my award shelf," said Andy Daniels, bustling into the room, not bothering with *hello*.

I looked up and he gave me a big grin. He was short and slight, with long curly hair, Levis, cowboy boots, and an open-necked shirt. He must have been in his late thirties, but something about his impish size and the gleam in his eye made him seem more like a kid.

I held up one of the dolls. "What do you win these for?"

"Everything," he said, sauntering over to join me. "I never get Emmys, so when I do a great show, I buy myself a bobble-head. Smart, right?"

I smiled. Andy's shows earned huge ratings and made him

millions. But they often caused newspaper columnists to declare the end of civilization as we knew it.

Andy reached over and took the "trophy"—a tough-looking guy on a motorcycle—out of my hand. "I bought this one after *World's Worst Ways to Die*," he said, rolling it around on his palm. "The show got a twenty-two share—considered by the networks to be ratings heaven. But *The Washington Post* suggested I go straight to hell."

"I'm glad you're still here."

"Me too." He grinned, and despite still being irritated from cooling my heels for an hour, I grinned back. My annoyance disappeared. Andy Daniels was one of those guys you just had to like.

He put the substitute Emmy back on the shelf and headed to his desk, a rough-hewn piece of wood propped up on two iron T-bars. Then he stopped and turned back to me, his eyes opened wide.

"Wow, I just remembered Dawn Rose said you wanted to talk about Cassie. And here I brought up *World's Worst Ways to Die*. How's that for irony?"

"Ironic," I said.

Cassie's first job, the one in television, had been working for Andy Daniels. She'd been hired right out of college as a production assistant—a glorified go-fer. Hundreds of eager grads would have been begging to bask in Andy's shadow, and Cassie had snagged the prime post. She'd lasted only about six months on the job.

"Did Cassie do *Worst Ways to Die* with you?" I asked.

"I think so. Geez, hard to believe she's dead." Andy shook his head. "We must have been in production on that one about the time Cassie worked here."

"A scary show?" I asked.

"Plenty of blood and gore, as I remember." He laughed, his good cheer at odds with the subject. Though, come to think of it, he had a right to be happy. The show had probably scored with viewers and earned Andy a big enough bonus to buy another dozen pinball machines.

"So what are the world's worst ways to die?" I asked.

"Hmm, let me think." He tapped his foot. "My favorite involved a rare South American spider. After the sting, the venom rushes into your blood and travels up your body." He twisted his fingers as if he were playing "The Itsy Bitsy Spider." "First you have no feeling in your toes. Then no feeling in your legs. Pretty soon you have no stomach, no arms, no talking, no breathing, and finally"—he clapped his hands sharply and then raised his palms toward the ceiling.

"You die," I said, interpreting.

"Die dead. Doesn't take long." He gave a slightly maniacal grin. At least the man enjoyed his work.

"You know Cassie died of poisoning," I said.

"Really? Whoops!" He put a hand in front of his mouth, as if wanting to push the previous words back in. "Not a South American spider, I hope."

"Arsenic."

Andy wrinkled his nose. "Arsenic? Isn't that kind of . . . ordinary?"

"Real life happens that way."

"Poor Cassie. Beautiful, beautiful, rich, rich, rich. If it were my show, she'd have died from ingesting gold dust." He shook his head slowly, his producer's instincts offended by the lousy last act. It was as if *The Sopranos* had ended with the screen going blank. Oh wait—it had.

Andy went over to a bright orange exercise ball in the middle of the room and plopped down. He put his chin into his hand like Rodin's *Thinker*—only Andy's Thinking also involved bouncing up and down. He bounded higher and higher off the rubber ball, then gave one sudden spring and rocketed onto his feet.

"I think I've got an idea for a new series," he said cheerfully.

"Don't tell me you're replacing *American Idol* with *Death by Gold Dust*."

"Not yet." He laughed. "There are a lot of reality shows on the air right now about singing and spelling bees. But gruesome will come back. It always does."

"What other shows did Cassie work on with you?" I asked.

"Let's see, she would have been around for *How to Bed a Billionaire*." Andy gave a knowing chuckle. "Guess she paid attention to that one."

"Good show?"

"Killer concept. We sent five gorgeous girls into an ultraexclusive club in New York that only admits billionaires. Whoever got her Richie Rich into bed first won a million bucks." Andy grinned happily.

"I must have missed it."

"Never aired." His cheerful face crumbled, the sting of rejection still fresh. "The network got nervous. First problem was we filmed undercover at the club without permission. Second, the whole idea of having sex to win scared the top brass. And third"—he held up three fingers for emphasis—"the billionaire who first went to bed with one of our girls turned out to have a spanking fetish."

I saw what made Andy such a master. Just hearing about the show left me slightly appalled—and eager to see it.

"I don't know what's happened to network television," Andy complained. "A little spanking is not a terrible thing."

"No spanking, and then they fire Molly," I said sarcastically. "What's going on?"

Andy made a face. "Sorry about Molly. I like her. In fact, I introduced her to Cassie." He paused to consider. "Hey, so if Molly killed Cassie, I'm sort of responsible, aren't I?"

"Molly's not the culprit," I said firmly.

Andy sat down at his desk, then got up again almost immediately. I could see why he didn't spend much time in the office—he had way too much energy to contain within four walls. He walked over to a big gumball machine that tottered on top of a bookshelf. A pile of nickels stood beside it, and he took one, put it in, and grabbed the green gumball that clattered down.

"So if not Molly, who?" he asked.

"I was hoping you might have an idea."

Andy seemed to ponder the possibilities as he tossed the gumball from hand to hand. Then he lunged forward like a puppy going for a Frisbee and caught the candy in his mouth.

"If only Cassie had listened to me," he moaned, chomping down on the gumball. "Right after she got married, I proposed we shoot a reality show about her. I wanted to follow her around with cameras for a few weeks to find out what it's like being rich. Do you drink the rare, sixty-thousand-dollar vintage Macallan scotch every night? Take the private jet to Paris if you want a good brioche? Buy the diamond-studded bra from Victoria's Secret?" He paused to blow a bubble with his gum, then added excitedly, "This is what America wants to know. What America *deserves* to know. The big question facing our nation: If you don't care what's on sale at the drugstore, which brand of toothpaste do you buy?"

I smiled. Only Andy could make it a matter of national urgency whether Cassie used Colgate Total or Crest Tartar Protection. But his enthusiasm was catching. I kind of wanted to know myself.

"Cassie turned you down?"

"Nope. She liked the idea. But Roger threw a fit. He said he had too much dignity to allow that kind of attention. If she wanted a rich guy with no class, she should have married Donald Trump." Andy's eyes twinkled. "That argument alone would have gotten me a twenty share."

I laughed. "Do you know much about Roger?"

"We did some research on him," Andy said. He looked toward his door, and as if on cue, Dawn Rose came in. Come to think of it, she really had taken the cue. Her cubicle was within earshot, and she'd been listening avidly from her desk.

"The background on Roger," she said, handing him a folder. "I pulled it just in case you'd need it."

The girl got extra points. It couldn't be easy staying a step ahead of Andy—or even a step behind.

"Thanks." He quickly flipped through the pages as Dawn walked out again.

"Anything interesting?" I asked.

Andy shrugged. "All that's interesting about him is the dollar signs. He earned a fortune in investment banking, then started a hedge fund that made him seven hundred million in one year. He paid off his first wife big and they divorced amicably. From everything I see, they still say nice things about each other. He moved to LA and played the playboy for a while with starlets. Second wife, a model from Brazil, lasted two years. Had a solid prenup there and got off easy. Then Cassie."

"Kids?"

"Two from wife number one."

"Maybe the kids wanted to get rid of Cassie to protect the inheritance."

Andy consulted his notes. "Teenagers. At boarding school in Switzerland." He slapped his thigh and grinned again. "See? This Roger's a piece of work. He would have been great TV. Who sends their kids to B.S. in Switzerland?"

"B.S. meaning boarding school?"

"B.S. meaning I wonder what this guy's full of." He turned a page. "Anyway, forget the inheritance motive. Their mom got the kids ironclad trust funds in the divorce."

"Still, there's always revenge," I said. "If my husband dumped me for a twenty-seven-year-old, I like to think my kids would have the courtesy to kill her."

Andy nodded. "I know you're joking, but that's the thing. Who'd kill Cassie? Everybody and nobody. Everybody because she was rich and made people jealous. And nobody because—" He paused. "Well, because outside of TV land, murder is serious."

Andy put down the folder and started playing the pinball machine. Neon lights flickered and the machine *bing*ed. But Andy Daniels, the genius behind *World's Worst Ways to Die,* turned away with a sigh. He seemed as puzzled as a kid who's spent too much time with video games and now can't understand why real life doesn't have a PLAY AGAIN button.

"If you're pissed at her and you really want to teach someone like Cassie a lesson, you plant a nasty story in the *Star.* You don't—"

"Kill her," I said, finishing his sentence.

Andy shook his head. "Geez, somebody killed her. How do you like that? On a TV show, I'll do anything. But real life should be different."

Andy went back to his exercise ball, this time lying across it and closing his eyes. I had the feeling I'd lost his attention for now. I turned for the door, then paused, wanting an answer to just one more question.

"How come Cassie lasted only six months with Genius Productions?" I asked.

Andy seemed to flinch but didn't open his eyes. "Who knows? Young kids are always a little flaky."

"So she just left? You didn't fire her?"

"Don't think so."

I hesitated a little longer. Andy probably got a hundred résumés a month from twentysomethings desperate to get a first foot in TV. Most would be grateful to get him coffee and take in his dry cleaning. Cassie had actually worked on shows.

"Strange that she'd leave," I said. "Seems like she had the proverbial job to die for."

Andy sat up. "She didn't die on the job."

"I know that. I'm just wondering what didn't work out."

Andy stared at me, his face an odd mix of anger and apprehension. "People move on," he said. "That's all. She moved on."

I drove west down Pico for a few blocks, took a left, and just before Wilshire Boulevard turned into a small parking lot next to Barneys. One of my clients demanded throw pillows for the Eames sofa I'd found for her den. I'd tried to explain that the designer's leather, teak, and polished aluminum gem didn't need anything to clutter its clean lines. But the modern vibe didn't sing to her. She wanted pillows, and she wanted them handmade, beaded, and one-of-a-kind ornate. I could either stop here or get on a plane to Pakistan.

Inside Barneys, I skipped by the shoes and paused briefly on the main floor to admire a buttery-soft Lanvin handbag.

"One of my favorites," said a saleswoman coming over. "It's called the Kansas tote."

I glanced at the tag. When did four figures become reasonable for a purse? For this price, I could make a down payment on a small ranch in Kansas.

"I could also recommend the Kentucky velour leather," she said, displaying another bag.

Two hundred bucks more. So maybe a horse farm in Lexington. At least I had options.

"They're lovely, but not today," I said, scurrying away. If I browsed bags any longer, I'd end up buying the entire state of Texas.

Years ago, I'd bought an expensive Givenchy purse and showed it proudly to Dan. From the baffled look on his face, I might have been flaunting a Ziploc sandwich bag.

"Doesn't turn you on?" I'd asked.

"You turn me on," he'd said, putting his arms around me. "What you wore to bed last night turned me on."

"I didn't wear anything to bed."

"Right."

If a bare shoulder had more appeal than a shoulder bag, I could save myself a couple of thousand dollars. Apparently no man had ever been attracted to a woman for her hot Birkin.

I left the accessories department and stepped onto the escalator. Too restless to stand still (Andy Daniels and I had something in common), I walked up the moving stairs and past a woman so skinny she probably hadn't seen a lettuce leaf since yesterday. I wanted to offer her a candy bar. Hadn't she heard that the average American woman wore a size 14?

My cell phone rang and I flipped it open.

"Is this Mrs. Fields?" asked a slightly gruff man's voice.

"Yes it is."

"I'm Joey Tartufo. Security officer for Anthropologie. I'm calling about your daughter, Ashley."

"Oh my God." I grabbed the handrail to steady myself. "Is she okay? Wh-what happened?" Had my baby been attacked? Accosted? Had the poor child gotten lost?

"We caught her shoplifting a pair of gold earrings."

"Ashley? Are you sure?" It didn't make sense. Ashley didn't even like gold. "She usually wears silver," I said.

"These are gold," he said calmly. "Listen, Mrs. Fields, I'm calling you instead of the police as a courtesy. If you'd like to come over, we're at 320 North Beverly Drive."

"I'm close by. I'll be right over. Please wait for me," I said, as if hoping to arrive before he served the soup. Or before he served Ashley with an arrest warrant.

I spun around on the escalator step and started racing down. The emaciated model looked at me in surprise but stepped aside. A moment later, I jumped onto the first-floor landing, rushed out of Barneys, and ran frantically down Wilshire. At the corner of Beverly Drive, I stood for a moment, but when the blinking sign didn't immediately change to WALK, I walked anyway.

"Hey, lady, you from New York? Cops give tickets for jay-walking around here!" a man called out.

He was right, but who cared? The real penalty right now involved my daughter's reputation.

Inside Anthropologie, a fresh-faced young sales clerk immediately greeted me with a cheerful smile. But before she could show me the colorful skirts, the unusual home accessories, or the jewel-studded shoes (the place seemed to be Barneys for the under-thirty crowd), I said, "I'm looking for Joey Tartufo."

Her face changed. "Right this way," she said, leading me to the back of the store. She knocked lightly on a door, and Joey Tartufo opened it almost immediately. Medium height and broad-shouldered, he had a bushy mustache and unexpectedly kind eyes. He reached to shake my hand, but I looked past him and saw Ashley and her friend Tara, sitting close to each other on two hard wooden chairs.

"Honey . . ." I said, starting over toward her.

"I'm okay, Mom," Ashley said. She crossed her arms in front of her chest as if warding me away.

Joey dangled a pair of drop earrings in front of us. "We found these in your daughter's backpack," he said. "Twenty-two karat gold-dipped silver with emerald drops. Price is two hundred forty-eight dollars."

"I don't need to steal," Ashley said boldly. "My mom buys me anything I want."

"I wouldn't buy those for two hundred forty-eight dollars," I admitted.

"Well, I wouldn't even want them," said Ashley irritably.

"They're probably not real emeralds," said Tara. "Maybe emerald-colored glass."

"The inventory sheet says emerald," said Joey Tartufo, all but stamping his foot, "and the point is Ashley left the store without paying for them."

"She didn't *leave* the store," said Tara. "When you grabbed her, she had her hands on the door, but her feet were still inbounds."

"This isn't a game," said Joey Tartufo.

"You have to play by the rules anyway," said Tara, tossing back her long blond hair. "My dad's a lawyer, and I know all about procedure. Why did you stop us, anyway? Did you have cause?"

"One of the sales people observed you two whispering and acting suspiciously."

"We're teenage girls. Of course we whisper," said Tara, rolling her eyes. "Duh. Duh-uh."

Ashley elbowed her friend, her own demeanor suddenly changing. "It doesn't matter," Ashley said, tears welling in her eyes. "The earrings must have fallen into my backpack without my knowing it." She got up and ran over to me, throwing her arms around my waist. "Mommy, I'm so sorry. You're always telling me not to leave my backpack gaping open. You're right! I forgot to close it and he thinks I'm a thief. I'm not a thief."

She burst into loud sobs. I held her tightly as her whole body shook and her wails filled the room. Joey Tartufo came over and put a comforting hand on her back.

"Don't *touch* her," Tara called out. "Illegal!"

But Ashley, gasping with sobs, turned around and grabbed Joey's hand. "My daddy will kill me if he finds out," she said. "He was charged with murder once, but this time he'll do it."

"Ashley!" I said, horrified.

"A murder charge?" Joey asked.

"He didn't do it," I said quickly.

"At least we don't think so," said Ashley. Still clutching

Joey's hand, she brought it to her cheek. Tears streamed down. "Please, I swear I'm innocent. My mommy's been through so much. Don't accuse me."

Thoroughly discomfited, Joey pulled his hand away from Ashley's. "Look, nobody saw you lift the earrings, so it's just circumstantial. If your mom buys your story, I'll go with it."

He looked at me, and I put my arm around my daughter. "Ashley's a good girl," I said. "She'd never steal. She probably brushed past those earrings and they fell into her bag."

Ashley beamed, her sobs turned off as quickly as a TV in an electric storm.

I conferred a few more minutes with Joey Tartufo and signed two papers.

"That's all," Joey said to the girls. "But please stay away from the store for a while, okay?"

"Unconstitutional! We have first amendment rights!" cried Tara as she headed to the door. But she didn't wait around to discuss them.

Back on the street a moment later, the girls scurried a few feet ahead of me, whispering to each other and giggling. I stared at the small Prada backpack slung over my daughter's shoulders and then stopped in my tracks. I felt my stomach turning upside down. Or maybe that was my heart.

"Girls, come over here," I called out. I edged under the awning of a store, out of the way and out of the sun. Ashley and Tara exchanged glances but joined me.

"I have a few questions and I want some straight answers," I said. "To start, what are you two doing in Beverly Hills?"

"I had an appointment with the dermatologist, and Ashley decided to come," Tara replied.

The dermatologist? Nothing for a skin doctor to do on Tara other than let her sit in the waiting room so other patients could admire her smooth porcelain complexion. Though I'd consider it false advertising.

"How did you get here?" I asked, not letting up.

"My mom dropped us off," Tara said. "She wanted to Zen out for a couple of hours, so she went for a massage. Some fancy day spa. I knew she'd turn off her cell phone, which is why the security guy called you."

Okay, not impressed. Tara's mother let two teenage girls wander aimlessly while a stranger rubbed oil into her back. But I lost some parenting points, too. With school closed for Faculty Planning Day (a day off to plan more days off), Ashley had agreed to catch up on French homework and read *Pride and Prejudice*. I wouldn't let her watch the miniseries instead—even though Colin Firth made a darn cute Mr. Darcy.

I cleared my throat, getting myself back on track.

"So you found yourselves bored in Beverly Hills and decided to give shoplifting a try. Is that correct?" I kept my voice even. If I turned judgmental, the information spigot would close.

"Not correct," said Ashley. "I'm innocent."

I went over and tapped the top of her tiny pack. "This isn't the big North Face you take to school that's always gaping wide. This one's miniature." I pulled the zipper. "It's not likely that earrings would fall off a display into a two-inch opening."

Ashley exchanged a look with Tara.

"You're a good detective, Mrs. Fields," Tara said, tugging self-consciously at the bottom of her pink cotton sweater.

I eyed her critically. "Why don't you take off the sweater," I suggested. "It's warm enough."

She shrugged and pulled off the top, revealing a ruched and ruffled scoop-neck T-shirt underneath. If that didn't belong on the shelves of Anthropologie, I'd eat my vintage cashmere.

Now Ashley started giggling. She covered her mouth, but the laughs turned to guffaws.

"You had the shirt on the whole time and that Joey dude never guessed," said Ashley. "How hysterical is that."

"You just have to know how to stay cool," said Tara, dropping her previous posturing. She reached over and locked pinkies with Ashley. "We did it. Girlfriend bond."

"We did it, but it almost fell apart," said Ashley. "You said if anything happened, you'd get us off by spouting legal stuff and talking about your dad."

"Instead, you talked about *your* dad," said Tara, giggling. "So brilliant. Plus all the sobbing. Omigod, Ashley, I almost believed you myself."

The pretense of innocence gone, Ashley's face glowed in triumph. Maybe the girls had forgotten that I was standing there or figured I wouldn't care. But I did.

"You lied," I said softly to Ashley. "And you got me to lie for you. That's wrong."

"Oh, Mom, lighten up," she said. "You defended Daddy on a murder charge, and now Aunt Molly. You had to support me."

"But Daddy and Aunt Molly weren't guilty," I said.

"How do you know?" Ashley asked, her voice rising.

"I know. In fact, I'm *sure*," I said firmly.

"And I'm *sure* the earrings fell into my backpack," Ashley said, mimicking me. She laughed rudely. "Come on, Mom, it's pretty easy, right? Go for what you want and screw the truth."

Chapter Six

— • —

I tossed and turned so much that night I could have starred in a Lunesta ad. By the time Dan got home from the hospital, I'd kicked off the comforter and gotten totally tangled in the pale beige one-thousand-thread-count sheet that I'd had hand-embroidered by a Swiss seamstress. For all the comfort I felt tonight, I could be sleeping on burlap.

"Everything good with you?" Dan asked, falling into bed next to me. His voice sounded weary from a long day in the operating room.

"Not all good," I admitted. "But we can talk in the morning."

"I have another surgery at six A.M.," Dan said. "Better tell me now."

I put my head on his shoulder, then decided to give him the bad news quickly.

"Ashley shoplifted a pair of earrings, and I got her off, which I shouldn't have, but I did because she cried and convinced me she hadn't done it," I said in a rush. Then, picking up the pace even more, I continued, "If she's such a good actress, maybe she should try out for the school play. It's *South Pacific* this year, and always liked Nellie, the cockeyed optimist. Anyway, her friend Tara stole a T-shirt and wore it right out of the store. I called Tara's mom, even though Ashley threw a fit and said that would ruin her life, but the mom was in the middle of a manicure and she couldn't have cared less. So I hung up and talked to Ashley about peer pressure and having an internal moral compass and knowing wrong is wrong."

I finally stopped and took a deep breath.

Dan lifted his head from the double down pillows. "Good lung capacity," he said. "But I'm not sure I completely followed."

"Where'd I lose you?"

"Somewhere around the cockeyed optimist."

I sighed. "Ashley's complicated. Sometimes I think she doesn't know whether to be bad or good."

"So tell her to be good for goodness' sake," said Dan.

"If she still believed in Santa Claus, maybe that would work."

Dan put his arms around me. "Thank you for dealing with all this, Lacy. I don't say it enough, but I appreciate you. I really do. I'm sorry about how busy I've been."

I hugged him tightly. Dan spent more hours than I liked at the hospital, but I'd never be able to change that. I'd fallen in love with a man who happened to be good and kind and generous. He got his sense of self from taking care of his patients and staying busy. Like every man, Dan needed action, not analysis.

"Can I share two more family headlines before you fall asleep?" I whispered.

"Go for it."

"Grant's taking a college physics class after school. Our very own Presley Prep didn't have any science classes left to challenge him, so the headmaster made all the arrangements at UCLA."

"When did that start?"

"The morning after Cassie died. Molly had been questioned by the cops all night and she popped over for breakfast. I was so distracted I didn't even notice that Grant had spiffed up in nice jeans. Anyway, we talked that night. I apologized."

"I'm glad," said Dan. "Men like their mothers to notice their nice jeans."

"You're teasing me," I said, rolling over.

"Teasing you but loving you," Dan said, spooning behind me. He pressed his strong chest against my back. "By the way, you look way too young to have a son in college."

"Flattery will get you everywhere," I said, as he cupped his hand against my hip.

"You said two family headlines," Dan said. "What's the other?"

"Jimmy lost another front tooth."

"Did Toothman come?" Dan asked, stroking my bare skin. When Jimmy announced one day that he didn't believe in the tooth fairy, Dan told him he was right. No fairy flew through the sky to leave money under a pillow. But a superhero did. To the pantheon of Superman, Batman, and Spider-Man, we introduced—Toothman!

"Toothman left him five dollars."

"Wow—is that for a tooth or an arm?"

"It's the superhero minimum in this zip code."

"Well, I'm glad Jimmy still believes," Dan said, letting his fingers flutter upward from my waist.

"Willing suspension of disbelief. I wouldn't mind if someone left five bucks in my bed."

"Would you mind if someone made passionate love to you in your bed?" asked Dan, kissing the back of my neck.

I turned my head so our lips met and we were face-to-face

and skin-to-skin. "Come be my superhero," I said, snuggling closer. "Make me believe."

The next day, Molly wanted to talk and suggested we connect at the quilting store on Melrose Avenue.

"Quilting?" I asked, when we met on the corner at noon and exchanged a hug. Despite everything, Molly looked fashionable in a white Helmut Lang blazer and black cropped pants. Her python skimmers weren't exactly tame, but at least the flat heel meant she wouldn't break an ankle.

"Quilting's the craft du jour in Hollywood," she assured me.

"I thought all the chic people took up knitting. All those articles about Julia Roberts and Reese Witherspoon clicking their needles on set and giving cameramen handmade scarves at Christmas."

"That's so last week. Once middle America started copying, the celebrities had to move on."

"I hate to break it to you, but the very lovely and talented women of middle America were knitting long before Julia Roberts."

"Oh please," Molly said with a groan. "It's the old tree-falling-in-the-forest question. If a schoolteacher knits an afghan in Iowa but *US* magazine doesn't report it, does the blanket really exist?"

I laughed. "Only if Rob Reiner buys the rights."

"And he turns it into a touching movie starring Meg Ryan that wins a Golden Globe and revives her career."

Now we both laughed. Molly, the successful Hollywood insider, could still see an outsider's view.

Halfway down Melrose, we stopped at Jenny's Crafts, a tiny store with classic Americana quilts festooning the window. A handwritten note, hung on the door, said: CLOSED UNTIL 2:30. I'M AT AGO FOR LUNCH. JENNY.

"I have a feeling she's not living off the proceeds of the

store," I said, laughing. The restaurant Ago happened to be nearby, but with Robert De Niro as one of the owners, it attracted an A-list power-lunch crowd.

"The store's probably a hobby," Molly admitted. "Jenny's married to someone well known, but I forget who. Everyone successful is connected to someone rich and famous in this town, haven't you noticed? Makes life easier."

I put my arm around her. "I know lots of other ways for women to succeed. You've done it. You don't need to marry rich."

"Not marry. But maybe . . ." She shrugged. "A friend in the business, as they say."

"Is that how you saw Roger?"

"He's been helpful," Molly said without elaborating.

We stood silently for a moment, staring into the window.

"I'm glad the store's closed," I said as we walked away. "The whole quilting and knitting craze feels creepy to me. Why would women who could be running movie studios or programming computers act like Amish housewives?"

"They can do both. Handcrafts are just a way to calm your nerves, and mine need calming. Let's go find a Starbucks."

"Cappuccino's not calming."

"I'll get a decaf."

"According to one study, what restaurants label *decaf* still contains caffeine seventy-two percent of the time. You'll feel better if we just walk."

"That's why women have sewing circles," Molly argued. "So they can *sit* and talk, rather than *walk* and talk."

"Walking arouses endorphins. Improves your mood."

"My mood can't be improved." Molly took a few steps, and then flopped onto a bench outside a small Mexican restaurant. At night, throngs of rowdy patrons spilled onto the sidewalk, salted margarita glasses in hand, but now all remained quiet, and the bench did look appealing. I sat next to her.

"It seems strange to be with you during the day," I said. "What's happening with Molly Archer Casting?"

"Nothing. Nada. Clients cancelled and nobody calls."

"You're being shunned?"

"Like an Anne Klein suit at the Oscars. I'd be willing to go the Mel Gibson routine and apologize. I'd even go into rehab. But what am I supposed to apologize for—having lunch with Roger the day his wife died?"

I sat back and looked at Molly, then tapped my fingers on the back of the bench. "Look, sweetie, I'm here for you. I know you're innocent. I want to solve the case and get your agency running again. I like you better when you're casting shows than casting stitches. But the LA police are asking questions, and you've got to tell me the truth. All the dirt. If I hear the worst from you, I can ignore all the other innuendo."

Molly ran her fingers through her hair, spinning a smooth lock around and around with her pinky.

"Okay, I'll tell you. I'm guilty of DWI."

I jolted forward as if someone had pulled the back off the bench. I had certain lines that could never be crossed, and that was one of them.

"Molly," I said slowly, "you were Driving While Intoxicated?"

"Of course not," she said. "Dining While Infatuated."

I put my head into my hands. "Could you be serious, please?"

"I am serious. I'm thoroughly besotted with Roger Crawford. Modestly, I think he's kind of smitten with me, too. But we're all business—not what you think. He's intrigued because not a lot of people talk honestly to him, and I do."

"He never tried to take you to bed?"

"Never, I swear. If this were a 1950s movie, the censors wouldn't have a thing to cut. He likes that I'm introducing him to Hollywood, and we have fun together. Before all this happened, I think he had some business plan in mind for us. By the way, he once told me that closing a great deal is better than having sex."

"You could teach him otherwise."

"You bet I could. But as long as Cassie was around, there wasn't a chance. Now that she's dead, who knows. I have my fantasies."

I clamped my hand over Molly's mouth. "Don't say that out loud," I whispered. "It just confirms what everyone's thinking."

"Oh, for heaven's sakes, if every fantasy ended in murder, the George Clooney Fan Club would hold its meetings at San Quentin," she said, pushing my hand away. "I thought you wanted the truth."

"I can't handle the truth," I barked, in my best Jack Nicholson imitation.

"Well, try this. The more likely scenario is that now that Cassie's dead, Roger won't even speak to me. If the cops are asking questions, he'll want to keep his distance."

I sighed. "Give me some background. How did you meet?"

"His company put about ten million in a movie I cast. Roger had never gone Hollywood before, but a lot of guys who've made fortunes in Silicon Valley or Wall Street come here. Investing money in movies is more glamorous than trading pork bellies and coal futures. HBO beats IPO for wooing women, and at cocktail parties you can schmooze about Leo DiCaprio instead of leveraged buyouts. Anyway, Roger showed up on the set a few times, and we talked. After that, he started calling and I'd give him the inside scoop that investors never hear. I introduced him to some hot directors and found him a terrific script to back."

I smiled. "So he likes you because you could make him money. Cassie wasn't your competition—it was his broker at Morgan Stanley."

Molly shrugged. "Roger appreciates that I'm smart and

savvy and built my own company from scratch. He calls me B&B because I'm bright and beautiful."

"And you call him B&B because he's so full of baloney."

"You mean I'm *not* bright and beautiful?" Molly asked, making a face.

"Of course you are," I said soothingly. "But when a guy like Roger coins a phrase, he spends it liberally."

"Maybe," said Molly reluctantly. "In business, Roger's a master manipulator. He's used to getting what he wants."

"Could he have killed Cassie?"

"Why would he? He could end the marriage without poisoning the tea."

"Arsenic's definitely quicker than divorce. And cheaper."

"Roger doesn't behave that way. Doesn't act just for money." She shook her head emphatically. "No way."

"Maybe he worried about more than money. Say Cassie threatened him with something that made divorce dangerous. For example, if he left, she'd let the whole world know that he wears women's pajamas to bed."

Molly shuddered. "I confess my great infatuation and you have to ruin it. What an awful image. Next time I close my eyes, I'll picture the man of my dreams in a Natori nightgown."

"I'm not saying he has a lingerie fetish. But wives know things. Maybe she picked up on some shady deal at his business that he didn't want exposed."

Molly stood up and paced back and forth on the cement sidewalk. I'd obviously been right about the calming effects of walking. But many years of marriage had taught me not to point out that she should have listened to me in the first place.

"Roger's a self-made man from a working-class family," Molly said. "He earned everything he has without cheating, stealing, or killing."

"I'm sure he's a model mogul," I said impatiently. "A prince among men. But if Cassie resorted to emotional blackmail, how would he respond?"

"How would any of us respond?"

"Badly," I said. "Hence, arsenic in the tea isn't that crazy. All he had to do was go into his own penthouse the night before."

Molly stopped pacing and gazed off in the distance, as if she'd just thought of something. "Possible, I guess. I don't know. I really don't."

I stood up. "One other thing. The police say they found your fingerprints on the refrigerator."

Molly pinched her lips together. "Wow," she said finally. "They told you that?"

"They did. That's direct from the duo of Wilson and McSweeney, no less."

"All these distortions." She shook her head. "That first night, they told me you'd already pointed the finger at me. Now they tell you . . ." She let the sentence drift away. "I'm their favorite target."

"Then it couldn't be true?"

Molly didn't answer. At least she wouldn't lie to me.

"If true, it needs an explanation," I said softly.

Suddenly Molly smiled. "I was at the penthouse *after* Cassie died, remember? When I saw you. In all the confusion, I probably touched the refrigerator."

Possible. Maybe she got thirsty and wanted a Poland Spring. Of course, Molly usually argued for tap water instead of bottled, but who'd be thinking about saving the world from plastic bottles in the midst of a murder?

"Sure," I said. "Simple enough."

Molly put a hand on my arm, "Lacy, darling, I'm trying to stay sane, but this is all too strange. I can't stand the suspicions. You've got to help."

"I'm trying, I swear."

"I know. I really do." She paused. "But could you please find a killer other than me or Roger?"

I rubbed my nose thoughtfully, wondering how far I'd go to help my friend. I had a daily life crammed with people: neighbors who shared carpool duty, fellow parents from the PTA, moms I met at swim meets. Then came colleagues and clients, yoga buddies and couples friends, and the seventy or so chums still on Dan's Christmas-card list. (Maybe we'd try eCards.com next year.) But nothing matched having one person who understood your deepest soul—and did everything to protect it.

When I got my heart broken in college by a boyfriend, Molly came to my room at 4 A.M. and held me while I cried. Then she produced a box of chocolate-covered cupcakes and swore that while boys might come and go, we'd have each other's backs forever. A promise sealed in sticky icing had endured. The day Ashley was born—six weeks earlier than expected— Molly arrived at the hospital within an hour, giving me a hug and a tiny pink cardigan and footie set from Petit Bateau. "She'll wear it home," Molly said confidently as we stood in the neo-natal ICU and I gazed in horror at the tiny tubes and wires at-tached to my baby. "Until then, don't leave her for a minute."

While Dan and I floated in a haze of anxiety for the next weeks, hovering day and night over our wrinkle-skinned daughter, Molly moved into our house to be pal, parent, and playmate for two-year-old Grant. She read him his favorite *Frog and Toad* stories before bed and raced him on his tricycle in the park. She taught him the words to "Frère Jacques" and held his hand the first time he came to meet his sister. Molly never wavered in her good cheer, so the rest of us didn't either. When Ashley finally left the hospital, pink-cheeked and perfect in her Petit Bateau, we were all ready to be a family. Molly would forever be part of it.

Now, standing on Melrose and looking at my best friend, I

gave a little smile. How far would I go to help Molly? The ends of the earth, probably. But she didn't need to know that.

"A suspect other than you and Roger won't be easy to find," I said grumpily. "But I'll do what I can."

"Thanks, sweetie," she said. "I can't ask anything more."

Of course she could. A vow of friendship made on cupcakes (even store-bought) should never be broken.

As soon as I got home, I made a list of possible leads. I called UCLA and managed to get through to the dean who had spoken at the memorial service. He was polite but not forthcoming. He suggested that if I had any further questions, I might talk to Cassie's former boss at the development office, Elsa Franklin.

The next day, I drove over to Westwood, passing by a gallery that specialized in modern American artists. Many years ago, I'd bought an unusual glass vase there for about fifty dollars. Recently, an art dealer who'd come by to see my Liza Lou beaded teacup (worth a stunning twenty-five thousand now, though you could find copies on the Internet for fourteen bucks) spotted it. Without asking, she'd lifted the vase from the shelf to check out the signature on the bottom.

"Just as I thought," she said, pleased with herself. "An original Dottie Mather. Her work has skyrocketed since she died."

"Mmm," I said. Dottie Mather? Never heard of her. But I shouldn't sound ignorant in front of a dealer. "So sad she died."

"Not so sad. She'd just turned ninety-three. Didn't start with art until she was eighty. A modern-day Grandma Moses." The dealer smiled. "How much can I pay you for the piece?"

Uh-oh. Like the beaded teacup, the vase had clearly appreciated from object to Art. And Art was worth—well, whatever someone would pay.

"Fifteen hundred?" I ventured, pulling a number out of the air.

"Done," she said, with a glint in her eye.

Darn. She'd probably resell it for twice that.

Now I continued driving through Westwood Village and up Hilgard Avenue to the corner of Westholme. At an information booth, a friendly guard handed me a campus parking permit and directed me to a nearby lot. I stowed the car and walked onto the leafy UCLA campus.

Sun streamed through the trees, and students ambled easily to class. A pack of prettily tanned girls with long hair, long legs, and short skirts rushed by, chattering happily. Nearby, two shapely young women dressed more for a lake than a lecture hall lay on a blanket. No wonder Grant liked taking physics classes here. On this sunny, sybaritic campus, one explanation of string theory involved Brazilian bikinis.

I strolled along Bruin Walk, the main campus path. Two students offered me free movie tickets and another urged me to sign his petition against hunger. I stopped and signed, wondering if anybody was *for* hunger? I walked on, looking up to admire the stately architecture. Maybe no ivy grew on these walls, but I couldn't imagine a more majestic campus.

But enough meandering. I hadn't come here to be a tourist. I asked directions from a friendly student who pointed me toward the building I wanted, the one where Cassie Crawford had worked. Stepping inside, I tugged at the cashmere sweater tied at my shoulders. After the warmth of the campus, the overly air-conditioned office seemed unexpectedly chilly.

I gave my name, and the young woman at the front desk stopped reading. "Elsa's expecting you," she said, picking up a pair of red-framed glasses from her desk and putting them on. "I'm Kate. I'll take you back."

"Thanks."

She stuck a fringed leather bookmark into her library-bound edition of *The Wings of the Dove*. I smiled, glad that Henry James still made college reading lists.

"Great book," I said. "You have the same name as the heroine."

She made a face. "The book is way too long. I liked the movie better."

"You're not an English major?" I ventured.

"Film and television," she said proudly. "It's my opinion that no work of genius should take more than two hours out of your day. One hundred twenty minutes. The best directors get that."

"What about Cecil B. DeMille?" I asked. "*The Ten Commandments*. Two hundred twenty minutes."

"Sascha Baron Cohen. *Borat*. Eighty-four minutes," she said, as if proving the point. Who was I to laugh at the comparison? I could guess which movie she preferred.

I followed Kate down a short hallway and into an office with thick beige carpet, classically elegant furniture, and elaborately framed oil paintings, including a portrait on the far wall of a gentleman in eighteenth-century dress. A woman sitting behind an English writing table looked up from her paperwork, removed her reading specs and got up to greet me. I considered Kate in her red frames and realized everything flipped upside down as you got older. At age twenty, you stopped reading and put your eyeglasses on. At forty (or fifty), you took them off.

"I'm Elsa Franklin," said the woman. "How nice to meet you."

She extended a hand. Her long tapered fingers were ringless and her short nails neat but unpolished. She had hints of age spots on her neck and her gray hair was pulled back in a chignon. Dressed in a white shirt, tan trousers, and beige pumps, she looked sensible and serious, though a Gucci scarf tied at her neck gave a hint of sophistication.

Elsa gestured for me to sit down. I picked a hardback chair, imitation Louis XIV, and we exchanged pleasantries about the beautiful campus and lovely day. Elsa brought over a silver serving set from a side table. Picking up the graceful coffee pot, she filled a delicate china cup and offered it to me.

"Such a tragedy about Cassie Crawford," she said, clearly done with small talk and getting right to the point of my visit.

I took the coffee and added milk from an engraved pitcher. "Awful," I agreed. "I'd known Cassie only a few weeks. I can imagine your shock when you heard."

"I knew her well. She worked here about a year."

"Doing what?" I asked.

Elsa settled down in a high-backed chair across from me. "The development office raises money for the university. We deal with alumni, parents, corporations, foundations—you name it. The professors on campus may get all the attention, but they couldn't do their work without us."

I heard a hint of defensiveness in her voice. Okay, so I'd discovered one fault line at the university. Probably at any university.

"I'm sure your work is well appreciated," I said.

"Not always. But we all understand that a large school requires a large endowment." She passed me a floral Wedgwood plate arranged with expensive chocolates and Godiva biscuits. I carefully picked out a Vosges truffle. Delicious. This must be the same routine Elsa used to pamper prospective donors. I understood how it worked. Much more upper-crust coddling and I might end up writing a check for a new library annex.

"How did Cassie do at her job?" I asked, taking another chocolate and popping it in my mouth. This one had a cherry-cream center. Yuck. Forget the library.

"Oh, I'd call Cassie first-rate. Really outstanding," Elsa said. "Many of the young women who start here want to deal with the biggest donors immediately. They're usually not experienced enough to warrant that. But Cassie had"—she paused—"a certain talent."

"What kind of talent?" I asked. Unlikely that she tap-danced in front of donors or played them *Moonlight Sonata*. Unless she wanted to become Miss America.

"Cassie had a very seductive way of talking to people. Gently wooing them. Men responded quickly to her."

"Did she ever step over the line?"

Elsa smiled tightly. "We don't have lines here. I assume the people I hire act appropriately."

"No need for moral codes? Lectures to the young fund-raisers on avoiding temptation?"

Elsa took her linen napkin and dabbed an imaginary crumb from her mouth.

"Wealth always has its temptations. Our job is to direct the money where it does the most good."

"And Cassie did good?"

"Very good. Or very well, I should say."

"I gather she met her husband working here."

Elsa nodded. "I knew he liked her right away. She had a number of private meetings with him and then brought in a big check. I hadn't expected them to get engaged." She paused, then hastily added, "But of course I was very happy for her."

Something about her tone seemed off. She sounded as credible as a late-night infomercial for Trim-Fast diet pills. But I couldn't quite figure out why Elsa wouldn't want Cassie married to Roger.

"So she gained a husband and you lost a fund-raiser," I said, taking a stab at one possibility.

Elsa shook her head. "Cassie asked to stay on part-time. She made it clear that Roger had to be her first priority, but she wanted to come in whenever he didn't need her. We worked it out."

Given the expression on her face, I gathered that Elsa didn't usually subscribe to the idea of flextime or "family first," but she hadn't had a lot of options. It would be hard to fire a fund-raiser who has dinner parties with billionaires. If Cassie wanted to keep the job to have some identity apart from Roger, Elsa had to cave.

"How much did she work?" I asked.

"Not much." Elsa took a large gulp of coffee, as if to wipe the sour taste from her mouth. "But Cassie had her connections. She always insisted it's not the time, it's the results."

"Did Roger continue to make donations? His friends?"

"I won't discuss that," Elsa said brusquely.

She put down her coffee cup with a noisy clink, and the tension level in the room suddenly soared. An awkward silence followed.

"You have such a lovely office," I said, hoping to get us back on neutral ground. I gestured to the oil painting on the wall. "Is the portrait a university founder? An early settler of California?"

Her shoulders relaxed just a bit. "Neither. He's my great-great-great—well, I can't remember how many greats—uncle from back East."

Well, that made sense. Nothing Californian about this office, and any guy who'd traveled west in a wagon train probably wouldn't be posing in knickers and a frilly shirt.

"So your roots are on the East Coast?" I asked.

"Connecticut," she said, fingering the pearl circle pin on her blouse. "My family's lived there for generations. I attended Connecticut College for my BA, then did graduate work at Columbia. I worked at both schools for many years."

"What brought you here?"

"Oh, you know," she said vaguely. She brought a hand up to her ear and adjusted her pearl-stud earring. "Life takes unexpected turns. We have moral responsibilities. I came about nine years ago."

"I'm also a transplant," I said, eager to find something we had in common. "I grew up in a small town in the Midwest and went to Ohio State. I came here on a whim after college with my best friend Molly and met my husband. Dan Fields."

"Dan Fields, the plastic surgeon?" she asked. When I nodded, she seemed to perk up, then raised her coffee cup as if making a toast. "Well, what a pleasure. We gave Dr. Fields an award at our Humanitarian Dinner two years ago."

"That was from this office?" I hadn't made the connection.

"I remember it well."

"Who could forget? He filled three tables at the benefit, at twenty thousand dollars each, and the hospital took several full-page ads in the program. He brought in quite a tidy sum. I'm always pleased when we honor the right person."

"Actually, I thought he got honored for providing free treatment to poor children with cleft palates," I said, a tad tartly.

"Of course." Two bright spots of color popped out on her cheeks as she realized her faux pas. "I mean, we certainly don't give honors to people to get money from them. We give honors to . . . um, honor people."

"Sure," I said.

Silence, as the tension in the room built again. But now it was Elsa Franklin's turn to do something about it.

"So how else can I help you with Cassie?" she asked, eager to talk about anything but Dan's dinner.

"I need some leads," I said. "Names of people who might have liked her—or disliked her. Donors she encountered. Problems she might have had. Any hints that could help us understand what happened."

"You're making inquiries on behalf of Roger, is that right?" she asked.

"More or less," I said. I'd dropped Roger's name when talking to the dean and didn't need to explain more now.

Elsa Franklin nodded briskly. "Roger Crawford has always been a very generous contributor to the school. I'd hate to think any suspicion could rest on him."

Sure. Not good to name a building after someone who could end up in jail.

"Who'd be on your list of suspects?" I asked.

"I hadn't really thought about it." She stood up abruptly and went over to her desk. Sitting down at her computer, she began typing, and after a couple of minutes I wondered if she'd forgotten that I was still there.

"One name that comes to mind is Billy Mann," she said finally. "Cassie had been seeing a lot of him when she started working here. I let her know he wasn't an appropriate companion."

I looked up, surprised. "I thought you said you didn't have moral codes or lines that couldn't be crossed."

"Meet him," Elsa said. She hit a key on the computer, waited as a page spewed from her printer, then handed it to me. I glanced down and saw Billy Mann's name, address, and phone number.

"Let me know if you find any line he wouldn't cross," she said.

Chapter Seven

—— • ——

Mann's Motorbikes was a graffiti-covered storefront on a grim stretch of La Cienega, south of downtown. I'd probably passed by here dozens of times, driving to the Los Angeles airport and trying to avoid the traffic on the 405 freeway. But just as the glitterati on both coasts referred to my home state of Ohio as "fly-over country," this was drive-by country. You ignored it on the way to someplace else.

But now I paid attention.

I pulled up at the address Elsa had given me just as a broad-shouldered man with long hair, gold-stud earrings, and a tattoo on his muscular arm burst out of the shop.

"Help you, lady?" he asked, rubbing his index finger against the side of his nose.

"Um, yes," I said, "I'm looking for Billy Mann."

"Well, lucky you. You're looking *at* Billy Mann."

Staring, more like it. He had the handsome, sexy appeal of Russell Crowe playing ultimate bad boy: worn black leather jacket, tight but tatty jeans, and scruffy beard. If Molly had been with me, she'd have cast him in something imme-diately.

"I'm Lacy Fields," I said, extending my right hand. Instead of shaking it, Billy grabbed my fingers and pulled them close to his face. Inspecting my pale-pink nail polish, now slightly chipped, he gave a loud snort.

"I skipped my manicure this week," I said, apologetically. "I've been busy."

He snorted again. Could he possibly be au courant enough to scoff because I liked natural shades instead of Chanel black satin? Really, that fad was going to be replaced faster than Justin Timberlake's girlfriends.

"What are you doing here?" he asked. "I run a bike store. You're not a biker." He ran his thumb across my fingers. "Soft skin. Long nails. No calluses anywhere." He dropped my hand and took a step back. "You a plainclothes cop?"

"Not a cop," I said. For his information, these weren't ex-actly plain clothes, either. My simple silk skirt happened to be Escada, and the ruffled blouse came from the first collection of a talented young designer with her own section at Fred Segal.

"Why would I be a cop?"

He shrugged. "I've been expecting one to show up since Cassie died."

I nodded. "I did come to talk about Cassie. But only as her friend."

"Lacy Fields?" He looked at me suspiciously. "If you're a friend, why don't I recognize the name?"

"I probably got to know her long after you two had split. She hired me to decorate her penthouse."

"Oh, sure. The decorator." He nodded knowingly. "We talked about you."

"You did?" I wondered what they'd said. Had Cassie men-tioned my talent for tracking down antiques? Vanity aside, the bigger point didn't escape me. They'd talked in the last couple of months.

"Yeah, Roger had recommended you, right?" He looked me over carefully. "She always got nervous when Roger talked about a woman, because she worried that he screwed around. It wouldn't have been with you, though."

"It *could* have been," I blurted, unexpectedly insulted.

He gave his sly, Russell Crowe smile. "Sure, it could have been. I didn't mean it that way. I'd screw around with you anytime."

Well, that was better. I mean, not really better. I didn't want to screw around with him. But I took yoga, waxed my legs, and highlighted my hair. I got rose-petal facials and never went to sleep with my makeup still on. I shouldn't be immediately dismissed.

"I'm just trying to figure out what could have happened to Cassie," I said, getting down to business. "I'm making some inquiries to get to the bottom of it. She collapsed in the apartment when I was there. Horrible."

"Goes to show you," Billy said, kicking a pebble underfoot with the edge of his square-toed boot. "I always say, 'Live fast and free, because tomorrow you may die.' But I'm the one who was supposed to die young."

"Why?" I asked.

Billy looked surprised. "Why? Because I ride hogs and compete in dangerous races where people smash and crash. I spent two weeks in intensive care once, but other than that, I've never had a scratch."

"Good for you." Then trying to be delicate, I said, "I understand you and Cassie used to date."

"Date?" Billy smiled, and his teeth were unexpectedly straight and white. Either he had good genes or biker dudes in LA went to cosmetic dentists.

"Not date," I amended, realizing I'd used a word that was, well, dated. "So how would you describe it?"

"Probably as mind-blowing, earth-moving, proof-that-God-exists sex."

"Now you're bragging."

"Just being objective. As I'd be glad to show you."

"No thanks." We both smiled, and the little flirtation didn't hurt. I'd been around long enough to understand that earth-moving sex didn't depend on positions, practice, or never-ending potency. Forget the Kama Sutra or even Viagra. Nothing could beat lying naked next to my husband, the man I'd adored for nearly two decades. We'd gotten married on a faraway beach, then come to LA, had children, and learned to deal with teething pains and teachers' meetings, bills and mortgages, disappointments and disagreements. But at the end of the day—okay, not every day, but enough of them—we still turned to each other for passion and sex. Nothing could be more mind-blowing than that.

Billy gazed at me with his green eyes and stroked the three-day stubble at his chin as if deep in thought. Then he stood up straight and snapped two fingers together.

"I'm going to do it," he said.

"Do what?" I asked.

"Show you the e-mails. I know we've just met, but I've got to trust someone and better you than the cops. You seem a lot like me—no agenda but the truth."

That sounded like a motto of the FBI. Or at least the local Cub Scout troop.

"No agenda but the truth, right?" he repeated. He raised his hand, as if taking an oath.

"The truth is always good," I said.

"High five!" he shouted. He stretched his hand higher, and when I didn't move, he said, "Come on, give me five!"

Not sure what else to do, I awkwardly raised my hand to reach his. Instead of just smacking palms, he clasped my hand tightly, then twisted his fingers in what I guessed served as some odd biker's salute. Could be we'd just become blood brothers—or else I'd pledged to be his Harley chick.

Maybe the latter, because he put his arm on my elbow and steered me toward the side of his shop.

"These e-mails from Cassie," he said. He stopped, hesitating. "Well, maybe I won't say anything until you see them. They speak for themselves."

"What do they say?"

"Volumes."

"Give me a hint."

"Casssie kept talking about how Princess Diana had worried that her husband might off her, and how after she died, nobody believed Charles had anything to do with it."

"He didn't," I said. "She got killed in a car accident, remember? Chased by photographers through a tunnel in Paris."

"Cassie wasn't so sure. She seemed scared."

Cassie as Princess Diana? My client didn't exactly arouse the passions of the paparazzi, but I got the not-so-hidden agenda. Cassie worried that she might die—and Roger would never be a suspect.

We were standing in front of a shiny motorcycle now, and Billy handed me a helmet.

"Come on," he said. "I'll take you over. Just a ten-minute ride. I really want you to see these."

I looked dubiously at the helmet. Riding a Harley made my list of "top ten most dangerous things to do," right up there with hang gliding, bungee jumping, and arranging blind dates for Molly. But what the heck. As Billy said, he lived fast and free—and still lived. Cassie, protected in her gilded cage, had died. Maybe I'd relabel my list "top ten things that could be darn fun to experience if I weren't such a chicken."

Should I launch those experiences right now? I didn't have to rush home. Dan had arranged to take the kids out to dinner tonight at Tijuana Taco. I rarely came along for his Mexican family feasts. Stated reason: Dan deserved bonding time alone with the kids. Real reason: Who wanted to eat refried beans? My thighs couldn't handle food that had been fried once, never mind twice.

Enchiladas or not, I had three kids who needed my attention and devotion. On the other hand, my client Cassie had been murdered and my best friend, Molly, had gotten herself entangled with Roger—and she needed help. Friendship mattered, and the kids needed to know that, too.

I held the helmet uncertainly. Billy obviously knew his way around a motorcycle, but I'd only trust him sane and sober. Mothers Against Drunk Driving had made vigilantes of us all.

"So, Billy, are you high?" I asked bluntly.

"Only on life," he said.

I rubbed thumb and forefinger against my nose. "I noticed you rubbing your nose when I first arrived, and you've been sniffling since I got here," I said.

"Allergies," he said. "Nothing more exciting than that. Do you think I'd be hanging out here if I had enough cash for cocaine?"

"What would you do instead?"

"Go clubbing with Britney Spears," he said snidely.

"Or club Britney Spears, which might be a better idea," I said.

He laughed and I decided to believe him. Maybe I was deceiving myself because I wanted to see if the e-mail messages gave a glimpse into Cassie's mind. Either way, I put on the helmet, and Billy reached over to help me adjust the strap.

"You okay riding in that skirt?" he asked.

I swished the prettily pleated silk Escada, which had plenty of swirls to settle around me without hiking up. Fortunately, I'd given up wearing pencil skirts long ago. No use pretending you were still a thin line Pentel when you'd moved to Uni-ball extra-wide.

Billy patted the seat and I climbed on. He put on his own helmet, settled in front of me, and revved the engine.

"Ready?" he asked.

He turned around and flashed a devilish grin. I grinned back, my excitement rising. My face flushed and my whole body throbbed with anticipation. No wonder good girls like Cassie fell for bad boys like Billy Mann. Dancing on the edge of danger—whether with men, motorcycles, or sex—made you feel alive.

"What do I do?" I asked.

"Hold on to me," he said, facing front again and grabbing the handlebars.

We took off down the road, and I felt a surge of adrenaline. Not the scary *I'd better fight that tiger* sensation, but the *Wow, I could soar forever* feeling. Wind in the face, hair blowing, world rushing by in a blur of color wasn't a bad way to get from here to . . .

Here to where?

Maybe I hadn't acted quite as responsibly as I thought.

I peeked sideways around my helmet and strained to get my bearings. Late afternoon and the sun glimmered to my left, so we were heading north. Good for me. But after that, my internal GPS gave up the ghost. Pressed up against the leather-clad back of a man I'd just met, I couldn't see very much, and I didn't dare let go for a better view.

Billy made a quick left onto a highway, and in just a couple of miles took an exit. I thought I caught a sign for Lincoln Boulevard, but now the pumping adrenaline had turned me into a heart-pounding, ears-buzzing, hands-trembling mess. I had to calm down.

I closed my eyes for a moment, trying to relax. When I opened them again, a boat basin came into view, the very blue water broken by long piers packed with vessels for sailing, motoring, and showing off newly minted money. Surrounding all of it, high-rise condominiums stood like glass-and-steel lighthouses, beacons of success for the smaller dinghies passing through.

I sighed. Admiralty Way in Marina del Rey. Not exactly South Central LA. The only gang warfare here involved faux gangplanks. Billy drew the bike to a stop and jumped off. He held out a hand and I climbed down, more tentatively. My legs felt stiff from the tension of straddling the seat, and I took a few bowlegged steps.

"Walking like that is the sign of a good ride," Billy said with a wink.

"My first time on a bike," I admitted.

Billy cupped his hand at my chin. "Do it a lot, and it gets better and better."

He turned around, and I expected Billy to head inland, toward one of the less-opulent apartment buildings. Instead, he began striding toward the water. At a gate marked BOAT OWN-ERS ONLY, he waved me forward.

"Boat owner?" I asked. "Sunfish or six-masted schooner?"

"You'll see."

We walked down the pier, where boats ranged from twenty-four-foot day-sailers to motor cruisers four times that size. The boats all had names gracefully painted on the stern, but the tradition of christening a ship after a beautiful woman seemed to have given way to showing off. A huge sailboat, clearly the toy of a Hollywood producer, boasted *Big Opening Weekend,* and another with shiny wooden detailing that must have cost a small fortune declared *Ain't I Smart.*

"I like this one. The *Lucky Duck,*" I said reading the name off a smaller sailboat halfway down the dock. "At least someone can count his blessings."

"The owner's a nice guy," Billy said. A moment later he swung onto a boat prosaically christened *DreamRide,* which didn't tell me much.

"Is this yours?" I asked, struck by the contrast between the grimy store where we'd just been and the clean, well-ordered boat.

"Nah, I just pick a different one to sail every night," Billy said. Then, seeing my shocked look, he laughed. "Of course it's mine. Help me rig and we'll get out of here."

I hadn't been sailing since age twelve, when I spent two weeks at a sleep-over camp on the shores of Lake Pashakee. Back then, we had a one-hour period for sailing and usually spent forty-five minutes of it trying to rig the boat. Since one of the older girls at camp had told me that Pashakee was Native American for "People drown in this lake all the time," I didn't mind staying close to shore.

"What do you want me to do?" I asked, trying to remember the difference between starboard and leeward.

"Grab this mainsheet," Billy said, handing me a thick rope. I figured I'd be pulling it to raise the sail, but instead he pushed a button and the sail began rising on its own.

"Neat," I said, smiling. Apparently boats had changed since my camp days.

With the sail raised, Billy tied down the rope he'd handed me, then hit some more buttons to start the engine humming. Within five minutes, we'd pulled out of the slip and cruised slowly into open water. If sailing had been this easy for Christopher Columbus, he'd have zipped to the Orient and never discovered America.

Billy's boat had a full-size steering wheel and the oceangoing version of cruise control. He set some dials that put us on a straight line to a distant point, and the wheel moved gently all by itself. With the steering under control, Billy disappeared underneath for a moment and came back with two frosty glasses.

"Beer," he said. "Hope you don't mind. It's all I have."

I took the glass, and Billy sat down next to me. I had about a

million questions I wanted to ask him, including how he managed to afford a getup like this. But I had more urgent business.

"So these e-mails from Cassie," I said, getting right to the
point. "I take it you keep them on the boat?"

"Yup," he said. "We'll get to them."

"Obviously, you two stayed in touch even after she got
married."

"Roger traveled a lot," Billy said, briefly checking the horizon and glancing again at his directional settings. "Cassie
needed a friend. Now that she was so rich, she didn't trust a lot
of the people who suddenly wanted to hang out with her."

"But you two had been hanging out for years."

Billy got up and leaned against the railing. "Old friends are
the best friends. You give each other whatever you each need."

I suddenly got it. "Cassie gave you the boat, is that it? And
you'd take her out whenever she wanted to get away?"

He shrugged. "Let's say she did. That'd make it pretty obvious that I didn't kill her, don't you think? I mean, you don't
knock off the goose that lays the golden egg."

I thought about it for a moment. His logic made sense. But
something didn't add up. Billy said he'd been waiting for the
cops to come since Cassie died.

"Why would you be a suspect in her murder?" I asked.

Billy slowly rolled up his shirt sleeve and pointed to a skull-
and-crossbones tattoo on his left bicep. He flexed the muscle a
couple of times, and the tattoo seemed to jump out and stare
down at the dragon that wound its way up his right arm.

"Tattooed biker dude with piercings, two drug arrests, and
a bad 'tude," said Billy. "Pin it on me and everybody's happy."

"Sure that's not drug-induced paranoia?" I asked.

"I told you I'm not high," he said irritably. The appealing
gloss of charm had evaporated, and his soft, warm eyes now
looked hard and angry.

"Did Roger know you and Cassie still saw each other?"

"Probably. When you're a billionaire, you know everything. Or you think you do."

I leaned back. "I'm sorry, Billy, you've got me confused. If Roger had been knocked off, I'd have you on my suspects list. On the other hand, I don't see what you get out of having Cassie dead, except maybe ownership of a very nice boat—but you had that anyway."

Billy looked relieved. "Yeah, maybe I'm overreacting." He walked across the deck and took a pair of binoculars from under a seat. "You can usually see some dolphins and porpoises in the water. Occasionally a whale. Take a look, and I'll go get the stuff we were talking about."

I took the binoculars and leaned over the railing while Billy went back underneath. The setting sun loomed large on the horizon. Grant had once explained to me why the orange ball that warms our planet seems so much bigger at the end of the day—something about the angle of refraction of light. Or maybe it's that at the end of the day everything looms larger: Small problems burn in importance and terror lurks in the darkening shadows.

Suddenly, the boat jerked, the bow lurching sharply to the left, and the sails began swinging wildly across the deck.

"Get down!" Billy called from underneath.

Before I could budge, the heavy boom smacked into the back of my shoulder.

"Oww!" I screamed, clamping a hand on the sore spot and ducking—but not far enough. The boom teetered back and forth and, gathering additional force in the wind, slammed terrifyingly into the back of my head.

"Help!" I yelled. My head reeling from the pain of the blow, I tottered forward and lost my footing. I tumbled over the railing, plunging through the air and . . .

Splat.

I landed in the water with such incredible force that it felt like I'd smacked into cement. Then the inexplicably hard surface gave way and I began sinking into the cold, dark ocean. Icy water pierced my clothes and covered my face. I hadn't had time to close my mouth as I fell, and now I choked on a mouthful of brine, coughing madly as the salt water penetrated down to my lungs. I kicked hard to get to the surface, but being completely disoriented, I instead forced myself down deeper. My eyes burned, and holding my breath was out of the question, because all the air had been forced out of me on impact.

Was this how people drowned? I'd been swimming all my life, but that hardly mattered. Now the water had turned into an enemy, fighting my efforts to escape from its cold clutches. I clawed at the water, desperate to surface but getting nowhere. Something slimy brushed by my face, and I slapped at it in panic. A jellyfish? Used condom? Slippery side of an electric eel?

I flailed my arms, as out of control as Ashley used to be when she threw tantrums as a toddler. Back then, I'd hug her arms tightly to her sides to help her calm down.

Something I could try now.

I crossed my arms in front of my chest and made myself stop kicking. I hoped to pop to the surface like a cork, but instead I hovered in the water. An image flashed in my head of the batches of brownies Jimmy and I made early every Saturday morning. Happy to be with him, I'd stopped counting calories and gained five pounds. If I sunk to the bottom and drowned now, the coroner could call it death by chocolate.

Wait a minute. Didn't fat float? Instead of dying from not dieting, I could be saved by Betty Crocker.

Sure enough, as my body became slightly more relaxed, I began to bob toward the surface. At least I assumed it was the surface, because I saw little glimmers of light. I turned upward, and in a moment my face broke through to air.

I coughed and spluttered for oxygen.

"Help!" I called into the gathering darkness.

I started kicking again, but this time to keep myself above water. The flowing Escada skirt, now a sodden mess, pulled heavily against my legs. No time for modesty. I put my shaking fingers to the waistband, found the zipper, and tugged. In a moment, the wet fabric slipped off and floated away. My shoes had fallen off long ago, and now I could swim freely.

But where to go? The current moved faster than I expected, and small waves splashed over my chilled skin. I could see the outline of Billy's boat, moving steadily away from me in the gentle evening breeze. I looked around frantically, but no other boat came into view. Where was the Coast Guard at a time like this? Or even a cruise ship. If I had to eat seafood buffets and play shuffleboard to be saved, I'd do it.

"Woman overboard!" I shouted.

Maybe I could flash an SOS. Though come to think of it, I'd heard that Morse code had been dropped on the high seas. Not that I knew it in the first place.

"*Bill-eeeee!*" I yelled. My voice was muffled by the waves but unexpectedly, the boat turned and began to head back toward me.

Now a new panic set in. Had Billy deliberately knocked the boom in my direction to send me into the water? If so, I didn't want to get anywhere near him. As the boat approached, I turned and started to swim fast in the opposite direction. Then I stopped. Not a wise decision. Did I really want to spend the night swimming desperately toward a shore I couldn't see?

"Lacy, *La-cee*," called a voice from the boat that was overtaking me now.

"I'm here," I shouted back to Billy.

He hadn't lowered the sails, but the grinding roar of the motor came closer. Then I heard a splash as a life preserver landed twenty yards away. I started swimming toward it, but Billy reeled it back in.

"Another try!" he called, and I saw him on the edge of the boat, hurling the ring again. This time, it plopped down ten feet in front of me.

"Nice throw," I said lunging for the round orange ring.

"Grab it and hang on," he directed.

I did exactly that, and in a minute I was riding the waves, being pulled gently back to the boat.

And back toward the spinning blades of the motor.

"Turn that off!" I screamed, over the roaring noise.

Billy must have complied, because a sudden stillness came over the water. Relief flooded through me as I passed inches from the motor, now mercifully stopped. Billy hung a metal staircase on the stern of the boat and drew me close enough to reach it. Anxiously, I put one foot on the cold metal and hefted myself up. When I got to the second step, Billy reached down, put his arms around my waist and lifted me into the boat.

"Are you okay?" he asked as I sat down shivering on the bottom of the boat.

I nodded dumbly.

"What happened?" he asked.

"You tell me," I said.

He reached down to the deck and came up with a dirty green towel that he bundled around my shoulders.

"You're shaking. You've got to get out of those wet clothes."

"I'm out of most of them," I said. I wrapped my arms around my bare, goosebump-covered legs and rubbed them to warm up. My hands quickly turned black and oily. I shuddered, not wanting to think about what had been with me in the drink.

"Jeez, what a weird accident," he said. "Good thing you can swim. I probably should have made you put on a life vest before we went out, but I didn't think of it."

"Do you even have them?" I asked, looking around the boat for the requisite orange jackets.

"Of course. It's the law."

I nodded, trying to convince myself that Billy Mann cared about following laws.

"You're right, I'd like to get into something dry," I said, unable to stop trembling. "Do you have anything I can borrow?"

Billy eyed me carefully. "Probably," he said. "Let's look."

He helped me stand up again, and with an arm steadying me at the elbow he led me belowdeck, past a tiny galley kitchen and a bathroom with a real shower—and into a full-size sleeping cabin. A big bed filled most of the area, tucked into the V-shaped front of the boat and expanding back. Pale peach sheets and a chenille blanket lay tangled over the mattress, though there'd been some effort to straighten up—the pillows were piled neatly, and a folded duvet rested along the edge. A small chest had been built into the opposite wall. One of the drawers stood partly open, and a hairbrush and travel-size tube of toothpaste rested on the bureau top. That they hadn't fallen suggested it had been a calmer ride belowdeck than above.

Billy reached to the far side of the bed and pulled up a bright yellow dress clumped into a ball. He shook it out. "You can wear this," he said, handing it to me. "In fact, you can have it."

I'd had my share of surprises today. I'd ridden a motorcycle, risked drowning, and ripped off my clothes in front of a man I barely knew. But nothing quite prepared me to see a vintage Nina Ricci couture cocktail dress with a wrapped bodice and delicate hand-sewn beading. It had to be worth thousands of dollars. I'd expect to see it on the red carpet at the Golden Globes, but not balled up under a bed.

"Where'd you get this?" I asked, holding the gown up to my shoulders. Whoever wore the dress before had been taller and thinner than me—and probably tanner, too. "Are you sneaking

into Renee Zellweger's closet? Making deals with Reese Witherspoon's stylist?"

He shrugged. "Someone left it here." Then, changing the
subject rapidly, he said, "At least it's something to wear home.
Get you out of the wet clothes." He tugged at the half-open
bureau drawer and produced a cashmere wrap in the same
shade of yellow. "This goes with it. A little warmer. Get dressed
and I'll come back."

He left again, and I slowly peeled off my wet shirt and
lace La Mystere cleavage-enhancing bra. The padded push-up
cups had absorbed the ocean water like sponges, thrusting my
chest up toward my chin. When I unhooked the now-heavy
bra, my breasts sagged but my spirit soared. I pondered the
matching panties for a moment, and then stepped casually out
of them. It felt strange, but I'd read about all the celebrities
going commando—i.e., wearing only a bikini wax under their
clothes—so I could give it a try. Though frankly, the expression
seemed odd. "Going commando" had a vaguely military sound,
as if army corporals defending America's freedom tossed their
Calvins before aiming their guns.

I pulled the dress on over my bare skin. It didn't hang badly,
but I couldn't reach the tiny corsetlike fasteners in the back.

"I can help," Billy said, coming back in.

I turned around and let him tug the dress into place.

"Don't worry," I said, when he couldn't get the fabric to
close at the waist. "Nobody will see." I wrapped the warm
shawl around me.

"You look good," Billy said, stepping back.

"I don't need to look good. I just need to get home."

"Yeah, the boat's set on course back. We'll be at the slip
soon."

A few minutes later, he docked the boat and helped me
onto the pier. I called a taxi to drive me back to the shop so I
could retrieve my car. No way I'd get back on the motorcycle.

"Let's walk a little to keep you warm until the taxi gets here," Billy said. He tucked his hand into my elbow and we strolled to the end of the pier and back, then down the next pier. A couple of boat owners waved to him, and he called out *hellos* to several others.

"You know a lot of people here," I said.

"Small community. See a lot of people, but I don't really know them."

We walked in silence. The expensive dress rustled at my knees, and as I brushed against the soft fabric, my mind whirled, trying to put tonight into context.

"Billy, about the dress I'm wearing. You said someone had left it on the boat. Was it Cassie?"

He shrugged. "Probably. I mean, I think so."

He thought so? Billy Mann might have a lot of women on his boat, but I couldn't imagine that many of them arrived in yellow beaded couture gowns.

The cab pulled up and Billy opened the door for me.

"Listen, I'm sorry about what happened. And in all the confusion, I didn't get to show you those e-mails. You have to come back."

"Sure," I said.

I'd almost forgotten about the e-mails, because now my mind was busy with something else. As we pulled away, I looked back at Billy, standing and waving at the retreating cab as if his true love were inside.

His true love in an unmistakable yellow gown.

Chapter Eight

— • —

B y the time I got home to our house in Pacific Palisades, the grandfather clock in the front hall had struck eleven and all seemed quiet. Slipping into our bedroom, I found Dan already asleep. Bless the man, he never even snored. He'd also thoughtfully left on a light—my favorite one, as it happened. For a bedside lamp, I'd made a shade out of an antique copper urn I'd found in a cluttered store on Third Avenue and had it refitted to sit on a round, gold-plated base. The combination of materials gave off a gently soothing glow.

Right now, I needed to be soothed. I quickly took off the elegant Nina Ricci and stuck it in the back of my closet. For some reason, I thought of Monica Lewinsky tucking away her blue dress. Could this frock also turn into evidence?

I heard a soft knock on the bedroom door and quickly pulled on a cotton bathrobe.

"Hi, sweetie," I whispered, opening the door to Grant and then stepping into the hall so we wouldn't wake Dan. "Did you have a good night?"

"Sure, but how about you? Everything cool? It's late." He glanced at his watch, and I could tell he'd been concerned. Funny how roles reversed.

"I got busy. A little over my head," I said, making a joke that only I would get.

"Solving the Cassie case?" Grant asked as we walked into his room.

"I don't really have cases," I said.

"Sure you do, Mom," Grant said. "The police should put you on the payroll."

"The police would prefer that I only solve decorating problems. Like what to tell my client in Malibu who wants a coffee table made out of seashells."

"Too tacky for a million-dollar mansion?" he asked, making a good guess.

"Exactly. But she thinks tacky is the new chic."

"I never know what that means," complained Grant, rolling his eyes. "I asked a girl in my math class why she wears purple all the time, and she said, 'Purple is the new black.'"

"And women my age say 'Forty is the new thirty.'"

"Okay, then, how's this?" said Grant gamely. "College is the new high school."

"Only for you, genius boy." I grinned and poked his arm affectionately. "By the way, how's your class going?"

"Good. Oh, and I met some people at UCLA who knew Cassie." He looked at me expectantly, and I had a feeling he'd been waiting all night for this conversation. "Don't get mad when I tell you how I know them."

"I'm never mad at you, sweetie." How could smart, steady, good-hearted Grant do anything that would upset me? "Tell me everything."

"I got tapped for a secret society at UCLA."

"Wow." I tightened the belt on my robe, taking a moment to think. "That was fast. Do they know you're still in high school?"

Grant shrugged, then pointed to his blue T-shirt with a logo I hadn't noticed before: a triangle, followed by ij.

"It turns out to be a big-deal club," he said. "Delta ij. A club for geeky science types."

"Geeky is definitely the new cool," I said, trying to keep my tone light.

Grant nodded. "Weirdly enough, it is. *Revenge of the Nerds* and all that. I don't really know much about the club yet, but I got invited to a meeting this afternoon, and they gave me the T-shirt."

"How did Cassie come up?"

"A physics professor at the meeting mentioned her. He runs the whole secret society, from what I can tell. He said that since Cassie had friends in Delta ij, the police might come around to ask questions. We could politely say we didn't have any information." He looked at me. "Maybe you should talk to him."

I raised an eyebrow. "Why? Sounds like he won't tell me a thing."

"Everyone confides in you, Mom. You have that trustworthy look."

Probably more like a lined, tired look, but I'd take compliments where I could get them. "Thanks," I said simply.

Grant scribbled on a scrap of paper and handed it to me. "His name's Professor Hal Bohr. He has office hours tomorrow afternoon from three to five. Schedule an appointment through your Google calendar."

I sighed. "Whatever happened to Sierra Club calendars? They looked so pretty on the refrigerator and they never scheduled appointments for you."

Grant laughed. "I'll teach you how to do it on Google. The Sierra Club wants you paperless."

"Not as much as they want my twelve bucks for a calendar." I took the page of information from him. "If I come over, I'll try really hard not to run into you. I know the campus is your territory now."

"Thanks, Mom, but it's okay." He smiled. "I'm not embarrassed by you anymore."

"Anymore?" I tried not to feel insulted.

"You've got to be humiliated by your parents when you're a kid. Like Ashley's age." Grant pulled the quilt off his bed, getting ready to turn in. "But eventually you figure out parents aren't so bad. Nice to have, in fact. They're around for a reason."

"Hard to grow up without them."

"Even harder to pay for college without them." He grinned. "Not to mention cars, cameras, and late-night pizza."

"At least I know my use," I said with a sigh.

"Just joking, Mom." He checked his cell phone and turned it to vibrate for the night. "I don't love you because you buy me stuff. I admire you. I like it when my friends meet you."

"So I can visit this Hal Bohr and you won't mind? I can ask him about Cassie and Delta ij?"

Grant looked slightly uncomfortable. "Ask about Cassie. But Delta ij is supposed to be a secret society, so he won't talk about it. I'd hate to get thrown out before I'm even initiated."

"I hear you."

Grant sat down on his bed and I went over and kissed the top of his head. Joe College or not, he deserved to know his mom loved him. I ruffled his soft hair. The appealing smell of baby shampoo and talc had long given way to his own enticing tang of hemp shaving cream and Rainforest bamboo soap. Any more ecoconscious products and he'd have a green halo around him.

I looked around his room. Grant might be growing up, but I still liked being his mom. And moms liked to be needed.

"Anything I can do for you?" I asked, thinking I might iron his tennis shirt or pack him lunch for school.

"You don't have to do everything," Grant said. "Go to sleep."

"You too, honey. Sleep well."

I left the room and closed the door, then went downstairs to make sure Jimmy had put his book report into his backpack. Inside the L.L. Bean bag, I found a torn Skittles wrapper and two broken pencils. I threw them away and put in a granola bar and newly sharpened pencils. Sometimes I felt like the hamster running on the wheel. I kept going, thinking only I could keep the world turning.

The next morning, Molly arrived just after the kids left for school. I made her a banana-yogurt protein shake with blueberries and wheat germ and fiddled with the new espresso machine for her requested double decaf half-skim cappuccino with extra froth. If Molly didn't get back to work soon, I might start charging for breakfast.

At least she listened intently while I described my adventures with Billy Mann.

"Wild night," she said,

"Can you make any sense of it?"

"Maybe he wanted to seduce you," she said taking a sip of the cappuccino. Too much froth. She wiped her lips with a napkin. "A ride on the bike and then onto a boat—it all sounds pretty alluring. Unless you've been married too long to notice."

"Married isn't the same as dead," I said. "Billy Mann has a sexy side, I'll give you that."

"So as you asked me with Roger—did he try to get you in bed?"

I groaned. "Molly, may I remind you he knocked me into the water with the boom?"

"You don't know if he meant to. Maybe he's just a lousy sailor who made a mistake. Then he brought the boat around and rescued you, thus becoming your savior, redeemer, and knight in shining orange-life-jacket armor."

"You're suggesting he thumped me into the water so he could haul me out? Sounds like some nautical version of Munchausen-by-proxy syndrome."

"Oooh, I saw that on Maury Povich once!" Molly said enthusiastically. "A woman secretly hurting her child so she could be the center of attention and make her better."

"I don't think that's what happened here," I said. "Billy already had my full attention."

"Then he had some deeper motive," said Molly. "Think about it. A ride on the Harley to get you revved. Then the romance of a boat set against your panic in the water. When he brings you to safety and into his arms, you're nothing but nerve endings."

"He did get me out of my clothes," I admitted.

"What?"

"I'd gotten soaked and kicked off half my clothes. He handed me a Nina Ricci vintage gown. Funny thing to keep on a boat, right? Bright yellow, by the way."

"Reminds me of a hit show at Lincoln Center in New York a few years ago with a lead character known as The Girl in a Yellow Dress. Audiences fell in love with her. She got so famous in Manhattan, she had to wear black to leave the theater and go outside."

I laughed. "So you brought her to LA and cast her in a movie?"

"Nope. Turned out everyone knew the role, not her."

I could identify with Molly's Broadway riff more than she realized. Anybody who saw me at the pier yesterday would remember me as The Girl in a Yellow Dress. Like the Broadway star, I'd be recognized only because of the bright yellow gown.

"I bet the vintage Nina Ricci belonged to Cassie," I said

to Molly suddenly. "It fits with everything I know about her style."

"Why would Billy have it?"

"Let's say Cassie came to his boat one night and stayed over. The next morning, she couldn't leave in her evening dress. Billy lent her a long sweatshirt, or maybe she had a pair of jeans along. She didn't want to take the dress with her, so she left it behind, figuring she'd get it next time."

I heard Molly inhale sharply. "You think Cassie married Roger and was still seeing Billy?"

"Seeing, yes. Screwing, I don't know."

"Could she have been that stupid?"

"Maybe she loved Billy but needed more money. So she married Roger, figuring she could get his money and go back to Billy."

"I think Henry James already tried that plot," Molly said.

I laughed, remembering the student in Elsa Franklin's office reading *The Wings of the Dove.*

"You're right," I said. "Big mess that didn't work out at all. Love and money and death, with all the needs getting confused."

"How could Billy and Cassie screwing lead to murder?" Molly asked.

I let the question linger in the air. Molly knew the answer as well as I did, but neither of us wanted to think about it. "Roger could have found out about her night on the boat and drawn his own conclusions," I said finally. "He would have been furious."

"Not furious enough for murder," said Molly sharply. "I already told you Roger's a smart businessman. If he tracked infidelity, he'd probably have grounds to void the prenup, get a divorce, and pay her nothing."

I sighed. Molly would defend Roger to the end. I could only hope he'd do the same for her.

"Let's get back to the yellow dress," I suggested, ready to try out my newest theory. "Think about this one. Cassie comes to the marina one night and various people notice her as a figure in a yellow gown, walking along the pier. Then they see me last night—same gown, same pier. They assume it's the same person, right?"

"Your butt's a little bigger, darling, and tits smaller. But you're right—nobody's measuring."

"The point is that if the police come by tomorrow and ask questions about a woman who died a couple of weeks ago, nobody makes the connection that the murdered girl is The Girl in a Yellow Dress. Unless they believe in ghosts. Because they've seen her too recently."

"I'm following you," Molly said thoughtfully.

"Billy doesn't have to worry about the cops finding Cassie's dress in his boat, because I've taken it away. I have no reason to give it to the police. Hiding it in plain sight."

"So you figure Billy dumped you in the water to get you wet and out of your clothes—but only to parade you in Cassie's dress. Not romance, but intrigue."

"Right."

"Do you think Billy's smart enough to have concocted such an elaborate plan on the spot?"

"Desperate men take desperate measures," I said direly.

Hal Bohr's office, on the third floor, up a well-worn staircase, had a handwritten sign on the wooden door: FRIENDS ENTER, FOES AWAY. Figuring I counted as neither, I knocked gently. Getting no answer, I turned the knob and stepped inside.

The room could have been the set for *Scary Movie 3*. Cobwebs hung from the ceiling while scattered newspapers and open books fell off dusty shelves. A broken laptop sat in the center of the room and a squealing rodent—mouse? rat?—ran around and around in a cage that stood propped on stacks of bound folders and science journals. Though I didn't see anyone, a voice suddenly broke in out of nowhere.

"Wassup?"

Not exactly a threatening expression, but it was creepy in the seemingly empty room. Then I noticed a flicker of motion. Two feet clad in orange socks banged against the far wall at about eye level with me, sticking straight up from a pair of green corduroy pants. Curious, I started to make my way through the obstacle-course room to get a better look.

"Are you standing on your head?" I asked.

"Yes, just a few more minutes. Blood to the brain is important."

I wended my way around a faded leather chair that had filler dribbling out of a worn spot on the back and came face-to-toes with Hans Bohr.

"Hi, I'm Lacy Fields," I said, as if unsurprised to be encountering an upside-down man.

"Nice to meet you. You're right on time." Removing one of his three anchor points, he extended his right hand and swayed slightly. I crouched down but, concerned that I might pull him over if we shook, stood up again.

"I could come back," I said.

"Don't bother. This is a good time. I hear you've already talked to Elsa. You want to know about Cassie Crawford."

Word traveled fast on campus.

"Right. Did you know Cassie?"

"Not in the biblical sense. I never slept with her."

Hmm. A real conversation stopper. What could I reply? *Too bad* seemed silly and *Why not?* over the top. Somehow, I'd inched a bit too close to his crotch, so I took a giant step back.

"Cassie never took my class," Hal said emphatically.

"What do you teach?" I asked, as if soliciting his syllabus was the key point of my visit.

For an answer, Hal pushed off from the wall, did two som-

ersaults, then stood up, arms above his head, as if he'd just finished his floor-exercise routine at the summer Olympics.

"I teach quantum mechanics, thermodynamics, and Newtonian mechanics," he said in a singsong tone usually reserved
for *The Cat in the Hat.* "Plus electricity, relativity, and gravity."

At the last word, he leapt into the air in the kind of split-
jump that cheerleaders do after a touchdown. He spread his
arms to touch his toes, then landed hard on the ground.

"As you can see, the laws of gravity are still working. I like
to check now and then." He smiled broadly and a little dimple
appeared on his right cheek. His thick curly hair had popped
back into place after his acrobatics and a gold stud glimmered
in his ear. I couldn't decide if he belonged at Cirque du Soleil
or the fifth-floor psych ward at Cedars Medical Center.

"If she didn't take your class, how did you get to know
Cassie?" I asked, trying to bring him back to the subject.

"We never had sex," he said.

"So you mentioned."

"Standard logic sequence. I don't have sex with any students. But that doesn't mean I *do* have sex with everyone who's
not my student."

"Of course not."

"Who'd have time?"

"You're a busy man," I said, thinking the fifth floor sounded
more and more reasonable. "Teaching quantum mechanics and
gravity and . . . um, everything."

"The Theory of Everything!" he said brightly. "Right there
at the intersection of quantum mechanics and gravity. If I have
sex too often, all I'll ever discover is the Theory of Nothing."

Oddly enough, I actually followed his rant. To try to
keep up with Grant, I'd kept a popular physics book by my
bedside for a year now. Frankly, I didn't understand a word
of it. Grant teased that I didn't need a bookmark—I could
open to any page, any night, and never realize that I'd read it

before. But I had picked up the fundamental conflict of modern physics. Einstein's relativity theory described how the vast universe of stars and galaxies worked. Quantum mechanics offered a way to understand the tiniest particles, like quarks and muons. *But they couldn't both be right.* So physicists had been searching for a way to put them together, understand the big and small with one theory that could explain the universe in all its extremes.

"You're working on the Theory of Everything?" I asked.

He sighed. "I'd like to understand even one photon of this vast intergalactic world that we call home."

"A good reason to study physics," I said, encouragingly.

"I hope to learn something before we're all pulled into some formless black hole that sucks the substance from our very being," he said ominously.

"Hopefully, that won't occur too soon."

"You never know," he said portentously. But then he spun around and climbed onto the seat of a wooden chair. "The best part of physics is that it's fun, fun, fun!" On the last word, he jumped off the chair, doing a double twist on his way down. His foot hit the chair back, which clattered down on top of him. Only slightly abashed, he brushed himself off and stood up again.

"You okay?" I asked.

"Always," he said.

Before he could vault off to some bizarre fifth dimension, I quickly said, "Do you mind if I ask you a couple of things about Cassie?"

"Ask away. Whatever I can tell you about"—he threw his arms wide and got down on one knee, singing— *"Cassie, Cassie, bo-Bassie, banana-fana, mo-Massie. Fi-fi so sassy. Cass-ie."*

I cleared my throat. Sassy Cassie. Hey, I could do this. I had a six-year-old.

"It sounds like Cassie made a strong impression."

"Impression? You mean like when you make a snow angel?" He lay down flat on the floor and flapped his arms, like a child on a wintry day in Maine.

"Um, this is Los Angeles," I said.

"Right. We never made snow angels." He jumped up again. "She liked to come to my office and have me talk string theory to her. Tsk, tsk. Such a bad girl. I say too many people have already been seduced by that theory."

"You don't believe it?" I asked.

"Plink. Plink. Plink." He plucked his fingers in the air, as if pulling at imaginary violin strings.

"Was she seeing someone at the time?" I asked.

"Time is a human construct, meaningful only as a comparative measure, not an absolute one," he said. "Go on, time how long it takes me to do these, and then interpret."

He dropped to the floor and did ten push-ups, counting each out loud with a sharp bark. His arm muscles rippled under his T-shirt. For the next ten, he lifted himself off the floor each time and clapped his hands. He finished by pushing himself up into a handstand, then springing upright.

"Yah!" he called, winking at me. He put his foot against the back of the chair, stretching out his hamstring. Then he looked at me and twisted his face into a silly expression, like Jim Carrey in *Mask*. His face was as elastic as his body.

How could I possibly get information from this crazy man? I took a step back and realized that Professor Bohr couldn't have been much more than thirty years old. To have a tenured professorship at that age (as I'd learned online that he did) put him in a rare stratosphere. He had to be a top-of-the-line genius.

In other words, smart enough to play dumb. Hal Bohr had happily figured out how to play into the stereotype of physicist as crazed iconoclast.

I pushed some books and newspapers aside and sat down on a broken-legged chair.

"You're very clever," I said. "Clever enough not to give me a straight answer on anything. What are you hiding?"

For the first time since I'd come in, Hal Bohr hesitated, and a shadow of uncertainty crossed his face. Then he pulled himself back into his wild-scientist role. "To hide in this vast galaxy is . . ."

"I know all about this vast galaxy," I said, interrupting. "What I don't know is enough about Cassie Crawford. Your Cassie Cassie bo-Bassie. The one you didn't sleep with."

"Not having sex sounds like I'm hiding something?" he asked.

"Classic misdirection," I said with a shrug. "You get me thinking on a personal level because there's something else you don't want to reveal."

His face twisted into such an expression of surprise that I figured I'd hit on something.

"Come on," I said. "You've got to help me. Let's do this scientifically. I ask you four straight questions and you give me four straight answers."

"I do science all day. Let's make it more fun than that." He licked the edge of his lips with his tongue and came over next to me. "A reflex game. Do you like games?"

He put his hands out in front of him, palms up, and gestured for me to put mine on top of them, palms down. Yup, I knew this game. I'd played it endlessly with Jimmy. He'd try to flip his hand over and slap me, while I tried to pull my hand away.

"Four questions," said Hal. "Each time I win, I don't answer. Each time you win, I tell the truth." His childish exuberance had melted away, replaced by an almost frightening intensity.

I nodded and put my hands out, holding them lightly over his.

"First question . . . How did you meet Cassie?" I asked.

Hal stared down, moving his hands imperceptibly beneath mine. I pulled away slightly, put them back, pulled away . . .

Slap.

He got me.

"I don't have to answer that one," he said happily.

I nodded. "Okay, question two. Can you tell me anything from her student days—anybody she might have known—that could have led to her death?"

"That's two questions," Hal complained. "Anything or anybody."

"Take it or leave it," I said.

"Take it." He flipped the other hand for a quick slap, but I got away before any contact.

He looked me straight in the eye. "While Cassie was an undergraduate, a physics student died coming home from a lab. She'd known him. The incident haunted her and lately she'd been asking a lot of questions about him. Still, I don't see how his death could have led to hers—despite the interconnectedness of the universe."

I nodded. Hal's eyes bored powerfully through me—as if seeing something I couldn't. I gave a slight, involuntary tremble.

"Next. Why would you answer my question about what might have led to her death by telling me about something that didn't?"

Almost before I finished talking, I felt *Slap, slap!* He flipped both hands and got both of mine.

"No answer," he said.

Final chance. I didn't hold out much hope—that I'd either have fast enough reflexes or an insightful enough question.

"Last question," I said. "Did you try to seduce her and fail?"

Hal tipped his hands, I pulled mine away.

His expression changed yet again. He tried to keep his features straight, but I saw a little smile playing on the edge of his lips.

"Try with Cassie? No, definitely no. Not my type."

"Who is your type?" I asked.

"Sorry, Ms. Lacy Fields, we're done," he said, dancing away. "We tied, two–two. I like this game. But I hate ties. Come back some time and we'll play again."

With that, he went back to the wall and threw himself back into a headstand.

I went out and closed the door behind me. I didn't have a Theory of Everything. But I had the feeling that if I spent a little more time with Hal Bohr, I'd at least start to have a theory about Cassie Crawford.

Chapter Nine

—— • ——

Molly invited me to a gala beach party at Roger's house.
"His wife's barely buried and he's whooping it up?"
I asked. "How's that going to look on the style page? Not to mention the police blotter?"

"It's a charity event," Molly said hurriedly. "Roger has decided not to let his personal grief get in the way of good works."

"Wallet of platinum and heart of gold."

"He wants to *help* people," Molly whined.

"You know who really gets helped by rich people's parties? The caterers, florists, bartenders, and DJs."

"No DJ. He's having a harp quartet. It's the next fad," said Molly, who always knew the latest trends before they even happened. She'd predicted the comeback of bell bottoms when the rest of us were still in boot-cut. But a harp as instrument of choice for dinner music? Molly had hit it again—harps were unusual, expensive, and difficult to handle. Perfect to show off at a Hollywood party. I thought briefly of Elsa Franklin's

Humanitarian Dinner honoring Dan. Next time we'd write a check and then eat take-out lo mein at home.

"Where's the party?" I asked. The penthouse on Wilshire probably still had too much yellow police tape for entertaining, and unless Roger planned to cart in busloads of sand, it didn't have a beach.

"Roger has his house in Malibu, but this will be in the event cottage next door. He bought it to be a separate bash abode." She smiled, pleased to be in the know. "He got the idea from Melanie Griffith and Antonio Banderas. We went to a dinner at *their* party house."

Instead of focusing on the decadence of a second residence kept just for merrymaking, I had a bigger concern.

"*We* went to a dinner at Melanie Griffith's?" I asked. "*We* as in you and Roger? *We* as in you and Roger who was probably married at the time?"

She didn't answer for a moment. "Roger and I have a connection that's hard to explain," she said finally.

"Roger feels like bad news to me. I think you should get away from him."

"And you know I always listen to you," Molly said tartly.

"You should."

"Really? How about that comic I dated when we first got to LA. You figured he had no future and hounded me to break up with him."

"Which you did."

"Correct. I broke up with Ben Stiller. His last movie made two hundred million. Same with the one before that."

"Would you really want to be with Zoolander?" I asked defensively.

"Maybe," said Molly. She paused meaningfully, then smiled. "But maybe not. Never would have worked. He married that actress from *The Brady Bunch Movie*. Nobody would ever confuse me with Marcia Brady. But give me some credit, Lacy. I do have an eye for good guys."

"You're convinced Roger's a good guy?"

"A good guy. But the police had him in for questioning again," Molly said.

"He's their suspect?"

"No," she said softly. "His lawyer says all the questions were about me, and whether Roger led me to think I'd be wife number four."

"Number four. Can you imagine? He collects wives like I collect handbags."

"That's me, an old bag," said Molly grimly.

"If that's true, you're an ostrich Kelly. Classic and classy and distinctive. The one everyone wants."

"The police want me, too. It's all circumstantial, but they don't care. I'm close to Roger, who owned the penthouse. I'm close to you, who had the key to let me in. Fingerprints on the fridge. I'm the center of the intersecting circles. Case closed."

"So what are you going to do?"

"I don't know. Roger and I had so many plans." She shrugged. "For now, I'm just going to his party. Will you come? There'll be fireworks."

"Emotional or pyrotechnic?"

"Definitely the latter," she said with a laugh. Then with more menace than I would have expected, she added, "And with Roger, you never know what will explode."

Not versed in what to wear to a Malibu beach party, I wandered into Ashley's room to consult my fashionista daughter.

"Bathing suit or little black dress?" I asked, after explaining the situation.

"Neither. A swing dress," she said, obviously ready to edit *Teen Vogue*. "Empire waist and not too many pleats. Bright color, like pink or orange. Go for a designer like Stella McCartney or Alexander McQueen."

"Aren't their styles a little young for me?"

"You could get away with it," she said looking me over

carefully. "Tara has a swing dress from Derek Lam with a corset top. My God, it must have been *so* expensive."

I raised an eyebrow. "Are you sure she . . . um . . . bought it?"

"I sure hope so." Ashley twisted her mouth, slightly embarrassed. I remembered the two girls outside the store, giggling about shoplifting. At least now, Ashley seemed to take the situation more seriously.

"Her dad gave her a platinum AmEx card so that never happens again," Ashley said. "Though I guess it wasn't really about money the first time."

I raised an eyebrow but didn't say anything. Simple rule of parenting: if you want your kid to talk, just listen.

"Tara's parents fight and don't spend any time with her," Ashley said. "She's pretty sure they're both having affairs."

"That must be awful for her."

"Awful, yup. And I'm the only one she tells about it," Ashley said, with a hint of pride. "Her mom is always off getting laser treatments for her legs and Restylane for her wrinkles and Botox on her butt."

Botox on her butt? If I were going to waste time (and money) on beauty treatments, I'd at least want to see the results in my makeup mirror.

"Sounds like shoplifting is Ashley's way of acting out," I said, sticking to the subject. "She's trying to get her parents to notice her."

"I guess," said Ashley with a shrug.

I sat down at the edge of her bed, pushing aside half a dozen stuffed animals to make room. At fifteen and just starting high school, Ashley was still caught in that awkward, in-between phase: cool and grown-up one minute, but needing her security blanket the next. Right now, the only boy in her bed (thank God) was the beat-up purple Barney she'd had since age two. I wanted to preserve the wedge of innocence as long as possible.

"Do you remember when you were little and I used to tell you that you never had to cry to get what you wanted?" I asked. "If you needed me, you just had to say . . ."

"*I want attention,*" Ashley said, in a three-year-old's wail.

"And I'd drop anything else and give you attention."

Ashley sat down next to me, comfortably tucking her legs under her. "You always kept up your end, Mom. You'd stop talking to Molly or Daddy or whoever else and play with me."

We both smiled, remembering the toys and dolls spread across tables in restaurants and the dressing room at Saks. I never had any doubt that connecting with my daughter was priority number one.

"Sometimes we'd take your Barbies and have conversations with them," I said, thinking of the lessons I tried to teach.

"One time you held up a Barbie in a bathing suit and insisted she'd just won the Nobel Prize for Economics," giggled Ashley. "We had to get her dressed so she could go to Sweden. Somehow it made sense to me."

"At least we didn't have Bratz. A doll in a thong might have put me over the edge."

We both laughed again, and I put my arm around my daughter's slight shoulders. "It gets harder to ask for attention as you get older. What you want isn't as clear. But I'm still here for you, honey. And always will be."

Ashley picked up the ragged Barney and put her head on my shoulder. "Sometimes I hate being a teenage girl," she whispered.

"All I can promise is that you'll outgrow it," I said, giving her a hug.

"Tara's having a secret party at her house on Friday night," Ashley blurted. "Her dad's out of town on business and her mom's going to Bacara for the weekend."

Bacara? The lush resort in Santa Barbara offered romantic villas overlooking the Santa Ynez Mountains. Given that they could cost a thousand bucks a night, it was unlikely she'd be heading there alone. Tara had probably guessed right about her mom having an affair. But right now the mother's morality didn't worry me nearly as much as the empty, unchaperoned house.

"What do you mean, a secret party?" I asked.

"Tara's allowed to have two friends over on Friday. Me and another girl. But everyone in school knows we'll be there alone. A bunch of junior guys told Tara they'll come by with beer, and the whole varsity lacrosse team's going to show up and do vodka shots."

My fifteen-year-old daughter hugging Barney and talking about vodka shots?

I needed to intervene. But given the reaction—or lack of one—when I'd phoned Tara's mom about the shoplifting episode, I knew she wouldn't cancel her getaway to supervise her daughter. Should I call the school? The police? Child Welfare?

I shook my head. So far, nothing had happened. I couldn't get carried away, but I still had to protect my daughter. My scared, confused, defiant daughter. She'd told me about the party because she couldn't handle this one alone. I had to help her save face.

"I guess it's up to you," I said carefully. "Tara's your friend and all. But a shame about the timing. I thought you might come with me to Roger's beach party Friday night."

Ashley opened her eyes wide. I smiled at her excitement—which, of course, immediately turned it off.

"Why would I want to go to some old people's party?" she asked.

"The Dixie Chicks are singing," I said, trying to recall some of the cool-factor details Molly had provided. (They hadn't seemed relevant at the time.) "And someone else. Joss Stone, I think."

"Oooh, I looove Joss Stone, don't you?"

"You bet," I said brightly, even though I wouldn't know a Joss Stone from a Rolling Stone. "I love him."

"Her."

"Did I say 'him'? I meant 'her.'"

Ashley crossed her arms. "Omigod, Mom, you've never even heard of Joss Stone, have you?"

I made a face. "Nope. It will be a cool party. The downside is that you'll have to go with your very uncool mother."

"You're cool, Mom. You are." She smiled. "Thanks for inviting me."

"Sure, honey." I hadn't even walked out of the room before she grabbed her cell phone to call Tara.

"Hey, listen, I can't come on Friday," I heard her say. "I'm going to a party with Joss Stone and a killer."

I closed the door quietly. A killer at the party? I didn't even want to ask.

Two days later, Roger's assistant Vince called to say his boss wanted me immediately at the penthouse on Wilshire. Vince didn't know the topic. And no, Roger couldn't wait. Now meant now.

I thought I'd passed the age when I'd drop everything because a man called. But I decided to make an exception. If Roger wanted to talk, I wanted to listen.

When I arrived, a large bald man wearing black pants, black shirt and the kind of earpiece that bouncers sport at bars opened the door of the penthouse. If I'd had to guess his previous profession, I'd go for football lineman or thug. His current role seemed to be a cross between butler and bodyguard.

"Your guest is here," he said.

"Pardon?" I asked.

He looked at me blankly and I realized he'd been talking into the wireless microphone attached to his earpiece, probably informing Roger of my presence. Technology had changed all our perceptions. If you saw someone walking down the street talking to himself, he could be crazy—or just have the latest Bluetooth connection.

"You Lacy?" he asked.

"Yes," I said, figuring that one had to be directed at me. "I'm here to see Roger."

"Raise your hands above your head."

I hesitated, but since Vince didn't seem the type to be fooling around, I tentatively bent my elbows, putting my hands at shoulder height.

"That ain't above your head," he said.

I pushed them up higher and he immediately clamped his own big, meaty hands just under my shoulders. I felt his hairy knuckles at the bare skin above the armhole of my sleeveless blouse, and I giggled.

"Something funny?" he growled.

"I'm ticklish. Particularly under arms. Sorry."

He twisted his mouth into a scowl and ran his hands down my side. When he got to my waist, I let out another yelp of laughter.

"Sorry," I said again. "You're tickling."

"I'm not tickling," he protested, trying to raise his status with me. "I'm patting you down and checking for weapons."

"Not really patting," I protested. "More like rubbing." Then, to distract myself as his hands continued down my legs, I continued, "Most women I know go to spas all the time for massages. Thai massage, rose-oil massage, full-body massage. But the way I see it, if somebody's touching me, he better be in love with me."

I'd barely finished the sentence before the thug/masseuse took his hands off me and leaped away. I snickered. Easiest way to get rid of a guy was to lament about love. The very word drove most men away faster than a Ferrari Spider.

"I guess you're clean. Not packing any weapons," he said.

"You should probably check my pocketbook," I suggested helpfully. "More likely I'd have something there."

He grabbed my bag and peered in. I thought of mentioning that the two-sided gold-tipped tube in the makeup case was an exact replica of the James Bond gadget that concealed a gun. This one hid matte lip color on one end and a touch-up gloss on the other. But he didn't seem interested. We'd had enough of each other.

"All clear," he said into his wireless. "Should I bring her back to you?"

Roger must have assented, because the bodyguard (as I'd now assumed he must be) lumbered ahead, leading me to the library.

Not much had changed in the room since the last time I saw it. I noticed the chipped edge on the Rothko frame and the ladder that Cassie had climbed. The floor had been refinished—a tone too deep—and all trace of stains removed. Two new leather chairs had been added to the decor, and Roger sat in one, in almost the exact spot where Cassie had lain dying.

"Hello, Roger," I said politely.

"Lacy Fields," Roger said, barely looking up. "Why have you been making inquiries about me and my late wife?"

I opened my mouth, then closed it again. I didn't owe Roger Crawford any explanations.

After a few seconds, the silence in the room felt awkward, and so Roger started talking again. "I'm very wealthy," he said, more as fact than boast. "People in all walks of life want to get on my good side. So of course I got calls about your little investigations."

Instead of asking who had called him, I ran through the possibilities in my head. Elsa Franklin, definitely. Andy Daniels, maybe. Billy Mann, no way.

Roger waited, but once again the dead air hung heavy. After

a few beats, Roger said, "I'm trying to figure out if you're looking for evidence against me," he said. "And if so, why?"

Not a bad interviewing technique I'd just learned. I could
get more information by keeping quiet than my usual babbling.

"Well, that's an interesting question," I said, finally. "I mean,
is there evidence against you to find?"

"Better people than you have looked," Roger said, an edge
in his voice. "I've been checked out by the SEC, the FBI, and
the Secret Service. All found me pure as snow."

"Why were they looking?"

Roger seemed to puff up in pride. He couldn't help bragging. "The SEC weighed in when I did a private equity deal
for a ten-billion-dollar public company. I had a standard FBI
background check after a major bank asked me to join the
board of directors. And the Secret Service weighed in before
my dinner at the White House."

He looked at me, waiting for a reaction.

"So how was dinner?" I asked. "Decent menu?"

"Small portions," he admitted.

"I guess nobody goes for the food."

"Or the company. I sat next to Justice Scalia of the Supreme
Court. Hard to say which is more insufferable—his politics or
his personality. At least he enjoyed the conversation. Gave me
his home number."

I laughed but also got the point. Roger hobnobbed in high
places. If I caused too much trouble for him, he'd call out his
buddies at the FBI, the SEC, the Secret Service and the United
States Supreme Court. Best-case scenario: I'd have my taxes au-
dited for years.

But really, what could anyone do to me? Roger Crawford's
threats didn't have to scare me. I obeyed laws, paid my taxes,
and didn't lie. Sure, I claimed the navy Akris suit as a business
expense on my last 1040, but I couldn't exactly wear T.J.Maxx
to meet wealthy clients, could I?

"Well, I'm glad you've been cleared by so many sources," I said. "Has anybody checked out your life with your wife?"

"None of your business," he said harshly.

"Of course it is. Cassie's dead and you're involved with Molly. It's pretty ridiculous that she's a suspect in your wife's murder, but she is. The bad publicity has already closed down Molly Archer Casting. I'm trying to help. She's my best friend."

"Pfft," Roger said, making a dismissive gesture. "I'm her best bet. I've told Molly not to worry about what happens to her company. I'll give her whatever she needs to get through."

"It's not only about money," I said.

"It's always about money," Roger replied.

I snorted. "Isn't it also about who killed Cassie?"

Roger nodded. "I want to find the real killer," he said, without a trace of emotion. I wondered if he had any idea how hollow his words sounded. Probably not. Roger had smarts, savvy, and sacks of money. But none of those necessarily added up to self-awareness.

"Look, maybe we can help each other," he said, softening. "We could share information."

"Fine."

He shifted in his chair, glanced down at his BlackBerry, and shot off a quick message. No reason his search for justice should interfere with any business deals.

"Tell me what you've found out so far," he said, putting the BlackBerry aside.

I tucked a stray hair behind my ear, then took a moment to disentangle it from my dangly earring—and to think. Roger wanted to know what I'd found out. He might be interested in my information from genuine concern. Or he could be trying to make sure that he'd covered his traces well.

"Go ahead," he urged.

Since I'd already decided that Elsa Franklin had spoken to

Roger, I could start there. Better to be straight and see where it led.

"I met with someone who used to be Cassie's boss," I said. "Name of Elsa Franklin." I sat down on a leather chair angled next to his and started filling him in on the details of our discussion.

As I talked, I watched Roger carefully. He seemed to relax just a bit—obviously relieved that my version of the conversation matched hers. It seemed unlikely that Elsa Franklin had mentioned Billy Mann, so I didn't either.

"Talk to anybody else?" Roger asked.

"Her other boss," I said. I gave him a quick summary of Andy Daniels and how Cassie had worked on a TV show called *World's Worst Ways to Die*.

"Thank you for your honesty," Roger said when I'd finished.

I had the feeling I'd passed some test, because he pulled an envelope out of his pocket.

"You're a good investigator. I'd like to hire you. Make this official."

He pushed the envelope across the desk.

"I'm sure you can find better investigators than me," I said, eyeing the envelope but not picking it up. "I'm an amateur."

"An amateur with good instincts and an eye for detail." He gestured around the room, taking in everything from the gold-serpent drawer-pulls on the desk to the eighteenth-century wall sconces I'd used as book lights around the library shelves. I'd bought the inlaid brass sconces at an all-comers flea market in Orange County, spotting their incredible quality despite layers of tarnish and mud. I'd bought them for twenty bucks each and had them polished and restored. An expert on Melrose Avenue appraised them for eleven thousand and begged to buy them from me. Old, rare, and museum quality, he said.

"Decorating's my job. Detecting is just sort of my hobby,"

I said now. But I had to admit that one skill had led me to the other. If I could search a flea market and find the unpolished gem, maybe I could march into an ordinary situation and find the unexpected killer.

"Open the envelope," Roger said.

I did. A bank check for ten thousand dollars had been clipped to ten crisp hundred-dollar bills marked "daily expenses." I stared at the pictures of Benjamin Franklin. How come he graced the big bucks and Honest Abe got stuck on a penny?

I closed the envelope again. I probably could be bought off—everybody's morality has a price. But mine happened to be many orders of magnitude more than this.

"Roger, I'm not taking your money," I said. "I can't work for you."

"Why not?"

Why not? I could think of at least three reasons. One: I didn't have a private investigator's license. Two: I'd gotten involved only to help Molly. And three, I couldn't be beholden to Roger Crawford. Not as long as I thought he might be the killer.

My face must have given me away—no World Series of Poker in my future—because Roger reached over and took the envelope back. But he hadn't become a billionaire by losing negotiations. He had his next bid ready.

"Here, then," he said, pulling a small box out of his pocket. "Take this. Not a payment. A sign of goodwill."

Not waiting for me to respond this time, he flipped open the velvet box. I looked inside and gasped. The bracelet coiled inside the jewelry case couldn't have been more perfect. Small diamonds in the shape of flowers, rimmed with gold.

Perfect—because I'd picked it out myself. The trinket glimmering in front of me happened to be the very one I'd joked about with Jack Rosenfeld that day at the jewelry store. The one I admired but hadn't even tried on.

"Who told you about this?" I asked softly.

Now Roger laughed, finally triumphant.

"You understand now, Lacy, right? You can't do anything without my knowing. You might as well take this. It'll just be a reminder."

He reached for my arm to slip the bracelet around my wrist, but I jerked away. The gorgeous diamond strand might as well have been metal handcuffs.

"Keep it," I said.

"Oooh, why, Lacy?" Roger asked, his voice a smarmy croon. He had dropped his professional veneer and seemed vaguely ominous now. "You know you want this. And I want you to have it."

"No." I felt a sudden fear coursing through me, as if taking the bracelet would bind me to evil and put Molly in even more danger.

"Last chance," he said.

"No. No, thank you," I repeated.

Roger's eyes turned cold and angry. He got up, opened the library door and motioned to his bodyguard, who stood outside. The thug took the bracelet and, in one swift move, yanked it in two. Gleaming bits of gold and diamonds scattered across the floor, and for good measure, Vince ripped it again. I gasped. I didn't care about the bracelet, but the violence of the act left me stunned.

Roger took a single diamond flower from his thug's meaty hand. He held it out to me on his palm.

"Don't make me take what's beautiful and destroy it," he said in that same sinister whisper. "Don't be so stupid."

I stood up straight and tried to get my shaking body under control. "You destroyed that all by yourself, Roger," I said. "You didn't need me. But what's the lesson I'm really supposed to take? That you don't mind obliterating something beautiful? Maybe even something as beautiful as Cassie?"

"Get out," Roger said.

Prepared to make sure his boss got his way, the thug grabbed my upper arm. But with unexpected strength, I shook him off.

"Don't ever touch me again," I said, striding toward the door on my own.

I yanked it open, and as I stepped out, I heard Roger and his bodyguard laughing, the snide, angry laughter of two nasty boys who didn't get their way.

Chapter Ten

——— • ———

I left Roger's place and came straight home, driving quickly down Wilshire Boulevard while I replayed the scene over and over in my head and pictured the broken gems gleaming on the wooden floor. Maybe I should have just taken the damn bracelet. Had I proven anything this way?

Well, sure. I'd found out that Roger had a dark side. Not getting his way elicited a swift and ugly response. I'd also discovered that he kept his own hands clean and let his hired bully do the actual dirty work. Nobody would ever find his fingerprints on a bottle of Kirin—but he might have written the check that bought it.

I pulled into the driveway and noticed Jimmy's skateboard upside down on the lawn and Grant's twenty-four-speed Trek mountain bike leaning against a tree. The kids were around, so it was time to clear my head and focus on them. My rule number one of being a mom: Work hard when you're working, but give 110 percent to family when you're home.

I'd barely made it halfway up the long flagstone walk when

Grant flung open the patio door and burst out, as eager as a race-horse bolting from the starting gate at the Kentucky Derby.

"Hey, Mom, look what I found for you," he said, rushing down the path and waving a piece of paper at me. He handed me the printout from a web page, showing a heart-shaped pendant necklace. Maybe it was karma. Turning down one expensive jewel just got me another.

"Pretty," I said. "What did I do to deserve it?"

"You're the kind of mom who should have a nine-hundred-thousand-dollar diamond," he said, grinning.

With it raining diamonds, maybe I should call Elizabeth Taylor. I handed the page back. "Is it real?"

"Certified twenty-carat yellow diamond. F grade for clarity, which sounds like failing but is apparently good. It's up for auction at Christie's in two weeks. I figure I'll buy it for your birthday."

"My birthday's not for months and you already promised me a gift certificate to Ben & Jerry's," I said. "Even the Chunky Monkey isn't as rich as this."

"And not as rich as Cassie Crawford," said Grant.

I looked from him to the picture. "It was hers," I said, making the connection. "She wore it the first time we met. I'd recognize it anywhere. There can't be two like that."

Grant nodded eagerly. "I figure you could use some help, Mom, so I have a computer program that alerts me every time Cassie Crawford's name gets mentioned online. That's how I found it."

"Where'd you get the program?"

"Jake and I wrote it," he said. "Don't worry, Mom. All legal."

Grant's best friend, Jake, the computer genius, had a blog, a personal website, and so many videos up on YouTube that he rivaled the Disney Channel. I sometimes worried about the kids creating tracks that would live forever online. But that was the new generation gap: Grown-ups fussed endlessly about identity theft and privacy; teenagers cheerfully invaded their own privacy and felt most alive when they lived online.

"Given all the news coverage on Cassie, you must be getting a lot of alerts," I said.

"Yeah, but I get through the junk pretty fast, and I never would have found this necklace otherwise. Cassie's name wasn't in the Christie's catalogue or anything, just in the fine print online that discloses provenance and stuff like that."

"Good for you," I said. Then, trying to figure it out, I added, "So Cassie put the necklace up for auction before she died?"

"Exactly what I wondered," said Grant. "So I called Christie's and asked about the whole history of the necklace—you know, blood diamond, conflict diamond, all that. Said I needed to know because I was interested in bidding."

I raised an eyebrow. "Very resourceful, but you shouldn't lie."

"I didn't lie. I would be interested in bidding if I had the money. True fact."

I tried to look stern but felt the corners of my mouth twitching. "Okay, so what happened?"

He shrugged. "It took a while, but they connected me to some expert appraiser who traced the diamond back to 1904 in Canada. Before he hung up, I said I wanted to ask a hypothetical question. If I ran a hedge fund and my fiancée had psychic powers, could I buy her this diamond?"

"A fiancée with psychic powers?" I shook my head. "I didn't even know you were dating."

"I said it was hypothetical," Grant said indignantly. "If he thought I meant me, well, that's his problem, right?"

I couldn't argue. Actually, I could, but why bother?

"So what did you learn?"

"He said I didn't have to worry about a blood diamond in the people-being-killed-in-South-Africa way, but there might be some bad vibes because the second-to-last owner had died. Cassie Crawford."

"Second-to-last?"

"Apparently Cassie had given it to some guy who contacted Christie's and put it up for sale. They verified the diamond's authenticity. No record of theft."

"Who was the guy?" I asked, not able to resist.

"Somebody named Billy Mann."

"Billy Mann?" I tried to keep my voice even, but as usual, my face gave me away.

"Wow, Mom, you know him, right? I can tell," Grant said, immediately reading my expression. Forget the World Series of Poker, I'd be out in the first round of gin rummy.

"I met him briefly," I said, deciding not to mention the ride on his motorbike and my little dip into the ocean.

"What do you think? Is he a suspect? I say Billy Mann stole the necklace and killed Cassie before she could report it."

I shrugged. "Maybe she gave it to him as a gift. They were friends."

"Some good friend. Jake's my friend—and he just gave me a used hard drive he found at the dump," Grant said.

"Maybe Cassie and Billy were more than friends," I amended, incapable of using the word *lover* in front of my son. But he immediately understood.

"Then it's easy," Grant said, already envisioning their romping. "Billy snagged the necklace after they had sex, and he killed Cassie before she could take it back."

"No way," I said, shaking my head. "Cassie must have gotten the necklace as a gift from Roger. So she would have been married by the time she had it. She wouldn't be having sex with Billy."

"Mom, haven't you ever heard of extramarital affairs?" Grant asked, with just a trace of condescension. "This is LA. Everyone does it."

Uh-oh. I didn't have a good answer for this one. I could get on my moral high horse and lecture Grant about love and honor. But my son was old enough to drive a car, go to R-rated movies, and join the Marines. He had surging testosterone and a subscription to *Maxim*. We could talk honestly.

"Let me just clarify that everyone doesn't do it," I said, hitting a middle ground. "If I'm having sex, it's with your dad."

Grant flushed. No kid wants to think about his parents in bed. Sunday school lessons about the Virgin Birth make perfect sense because we all figure it's how we got here, too.

"Fair enough, but all I'm saying is that it happens," Grant said, with more sophistication than he probably felt. "For all we know, Cassie and Billy Mann could have slept together the night before she died."

I sighed. I didn't want Grant involved, but at this point, I couldn't turn him away, either. He liked puzzles, and since he could solve a Rubik's cube in under three minutes and got bored with Sudoku, this was his next challenge.

"Billy lives on a fancy boat at Marina del Rey," I said, deciding to share some information. "It's too complicated to explain, but I think Cassie might have visited him there recently."

"Maybe a final fling," Grant said.

I nodded thoughtfully, envisioning the scene. Worried about losing Roger, Cassie came in her yellow gown and glorious jewels to end her affair with Billy. He took the news well but didn't like it. Somehow he got the diamond from her and then concocted a plan. Normally, you didn't kill the goose that laid the golden egg, but if it threatened to be the last egg you ever got, why not?

"I don't want to jump to conclusions," I said, thinking about the night the cops had come to the house. As I'd told them regarding orchids, don't pick a favorite until you've seen 'em all.

Grant nodded. "Well, Billy Mann must have some story

about how he got Cassie's twenty-carat rock. You could ask him." Then, suddenly concerned for my safety, he added, "Or maybe you should ask the police to ask him."

I took back the printout of the necklace, folded the page, and tucked it in my bag. "The police have enough on their hands," I said.

"Be careful, Mom. You have to admit that a million-dollar diamond is a pretty good motive for murder."

Dawn Rose, Andy Daniels's assistant at Genius Productions, called to say Andy needed to talk to me. Could we meet the next morning?

"How late will he be?" I asked, remembering our last meeting.

"Right on time," she promised. "He has something to share."

"Sharing" used to be reserved for kindergarten classes and AA meetings, but now it meant anything and everything. I didn't know if Andy wanted to share his deepest thoughts or a deep-dish pizza.

"Should I come to your office?"

"No, a different place. I'll e-mail you directions."

The next morning, I drove across the Santa Monica Mountains, then followed the directions I'd printed out. After about thirty minutes, the houses got sparser and sparser and gave way to horse farms and open rolling lands. This wasn't the parched, ragged countryside I remembered from growing up in rural Ohio. Irrigation sprinklers spread a gentle rain, and the grazing fields that extended as far as the eye could see appeared as perfect as the gardener-tended lawns of Beverly Hills. There was more green here than in a studio executive's wallet.

Though I hadn't traveled all that far from LA, my Lexus seemed to be one of the few cars on the road. I felt a moment of trepidation. Should I be venturing into unknown territory to encounter someone I'd met because of a murder? A silver-haired man driving a vintage Bentley passed me in the opposite direction, and I felt a little better. Oh, for heaven's sakes, Andy Daniels wasn't exactly a suspect. Just because he once knew Cassie didn't mean he'd poisoned her.

I turned up a long winding driveway lined with palm trees. The asphalt quickly gave way to gravel, then to a short dirt path surrounded by more of the tall, leafy plants. Funny how palms, a tree indigenous to the tropics, had become a symbol of Hollywood.

I pulled into a clearing, got out of the car, and walked slowly toward the low-slung white building in front of me. A rehab center? Spa? Buddhist retreat? I couldn't tell.

This time, I didn't have to wait for Andy. As soon as I walked in the door, he strolled toward me, wearing a white terry bathrobe and sandals. His curly hair jumped out from his head, wild and uncontrolled, but otherwise he looked calmer than last time. Somehow, he'd contained the hyperactive energy in his small, slim frame.

"You were my inspiration," he said when he saw me. "So you have to hear about my new show."

"Oh," I said, taken aback. Like last time, he hadn't bothered with "hello." But I'd come all this way to talk television?

"Right after you came to my office, I had a breakthrough. You wanted to talk about Cassie, so it suddenly hit me. How could I have missed it? *Doo-do DOO-do, Doo-do DOO-doo . . .*" He let his voice rise and fall in the singsong theme of *The Twilight Zone.*

"Weird, right?" he continued. "Cassie works on *World's Worst Ways to Die,* and then she dies. She's an assistant on *How to Bed a Billionaire* and she marries a billionaire. Something's going on. Must be energy fields."

"Or coincidence," I suggested.

"No such thing," Andy said. "Come on outside."

I followed him through the room—empty except for a sky-light and highly polished wood floors—to a back door.

Outside, we walked along a dirt hiking trail, then passed through a locked fence that opened when Andy punched in a digital code. On the other side, the scenery changed, the dirt path taking on a reddish glow and the vegetation becoming low scrub and cactus. We went up an incline, steep enough that I started breathing heavily, which then flattened out to a large, smooth surface, probably fifty feet in diameter.

Andy walked to the center and turned to face a free-form red-rock sculpture that towered over us. He lifted his chin so the sun shone down on his face, closed his eyes, and spread his arms to the side. I thought I heard a gentle humming from him.

Something about the area seemed familiar, but I couldn't place it.

"Where are we?" I asked Andy, not concerned about inter-rupting his meditation.

He dropped his pose and came back to me. "The Vortex," he said. "Can you feel the energy?"

"What energy?"

"From the Spirit Woman." He waved in the direction of the rock, and I remembered a trip Dan and I had taken a few years ago to the red-rock country of Sedona. While enjoying the brilliant scenery, we heard about the New Age locals who scoped out areas—the "vortex sites"—where special magnetic fields could provide spiritual energy. In search of one, we hiked to a popular area dominated by a rock dubbed Kachina Woman. About a dozen people stood in front of the spirit, meditating in that same head-tilted, arms-outstretched pose Andy had just assumed. I'd tried it and started giggling so uncontrollably that Dan grabbed my hand and pulled me behind the rock. Out of sight of the spiritualists, Dan put his arms around me and kissed me. "I'll show you what will really please Spirit Woman," he'd said, as we lay down on the red rocks.

"The only time I heard about a vortex was at a place just like this in Sedona," I said now to Andy.

"Exactly! I used to fly there on weekends when I needed inspiration. But my wife got tired of all the trips, so I had our own vortex built here."

I looked around, stunned. "You built this?" I asked.

"Not just me," he said modestly. "A few of us got together. Mostly other TV execs. Once I explained that all my show ideas came from the energy of the vortex, they wanted in."

"So this is . . ." I waved my hands, taking in the hiking trails, the red rocks, the towering sculpture.

"A spot to stimulate the brainwaves," Andy said, finishing my sentence.

The place must have cost a small fortune to build. But given the odds against having a success on TV, looking for encouragement from a fake rock didn't seem that strange. Every TV season brought thousands of pitches, hundreds of pilots, and maybe one or two that scored big. What other business gave you a bonus for a .010 batting average? Given the money that spewed from a hit, I could see why anxious execs would try anything. A few seasons of *Cheers* and you could have all the Kachina women you wanted. Produce another *Seinfeld* and you should sacrifice Prada-and-pearls to the statues every night.

"It's lovely here," I said looking around. "But if I remember from Sedona, you have a vortex at a spot where the earth's energy is increased."

"Right. Everything we created here increases the earth's energy." He spun around, as if being pulled by that very energy. Who was I to say it couldn't be transported? Some of the souvenir shops in Sedona sold containers labeled VORTEX IN A CAN.

Now Andy walked to the other side of the clearing and

motioned to me to join him. I noticed that six glass tea cups, each half-filled, had been lined up on a rock.

"I'll give you a demonstration of the new show I created with the help of the energy fields," Andy said. He picked up one of the cups and held it out to me. "To start, drink up. Chamomile tea with Ginkgo biloba. Very good for you."

I took a sip. The liquid was warm from the sun, slightly sweet and very pleasant. I drank a little more.

"Imagine you're a contestant on a game show," he said. "The more you drink, the more money you win. Drain five glasses, and it's a million bucks. But here's the rub. One of the cups is poisoned."

My mouth had started burning. I dropped the cup and watched it smash against the rock.

Andy grinned. "Arsenic. Cyanide. Diethylene glycol. All sorts of possibilities. I finally figured out the problem with most game shows. You don't really have anything to lose."

He reached down for another cup and handed it to me. I stepped back.

"You didn't really poison one of them," I said, with more certainty than I felt.

"Why not? Russian roulette is the greatest game of all time, and it's never been on TV. We'd have an antidote ready for contestants who cooperated." He looked at me steadily. "Get it?"

"What do you want me to do?" I asked in a scratchy voice. My tongue seemed to be swelling in my mouth and my throat felt ripped raw. Was it poison or sheer terror?

"How are you feeling?" he asked, looking at me carefully.

"Not good," I admitted. My whole head burned, and I put a hand up to my throat. No, it wasn't psychosomatic. Something other than sugar had been in that cup. If only I'd read the tea leaves.

"Wouldn't that be something if I accidentally gave you the

bad cup," he said, tightening the belt on his terry robe. "What are the odds? Just one in six, but you never know."

"Odds are one hundred percent," I said. "You filled the cups and put them out."

"Well, as I said, an antidote." He took a vial out of his pocket and held it in his hand.

I sat down, barely noticing as the red earth imported from Arizona stained my Tracy Burch white pants. Right now, I didn't care about clothes, Cassie, or Kachina. I just wanted to keep from fainting. I put my head between my knees.

"Tell me what you want from me," I said, feeling beads of perspiration popping out on my forehead.

Andy sat down next to me and folded his legs under him. He put a hand on my shoulder. "Don't worry, you're going to be fine. I just needed to get your attention. It's like the start of a show. Grab 'em and you've got 'em."

"Okay, you've got me."

"So here's what I want you to understand," he said, tossing the vial from one hand to the other. "You came to my office and asked a lot of questions about Cassie. But she worked for me years ago. She left years ago. And what happened then has nothing to do with . . . anything."

It suddenly came back to me how uncomfortable Andy had been at the very end of our conversation last time, when I asked why Cassie had left Genius Productions—just got up and left her perfect job. I hadn't thought to investigate any further, but he didn't know that.

"The whole scandal about Cassie leaving your company got nicely covered up," I said, taking a stab. How far off could I be? In LA, scandals ranged from a drug-driven orgy in the private room of a celebrity club to losing so much weight that the size 0 Versace didn't fit.

Andy flushed. "Maybe it would have been a scandal if we worked at Goldman Sachs, but this is television. The entertainment business. Late nights, close contact, a lot of adrenaline. Sex happens."

"You and Cassie," I said, catching on and trying to picture the two of them.

"I'm in love with my wife!" Andy said, springing up from his seated position to a crouch. He rocked back and forth on the balls of his feet. "Really. I swear. Nobody loves his wife more than me."

"So I've heard," I said.

Andy plopped down again and stared at me with his big blue eyes. "Everybody's entitled to one stupid mistake, but I don't want it coming out during a murder investigation."

"Your wife doesn't know?"

"Of course not. It had nothing to do with her."

"But you slept with Cassie." Was Grant right that everyone in LA behaved badly?

"More like we fell into bed together very late one night when we were out on a shoot. The next day we both regretted it."

"You regretted it because you felt guilty. What about Cassie?"

"Come to think of it, maybe she didn't regret it. I'm pretty good in the sack."

More than I wanted to know. "Anyway, you fired her."

"Never. I wouldn't have done that. Cassie decided she didn't want to put me in a bad position. She quit at the end of the week." Andy looked at me, concerned. "How you feeling now?"

"Lousy." I licked my bottom lip and felt blisters forming on my tongue. Is that what happened just before you died?

Andy stood up. "Everybody had forgotten about my dumb fling. But then you came to my office asking about Cassie and why she left." He shook his head and rubbed his sandal into the red sand. "After you left, I talked to one of the honchos at the network to get some advice. My shows make them so damned much money, he didn't want any scandal."

"So he told you to poison me?"

"He told me to do whatever it takes to make sure the story doesn't come out."

I wiped the back of my hand across my damp forehead.

"Only reason I'll spill your story is if I find some other connection between you and Cassie," I said. "Otherwise, your secret's safe. I'm glad you've got a guilty conscience, but that's between you and Spirit Woman."

"Thanks," Andy said, with the first hint of humility I'd ever heard in him. "So we have a deal?"

"Deal. Now can I have your poison antidote?"

Andy tossed me the vial he'd been playing with. "You'll be fine," he said. "The stuff in the tea just causes temporary symptoms. Same chemical that's in hot peppers. Capsaicin. I know it feels lousy, but there's no permanent harm."

"Then what's this?" I asked holding up the blue liquid that I'd thought would save my life.

"Listerine Cool Mint. In case my story left a bad taste in your mouth."

I got unsteadily to my feet and moved a few steps forward so we were eye to eye. "You seem to know an awful lot about poisons," I said. "Hobby of yours?"

"Just research for my shows," he said. "America likes to be revolted."

"Put that revolting Russian roulette show on the air and our deal's off," I said.

"It'd probably get a nineteen share."

"Go for that nineteen share and I tell everybody what I know about you and Cassie."

Andy shrugged. "Fine." He turned to the sculpted rock and steepled his hands in front of his face, as if in prayer. "I can always find another concept."

Chapter Eleven

— • —

By the time I got back to my car, I'd already started to feel better. I called Dan just to be safe and gave him a brief synopsis of what had happened.

"You'd better come by my office," he said gruffly. "Get here as soon as you can."

When I arrived, the nurse immediately whisked me out of the busy waiting area and into an examining room. Dan bustled in a moment later, his white coat crisp and spotless and a stethoscope tossed casually around his neck. His sandy-blond hair framed his elegantly patrician features, and his broad shoulders set off a body that had stayed lean and muscular from jogging and mountain climbing. After all these years, I still felt lucky every time I saw him.

"At least you're not looking sick," he said, which was not quite as complimentary as I might have hoped.

"The worst of it passed quickly," I said.

"Tell me the whole story."

I did, recounting the strange conversation with Andy as

well as I could. When I finished my narrative, Dan nodded, his impassive expression giving nothing away.

"Let's check you out," he said without any emotion.

I hopped on the paper-covered table, and Dan busied himself examining my mouth and throat, listening to my heart, and then feeling the glands at my neck. His strong, competent fingers prodded the skin just above my open collar.

"Mmm, I like when you touch me there," I said. "Your fingers feel good."

I might have been one of the seductive patients doctors learn to handle in medical school. He ignored my enticements and finished the exam.

"Your symptoms are consistent with capsaicin ingestion," he said in a professional tone. "Unless something further develops, I think we can assume you're in the clear."

"Nothing I need to do?"

"No. A glass of milk might neutralize some of the acid. If the tongue is burning, lick on an ice cube."

"How about a mango frozen yogurt at Pinkberry?" I asked, only half joking. I'd brave the crowds at the West Hollywood store only on doctor's orders. No matter how many branches of the dessert palace opened around LA, the lines kept getting longer. You'd think half of LA had been starving pre-Pinkberry. And given the number of women subsisting on spinach salads and Diet Coke, they probably were.

"Whatever soothes is fine," Dan said, not sounding very soothing himself. "As I said, you haven't sustained any permanent damage."

"Thank you, darling," I said. Then, sidling closer, I whispered, "Do you think a more complete exam would be a good idea? I can undress."

"No," he said, his voice as chilly as a dish of Pinkberry shaved ice. "I've seen what I have to."

I sat back on the exam table, mildly stung. "You seem angry."

"Not angry."

"What have I done wrong? Talk to me."

"Lacy, I have a busy schedule of patients. We can talk to-night. Short version is that I'm not thrilled when someone poisons my wife. I can't understand why you put yourself in these situations."

"To solve a murder," I said. "To protect Molly. You've got to admit I got some interesting information."

"Not as interesting as you seem to think," Dan said, irrita-tion in his voice. "A major TV exec hauls you out to a pseudo-desert and goes to elaborate lengths to scare you. And you believe all he wants to hide is that he had sex once with a dead woman?"

"You obviously don't believe it."

"A one-night fling is about as newsmaking as brushing your teeth. Tell me someone in this town who hasn't had one."

"Me," I said quietly. "And I'd hope you." I looked away, suddenly afraid to catch his eye.

The silence filled the room. I waited for Dan to come over, put his arms around me and say, "Of course I've never been with anyone else, sweetheart. Why would I want anybody other than you?" But Nora Ephron hadn't written him a script. And he'd never seen *Sleepless in Seattle*.

"All I'm saying is watch your back," Dan growled, an en-dearment that never would have made it to the first cut of *When Harry Met Sally*. "Trouble comes when you least expect it."

"I just discovered that," I said. And I picked up my pocket-book to leave.

Back in the car, I hardly noticed the burning in my throat be-cause a new pain had replaced it. Maybe Dan considered a fling just a fact of life, but I considered it a big problem. The solid foundation for our marriage seemed to be slipping away like a Malibu house in a mudslide.

Was Dan having an affair? Grimly, I gripped the wheel and hunched forward, visions of pretty nurses, grateful patients, and horny Hollywood housewives dancing in my head. I thought of my last conversation with Grant and wondered if he had picked up something about his dad. Maybe my detecting skills would be better used at home.

Suddenly a car coming toward me across an intersection blared its horn and swerved, missing me by inches. I slammed my brakes.

"Asshole!" the driver screamed. "You're supposed to stop at a frigging stop sign!"

Shaken, I waved my hand in apology and continued through the intersection, but then I pulled to the side of the road and touched my sweaty forehead to the cool steering wheel. Did I need a burning bush to make this any clearer? I prided myself on my perceptions, but I'd obviously been missing key sign-posts—on the road, with my husband, and possibly with the people I'd been investigating.

I grabbed my cell phone to call Molly for advice but got her voice mail. She'd probably tell me not to be so naïve. Boys would be boys, and as long as Dan came home every night, what more could I want?

Actually, a lot more.

Dan and I had our tiffs, but outside of a Hallmark Channel movie, marriage didn't get much better. We laughed together and still had fun. Sure, Dr. Dan could be unemotional, but his skill awed me. Wielding a scalpel in the operating room, he'd cut into a face without flinching, and he had to stay detached when confronted with deadly disease or disfigured patients. If that cool competence in the hospital sometimes felt like a deep freeze at home, I understood. The flip side of what you admired about someone also became what most annoyed you.

I eased the car back into drive and cautiously pulled away from the shoulder. Tonight, I'd ask Dan straight out what he'd

meant by dismissing one-night flings. If he said I'd misinterpreted, I'd demand that he tell me the truth about who and
when and . . .

Oh, heck—no, I wouldn't. Whether in murder or marriage, once you point an accusing finger, everything changes. I
wouldn't turn into Detective Wilson and risk the trust Dan and
I had built over all these years. I'd just pay more attention.

At the next light, I moved to the left lane and made a U-
turn. I needed something to distract me. I'd e-mailed Billy
Mann yesterday to ask if we could talk, and he'd sent a cheerful
message back that he'd be on the boat. Stop by any time. Well,
I'd do just that. Billy had been very close to Cassie. The necklace, the yellow dress—a lot of clues pointed his way. Maybe he
knew more about the murder than even he realized.

I traveled down Santa Monica Boulevard, got onto the 405
freeway, and zipped along at the speed limit for about five miles.
Then traffic came to a dead halt. I flipped on the radio to hear
the traffic report, which, sure enough, announced big back-ups
on the 405 South. Why listen just to find out what I already
knew? I turned to another station, featuring Dr. Phil. Since he
also seemed to be spouting the obvious, I moved on to a rap
station. Much more likely that Jay-Z had something new to say
than Dr. Phil.

For the next twenty minutes, I crawled along, barely moving a mile. Inexplicably, the traffic broke and I raced along—
then it stopped again. More frustration. Almost an hour later, I
pulled up to Marina del Rey. Out of the car at last, I stretched
my legs, went to the yacht owners' entrance, and tried to remember where to find Billy's boat. I wandered along the pier
until I recognized the yacht *Lucky Duck*. A portly older man
in madras shorts and an LA Lakers cap looked up from hosing
down the deck and waved at me. Billy's boat had to be nearby.
I sauntered down the pier, the sun warm on my face. Instead
of enjoying it, I immediately worried because I didn't have

on sunscreen. Most women I knew would rather run naked through the Staples Center than venture outdoors without a layer of micronized titanium dioxide to protect against wrinkles. My dermatologist had given me one that also contained licorice extract, chamomile, green tea, and Vitamins A, C, and E. If it didn't work on my face, I could always have it for lunch.

I found the *DreamRide* bobbing gently in its mooring and called out Billy's name. His jacket had been flung across the deck, but he didn't reply.

"Billy?" I called again.

I stepped tentatively onto the boat, the kitten heel of my Miu Miu mules sliding on the smooth surface. I kicked them off and walked across the small deck, then took the two steps that led down to the galley kitchen, the tiny bathroom, and a closed door.

"Billy? It's Lacy." I knocked on the door, then pushed against it.

A couple of beer cans and a half-empty bottle of Glenlivet rolled across the floor as I came in, and something wet seeped against my toes. Disgusting: spilled beer. Light crept in only through the edges of two small portholes, each covered by a white pull-down blind. Once my eyes adjusted to the dimness, I could make out Billy sprawled facedown on the bed. He had on a pair of jeans but no shirt, and a snake tattoo coiled its way up his bare spine. I sniffed. After a night of too much drinking, he was sleeping it off, dead to the world. I'd come back another time.

I left the dark room, stepped back through the galley kitchen, and started toward the brighter deck. As I looked down, my Revlon Perfectly Plum pedicure glinted in the sunlight. But oddly, the color seemed to have run. My toes, sticky from what I had thought to be beer, were now . . .

Bloodred.

I stopped in horror. The mess I'd stepped through in the

cabin hadn't come from a Michelob can. For a moment I stood frozen, one foot on the stair, deciding what to do. Leaving sounded good. But maybe Billy needed help. With gritted teeth, I went back to his room, grimacing as I stepped carefully across the sticky floor.

"Billy, are you all right?" I asked, knowing he wasn't. I yanked open the one drawer across from the bed and rifled through, quickly finding a small flashlight. I beamed the ray on Billy and saw what I'd missed before. At the very top of the tattoo, the snake's head was gone, pulverized by a bullet that had left a clean hole in the skin—and probably gone through to Billy's heart. Blood had seeped down through the blankets. I touched Billy's cheek. He wasn't just dead to the world—he was cold dead.

Panic seized me. Could the killer still be on board? I flashed the light around the room, but no intruder lurked in the corners. He'd probably escaped long ago, but I couldn't be sure. I glanced back at Billy and briefly considered the CPR I'd used on Cassie. But Billy had moved well beyond chest-pounding help. I knew I should leave, but curiosity got the better of me, and I made another sweep with the light. The room didn't seem any more disordered than when I'd been here the first night, changing into that yellow Nina Ricci gown. This time, no couturier dresses or even Juicy Couture Ts tumbled out. Shining the light into the top drawer again, I saw a jumble of tissues, hand cream, condom packets, and Vaseline. A purple hair scrunchy and a plastic bangle bracelet suggested a woman or two had been here—but neither remnant hinted at classy Cassie.

A banging noise intruded from somewhere and I knew I had to get out. I slipped along as quietly as I could, getting up to the main deck, then stepping onto the pier. Rushing along the slippery boards, I skidded to a stop when the man in the madras shorts climbed off *Lucky Duck* and blocked my path.

"Everything okay?" he asked.

I nodded dumbly, fumbling for my cell phone and deciding what I wanted to say to the police.

"I've noticed you here a couple of nights with Billy," he said, a little too jovially. "Hard to ignore you in that beautiful yellow dress. And I never forget a pretty woman."

There it was—proof that eyewitness identification couldn't be trusted. But instead of debating, I asked, "Are you and Billy friends?"

"We see each other on the dock. Sailing fraternity brothers, you might say. In fact, he borrowed my bailer. Seeing you before reminded me I need it back."

"I wouldn't try to get it now," I said softly.

"Isn't he on the boat?"

On the boat but dead. Not in condition to return your bailer. The obvious answer wouldn't come out of my mouth.

"He's a nice fella," the man continued. "Has that whole hippy-dippy look, but a good heart. Takes care of that disabled brother of his. Not everyone would do that."

Not the time for me to discuss Billy's finer qualities.

"I have to make a call. Excuse me," I said, making my way around his large frame.

As soon as I'd gone past him, I broke into a run, thinking how many times I'd told Jimmy to slow down on a slippery deck. But I kept upright until I got to a main area and found a shower—not unexpected at a boat basin—and let hot water pour down over my feet. I watched as the now-rust-colored refuse swished down the drain, removing any traces of where I'd been.

I had to call the police, but I didn't want to hang around. Sure, I knew you couldn't leave the scene of an accident. But a shooting where I'd found the body long after the fact and couldn't give any information anyway seemed different. I glanced at my watch and imagined the endless hours the cops could keep me at the station. I wanted to be a good citizen, but not at Ashley's expense. She'd been talking all week about going to Roger's party tonight. I had to get home to take her. No way I'd let her down.

Shaking, I looked around for a pay phone, but I might as well have been tracking the last living dodo bird. I went back to the car and dialed 911, hoping Los Angeles hadn't become efficient enough to track all emergency calls.

As soon as an operator answered, I started talking.

"The police need to get to Marina del Rey. There was a crime on a boat called the *DreamRide*. A man may be dead."

"Stay calm, ma'am. May I have your name."

I ignored the question and instead gave the boat location as best I could. "He'd already been shot when I found him," I said, disconnecting quickly.

I knew 911 calls got taped. So it's not that I disguised my voice. It's just that my great-great grandfather's Irish brogue took that moment to assert its DNA.

The moment I got back to Pacific Palisades, I went online and checked out half a dozen local news sites and blogs. But not one had a report of a dead man on a boat. Maybe Billy's body hadn't been found yet. More likely, another murder in Los Angeles—if the victim wasn't a billionaire's wife—didn't count as big news. More interesting to discuss Paris Hilton's flashing a bare breast at Bar Deux last night at 4 A.M.

I heard Ashley in her room and took a deep breath. I had to put Billy's murder aside for the night. No sense ruining the time with my daughter. As a mom, I'd long ago taught myself to compartmentalize. When you have too much to do and too many people who need you, you have to focus, focus, focus. Don't fret about the kids when you're at work or work when you're with the kids. Concentrate on where you are and who you're with.

Okay, I wouldn't think about Billy, dead, lying on his bloody bed. I wouldn't think about who might have killed him. In other words, I wouldn't think about the pink elephant in the room.

"Mom, you're not dressed yet!" said Ashley, strutting into my study.

"But you are," I said, looking up at my stunning daughter.

I smiled to myself. Looking at Ashley, I could probably forget Billy for a while after all. She'd pulled her long hair into a chic chignon as sophisticated as the Pucci sundress that outlined her increasingly grown-up body. Her long, tanned legs teetered on cork wedge-heeled sandals—so in style they'd be out of style in a week. But then, like the Pucci design, they'd probably make a fashion comeback in another four decades.

"You look amazing," I said, raising an eyebrow. "Sorry I lost track of time."

"Moooom, I don't want to be late," she wailed. "How could you get distracted? What were you doing today, anyway?"

What was I doing? Let's see. I'd been poisoned by a wacky TV producer, stumbled onto a dead body, and worried about my husband's fidelity. But I should have been ready for the party. I hated to think I'd hit the age where my cranial neurons started overloading. Though given today's input, the whole system had probably short-circuited. Smoke might be coming out of my ears.

"I'll be ready in a jiff, sweetie," I said, heading to my room.

Given how my daughter looked, nobody would notice me tonight anyway. I settled for Chloe ballet flats, a pink-and-white silk camisole, and a full white skirt. To my great relief, Ashley looked at me approvingly when I came out.

"Ooh, Mom, is that a petticoat?" she asked lifting the soft layer of cotton and touching the tulle underneath. "That's so right now!"

Right now? Was *Petticoat Junction* lost to the annals of bad TV? Come to think of it, women had spent centuries trying to shake off the burdens of corsets and petticoats. Now that we'd been liberated, we could finally enjoy wearing them.

We drove out to Malibu, and when we pulled up, a twentysomething woman in a plaid mini-dress and flat shoes rushed up to the car. Valet parking at private parties was de rigueur, but the name tag stuck to her chest said HI, I'M PENNY. YOU'RE LADY VALET!

I hesitated, unsure whether to trust my car to someone who spelled *your* wrong. Misinterpreting my qualms, she said, "Don't worry that I'm a woman valet. I've had practice with a Porsche and I'm a fiend behind a Ferrari."

"It's a Lexus," I said, getting out.

"I'd rather strip off my clothes than strip your gears!" she added brightly, a line that probably prompted extravagant tips from overstimulated businessmen.

I handed her the keys and Ashley and I headed to the beach, down a path lit by hundreds of twinkling overhead lights.

"Check out the Big Dipper," I said, pointing up. "And Orion's belt." We couldn't see stars in the real sky, but the artificial lights had been arranged to look like constellations.

Ashley craned her neck and her eyes sparkled. "Too much!" she said excitedly.

But *too much* never entered Roger's lexicon. At the end of the path, black-clad waiters stood lined up with magnum-size bottles of Dom Perignon. Ashley and I passed by them, but then stopped for another group of waiters who offered miniature bowls of Osetra caviar with mother-of-pearl spoons.

"Yuck," Ashley said, taking a taste and wrinkling her nose in disgust. "Why do people eat this?"

"An acquired taste."

"How's it acquired?"

"By having lots of money and wanting everybody to know it."

On the beach, hundreds of palm trees and flowering freesia transformed Roger's enormous stretch of waterfront into a tropical paradise. Small tables covered in silk voile and set with gilded china glimmered under towering candelabras. The star wattage circulating on the beach clearly outshone the Big Dipper.

"That's Nicole Kidman!" Ashley whispered. "And she's talking to Naomi Watts from *King Kong.*"

"Both Aussies. Very friendly," I said, as if we'd all gone hunting koala bears together.

Ashley nodded, her big eyes wide from excitement. At her age, she didn't need liner, mascara, shadow, and contouring cream to look naturally wide-eyed.

"Let's get something else to eat," I suggested. Noticing a man munching on a maki roll, I said, "There must be sushi."

A tight crowd of people had gathered nearby, hovering over what I assumed to be a buffet table. Most held polished ivory chopsticks, so I propelled Ashley in their direction. Strange that sushi should be so popular. Unless the fish were still flopping, it couldn't be too different from prepackaged pieces I bought at Gelson's.

The man in front of me stepped back, holding a piece of tuna roll in his chopsticks. One piece? Didn't Roger believe in providing plates?

A moment later, I realized plates weren't the only problem. Instead of being on a platter, the sushi had been carefully arranged on a long . . .

"No way!" Ashley yelped, suddenly glimpsing what had attracted everyone's attention.

A naked, well-tanned blonde lay perfectly still on top of a glass table, her arms stretched above her head. Pieces of raw fish and sushi rolls had been artfully arranged across her body, and only strategically placed flowers and banana leaves kept the scene from being X-rated. The model kept a serene smile on her face as guests plucked their hors d'oeuvres from her flat-as-a-serving-plate belly.

"This is the grossest thing I've ever seen," Ashley said, dropping her chopsticks. "I'm not hungry."

But most of the guests' appetites—of whatever sort—seemed to be stimulated. A throng wolfed down the sushi, ready to reveal what lay beneath.

"Is called *nyotaimori*," explained an impeccably dressed Japanese man standing by the model's feet. "In America, you say *body sushi*."

"Actually, in America we say 'Put some clothes on,'" I whispered to Ashley.

She giggled. "Good thing the model's not ticklish. If someone touched a chopstick to my tummy, I'd roll over laughing."

"And what about allergies?" I asked. "One sneezing bout and it's Big Macs for everyone."

"Gives new meaning to calling a woman a dish," Ashley said.

We both laughed loudly this time, and a woman nearby looked at us disapprovingly. "I believe this is an ancient Japanese tradition, like geishas, that deserves respect," she said, with just a trace of condescension.

"Really? An ancient tradition?" I looked at the Japanese man for confirmation.

"I think it's from the 1980s," he said. "Popular in men's clubs when the Nikkei boomed and everyone got rich."

"Come on, let's find something else to eat," I said, putting a hand on Ashley's elbow and steering her away. "At least caviar only exploits the fish."

We moved away from the crowd and I spotted Molly, standing alone and looking anxiously over at Roger. She waved and made her way over to us.

"Didn't I tell you it would be a fabulous party?" she asked, with more enthusiasm than she clearly felt. "You both look spectacular."

She took Ashley's hands and spun her around.

"You're the most beautiful one at the party," she said.

"Not the most beautiful, but maybe the youngest," Ashley said.

"In this town they're practically the same," Molly said, with just a trace of resentment in her voice. I followed her gaze back to Roger, currently standing with two young women who looked like they'd stepped out of the Disney Channel. Maybe Roger was holding auditions for the new Mickey Mouse Club.

"My god, that's Spider-Man!" Ashley said, her excited voice a little too loud.

I redirected my attention as Tobey Maguire gave her a small smile and continued strolling by, holding hands with his wife.

"Maybe having all the stars see you here tonight will get your business back on track," I whispered to Molly.

"Not happening," she said.

"Why not?"

"Roger's financing movies, so everyone has to be nice to him. But they show how moral they are by shunning me."

"That doesn't make any sense," I complained.

"Think of it as taking a private jet to Aspen and then renting a Prius. I'm the carbon offset."

"Well, I'm more worried about your neck than your business. You're smart not to seem connected in public."

"Smart?" Molly asked. "He's ignored me all night. If I killed Cassie to snag Roger, I'd be one pissed-off murderer about now."

I noticed a flurry of activity at one edge of the palm trees. Three huge bodyguards in black suits—including Vince, the thug I'd already met—circled quickly over to the area. I suddenly realized that the trucked-in border of trees effectively cut off our part of the seaside from any random beach walkers. Probably illegal—the beach remained public property—but what beachcomber would dare confront Roger's thugs? Confronting one of them the other day had been intimidating enough for me. Three of the steroid-packed brutes could empty the beach down to the Baja border. But oddly, all three now stepped aside, and one of them made a sweeping gesture of welcome as two people swaggered through the foliage. Something about their movements—and the thugs' deference—suggested one thing.

Cops.

Did they finally have evidence to arrest Roger? How perfect to do it here, at his own party. But they ambled past him. *Oh, no. Don't let them be coming for Molly.* I put my arm around Ashley and then I blinked a couple of times as the duo strolled in our direction.

Not just any cops. Detective Brian Wilson and Erica Mc-Sweeney.

A moment later, they stood in front of me, and Detective Wilson held out a plastic bag.

"Your shoes," he said. "You left them behind."

He unzipped the top of the evidence bag, and I suddenly remembered that I'd kicked off my gold-dotted Miu Miu mules when I got on Billy's boat to keep from slipping. Afterward, I'd fled barefoot. Back in my car, I'd reflexively slipped on the Tod's driving shoes I kept under the seat and hadn't thought about the missing mules again.

Now I tried to keep my expression blank as Detective Wilson held open the bag and displayed the gold-dotted shoes. Since they were evidence, he didn't touch them.

"We retrieved them from the crime scene where William Mann was found a few hours ago," he said, closing the bag again.

"What makes you think they're mine?" I asked.

"You wore them when we came to your house," Mc-Sweeney said. "I recognized them."

I must be the only woman in Los Angeles who could get arrested for wearing the same pair of shoes twice.

"I noticed them because they're so unusual," she continued. "But I figured they'd be too expensive for me."

"Forty percent off at Neiman's," I confided. "Miu Miu is Prada's lower-priced line. You won't see rip-off copies at Nine West the next week like you do with regular Pradas."

"Good to know," said McSweeney. "Shoes make the outfit, as everyone says."

"Are you both finished with the shopping tips?" Detective Wilson snapped.

"Sorry," McSweeney said.

Wilson tucked the bag under his arm, and puffing out his chest, swaggered closer to me. Sticking his face next to mine, he growled, "So, Mrs. Fields, from the discussion with my partner, I assume you can identify these shoes as yours?"

If Erica McSweeney had asked, I might have just said yes. But Wilson's blustering put me on edge—and made me cautious.

"No way to know, is there, Detective? A lot of women must have bought the same mules. Saks carried them. Probably Barneys."

"Size seven and a half," he reported. "Want to try them on?"

"I'm not Cinderella." And he'd never be Prince Charming.

"Good thing, because I don't believe in fairy tales. Just facts. And here's one. You were on William Mann's boat shortly before his death," Detective Wilson said, drawing his own conclusion.

"Wrong," I said. "Absolutely wrong. Even the Brothers Grimm wouldn't get away with that."

"We have evidence other than the shoes," the detective continued. "We found bloody footprints on the deck. By the way, footprints are as individual as fingerprints."

"Really?" I asked, surprised.

"Uh, usually," he said, momentarily embarrassed by his own fabrication.

"We also have eyewitnesses," chimed in Officer McSweeney,

helping out her colleague. "A man on the pier described you to a tee. Or more specifically, to a sheer white blouse with a ruffle down the front."

I sighed. Despite my average height, average weight, and average-length blond hair, the man in the madras shorts would be able to pick me out of a lineup in a flash. His confusing me with Cassie in the yellow dress wouldn't matter anymore. We'd talked in broad daylight, so he wouldn't have any doubts.

"Billy was dead when I got there," I said softly. "I hardly knew him. We'd met once before."

"So you admit that you did visit the boat earlier today," Detective Wilson barked.

"Complete coincidence. I have no idea who shot Billy. In fact, when I saw the blood, I worried that the killer might still be on the boat. I could have been murdered myself," I said, my voice rising.

"I'm glad you weren't hurt," said Erica McSweeney. I'd take the smidgen of sympathy, though she didn't sound too concerned.

Detective Wilson tried to hide his smug smile. "Really, Ms. Fields, it's dangerous being around you. First Cassie, now Billy. One dead body can happen to anyone. Two is just carelessness."

"I'm not dangerous," I sniffed. "But after all this, I might be in danger."

"Then we'll protect you," said Detective Wilson snidely. "You can come with us right now."

"Let's make it tomorrow," I said. "I'm with my daughter at the moment."

"No, you'll come now," said McSweeney, an edge creeping into her voice. "Someone else will have to take your daughter home."

"Are you arresting me?" I asked.

"We're bringing you in as a material witness."

"Leave my mother alone!" screamed Ashley, suddenly erupting. She'd been slowly moving forward and now she pointed an accusing finger at Molly. "She's the one you should be arresting! You've always thought she did it! Not my mom."

Detective Wilson gave Molly a long look. "Your friend is definitely on the list," he said. Then, turning back to Ashley he added, "But your mom's moved up to number one."

Chapter Twelve

— • —

I sat for over an hour in the police station, refusing to answer any questions. My friend Erica McSweeney stopped being so friendly. I didn't offer any more tips on where to find bargain Prada.

Jack Rosenfeld finally arrived at the station and rushed into the room in an Armani tuxedo and patent leather shoes.

I felt a surge of relief at seeing him—and then a surge of guilt for disturbing his evening.

"Did I drag you away from a party?" I asked, ready to apologize for making him leave early.

"Benefit night for the Los Angeles Philharmonic," he said. "Very impressive young conductor."

"What was the program?"

"Innovative combination. It started with an original composition and then . . ."

"I'm trying to run an investigation here," barked Detective Wilson, interrupting. "Beethoven hasn't been charged with anything."

"Neither has my client, I understand," said Jack.

Scowling, Detective Wilson sat back in his chair and played with his can of Dr Pepper. He'd offered me a Diet Coke, but other than that, we hadn't exactly been playing canasta together.

"I haven't answered anything," I said to Jack. "I told them I needed to wait for you."

I expected kudos but just got a curt nod.

"Detective, could we have five minutes, please?" he asked.

Detective Wilson made a face, slammed down his soda can, and stomped out of the small room.

"Give it to me fast," Jack said.

I did. A quick outline that covered all the basic points of why I'd been at Billy's boat. "But I don't know how they connected me to this so fast," I said, trying not to whine. "Or how Wilson and McSweeney got involved."

"I found that out on the way over," Jack said. "911 traced the call to your cell phone. The cops at Marina del Rey recognized your name and connected it to Cassie's investigation. So your favorite pair got called in."

"I didn't know the LAPD could be so efficient."

"They probably won't be so prompt getting you out of here."

I stood up. "Let's just tell them you need to be back in time for the encore."

Instead, Jack leaned against the edge of the table. He seemed calm, but tapped one shiny shoe against the floor.

"You ready?" asked Detective Wilson, pushing open the door. "I'd like to get the questioning started."

"Come right in," said Jack. "I know we'd all like to get home tonight."

Three hours later, I wondered why Detective Wilson had been in such a rush to start when he didn't seem in any hurry to finish.

"You getting tired?" he asked me finally.

"Sure. Aren't you?" I stifled a yawn.

"I'm never tired of looking for the truth."

In between asking questions, he'd left the room several times, each time coming back with new information. Or at least pretending to. Detective Wilson might be searching for the truth but he didn't bother sticking with it himself.

"The toxicology reports are positive for cocaine and marijuana," he said now. "So what happened after you and Billy got stoned?"

"You don't have to answer that," Jack said, parroting the comment he'd made a couple of dozen times already.

"I'll answer," I said, leaning back on my chair and crossing my legs. Unfortunately, channeling Sharon Stone in *Basic Instinct* wouldn't get me out of here. "I don't get stoned. I don't know whether Billy did—and you don't know either because drug test results take a lot longer than this."

I gave a smug smile, knowing I'd scored in this round. But Jack didn't look happy. Apparently you didn't win this game by knocking out your opponent.

Detective Wilson folded his arms across his ample chest. If one line of questioning didn't work, he'd go back to another. "So you're sticking to the story that Billy had a necklace you once saw Cassie wear."

"Exactly."

"Of all the necklaces in all the world, you recognized this one. A little unbelievable, isn't it?"

I didn't bother pointing out that Officer McSweeney had recognized a pair of shoes. "I don't see a lot of twenty-carat yellow diamonds in the course of a day," I said instead.

"How did you know that's what it was?"

Now Jack got restless, his foot tapping ever faster against the leg of the chair. "For heaven's sakes, Detective, you know LA. The women don't wear eyeglasses, they wear jeweler's loupes."

Detective Wilson looked at my eyes, as if expecting literal confirmation.

"Contact lenses," I said. "I've been considering Lasik surgery, but I just don't know."

"I had Lasik," said McSweeney from her perch across the room.

"Have you had a lot of dry eye? Halos? Trouble with night vision? I'm always worried about side effects," I said.

"No problems," she said amiably, renewing her role as friendly cop. Then moving on, she said, "But let's say you're right about the necklace. If Billy had something that valuable, why sell it at Christie's?"

"Where else would he go? He's not . . . I mean, he wasn't . . ." I paused, unable to get the tenses right—or take in what I'd seen. I'd hardly known Billy Mann and I didn't know if I trusted him. But dead? I cleared my throat. "Anyway, you don't sell something like that on eBay, and he's not the kind to have a lot of socialite friends who'd want to buy it from him."

Detective Wilson shook his head. "I'm sorry, Mrs. Fields, but your story doesn't add up. Not the socialite kind, fine. Then also not Cassie Crawford's kind."

"Wrong," I said. "He is . . . was . . . everybody's kind. Any woman would sleep with him. I would."

Every head in the room swiveled around to stare at me.

"You had sex with Billy Mann?" Detective Wilson finally asked, speaking very slowly.

"No, of course not. I'm married." I wouldn't let myself wonder if Dan shared my fervor for fidelity. "Are you married, Detective?"

He gave a barely perceptible nod, his jowly chin hitting against his barrel chest.

"How long?"

He looked over at McSweeney, who raised an eyebrow, as if telling him to humor me.

"Fourteen years."

"Good for you. Not quite long enough to be an applause line on *Oprah*, but better than many. Decent marriage?"

He nodded again and shot a nasty look at McSweeney, whom he now clearly blamed for getting him into this conversation.

"I'm glad to hear it, but I bet you look at the occasional copy of *Playboy,* right? Daydream about someone else?"

"I only look at crime reports," he grumbled.

"Really? Well trust me, Detective, your wife fantasizes now and then. Women do that. It's usually about someone manly, the kind who has a motorcycle and tattoo and will give her a great orgasm."

Detective Wilson turned bright red, a beach ball left too long in the sun. Across the room, Erica McSweeney snickered. Jack Rosenfeld turned away and propped his face against his hand so Wilson wouldn't see him smirk.

"We're not discussing org—orga—" Wilson cleared his throat, unable to say the word. "Sex," he concluded instead.

"Of course we're discussing orgasms. Cassie and Billy. Whether or not they hooked up recently, as the kids say."

"Roger Crawford happens to be a rich, powerful man," Detective Wilson said, finally.

"Rich and powerful are decent aphrodisiacs," I admitted. "But maybe not everything."

"You think his young wife would be unfaithful to him in the first year of marriage, just to have a good"—again the word caught in his throat—"a good roll in the hay?"

"Honestly, Detective, I don't know what went on between Cassie and Billy. I don't know how he got the necklace. And I don't know if any of it is connected to the bullet in his back."

Detective Wilson stood up. "Thank you for your insights, Mrs. Fields. We'll have further questions another time."

He left the room quickly, eager to get back to his wife before the Hell's Angels did.

Ashley didn't wake up until almost noon the next day, and I hung around all morning, waiting to talk to her. She finally came downstairs in frilly pink baby-doll pajamas that made her look more babe than baby.

"You're not in jail," she said snidely when she saw me. "What a shame."

"Honey, I'm so sorry. I can't apologize enough for ruining your night. I can imagine how embarrassing that was for you."

"Having my mother hauled off by the cops? What's embarrassing?"

She opened the refrigerator and took out two carrot sticks.

"Can I make you some breakfast?" I asked. "Pancakes? Scrambled eggs? Oatmeal?"

"You could," she said. "But why bother? I'd just go to the bathroom and barf."

Uh-oh. Go to the bathroom and barf? I had worried about this since she spit out her Gerber baby pears at eight months old. Eating disorders were like the common cold among privileged girls in LA—fast-spreading and hard to avoid. Now it had happened. I had to handle the problem right now.

I put my hands on her shoulders.

"I understand the pressure teen girls feel to be thin," I said. "We'll deal with it together. Thank you for telling me. That's the first step to being cured."

She took my hands off her shoulders and looked at me oddly.

"Being cured of what?" she asked.

"Bulimia, I assume."

"Who said anything about bulimia?"

"If you eat, you'll barf."

She sat down and put a hand against her tummy. "I have an upset stomach. After you left last night, I kept trying to develop a taste for caviar. Too much Osetra doesn't sit well."

"That's all?"

"Yuh-huh-uh," she said, turning her affirmation into a singsong censure of parental stupidity.

I sighed. "What else happened after I left?"

"Apologize a little more first."

My guilt returned almost immediately. "Oh, honey, I really tried to make it a special night for you. Better than Tara's party could possibly be. The last thing I want is to drag you into any unpleasantness. You don't deserve it."

She let a moment pass. "Is that all?"

"Tell me how I can make it up to you. I'll do anything."

Clearly what she'd been waiting for. "I need a new iPod."

"What's wrong with yours?"

"I lost it."

I grimaced. "You know the rule. Lose something and you have to replace it yourself."

"You said you'd do anything," she wheedled.

"If you need music, I could teach you to whistle," I joked. "Or I could sing. I was the only one in my sorority who knew the entire score to *Kiss Me, Kate.*"

Ashley sat back and crossed her arms in front of her stomach. "My life can't get much worse," she moaned. "Number one, my mother gets dragged off by the police and I'm humiliated." She raised a finger. "Two, I'm practically dying from eating bad caviar." Another finger raised. "And three, I had to beg a ride home after the party." She waggled the raised digits and groaned again. "Shame. Embarrassment. All of it your fault. And you won't buy me a crummy iPod?"

I put my fingers against my temples and gently massaged. Wasn't this what they should really teach in Lamaze class? All that time spent learning how to breathe during delivery, when talking to a teenage daughter turned out to be what took your breath away.

"All I can tell you is how sorry I am," I said, repeating my mantra.

"You can also buy me an iPod," she said, near tears.

I know bad parenting when I see it. I know no mother ever bought her daughter's good opinion with a checkbook. Children need love, support, and good values—not designer dresses and electronic toys.

"Sure, honey, an iPod. Any color you want." Why make a fuss? Every kid had an iPod. Maybe she'd teach me how to download Jon Stewart.

The tears disappeared and Ashley smiled. "Thanks, Mom. Phat."

"I am?" I ran my fingers down my hips.

"The other kind of phat. The one that's good."

"Sounds like we're back on eating disorders."

She laughed. "So after you left the party, I was mortified."

"And probably worried about me," I said, prompting.

"Mortified," she repeated. Her tears had disappeared, and she looked triumphant. "For about five minutes. Until Lindsay Lohan came over and said she knew how I felt to have a parent wanted by the police. Her dad had been in jail—whole big scandal—and she knows it's humiliating and I must want to die and she gave me a hug. Then Macaulay Culkin—remember him from *Home Alone*?—joined us to commiserate about *his* awful parents." Her eyes sparkled. "I mean, Mom, thank you *sooo* much for getting arrested."

"You're welcome," I said, completely confused by the turn the conversation had taken. I could have mentioned that I hadn't been arrested, but I'd hate to lower her status with the Kids of Bad Parents club.

She did a little pirouette. "It turned out to be the best night of my life! Hanging out with Lindsay Lohan and Macaulay Culkin, and all because of you."

"All that and an iPod, too," I muttered.

"Lindsay and Mac both ended up in rehab because of their parents," Ashley continued, unfazed. "But I had one glass of Sprite and called it a night."

Thank goodness for small things. I didn't look forward to visiting my daughter at Betty Ford. I took a deep breath. On the other hand, I could definitely use a Lamaze refresher.

Since Ashley would survive, I didn't cancel my appointment with a new client named Paige Hardy, who'd called and asked me to meet her at an auction showroom. I arrived early to survey the objects on display. And what a display! The pieces all dated from the Ming dynasty and seemed in as near-to-perfect condition as sixteenth-century chests, chairs and paintings could be. I could barely stop staring at an intricately engraved cabinet that glistened with rich reds and searing gold in an intricate mélange of dragons and phoenix decorations. I glanced at the auction price sheet and gasped. We'd practically have to sell our house to afford it, and while the elaborate drawers were exquisite, they didn't offer a lot of living space.

My client came in wearing short shorts and wedged espadrilles that showed off her long, tanned legs. With her blond hair pulled back in a simple barrette and a face that glowed despite minimal makeup, she looked like the captain of the college pep squad. But in LA, age is always inscrutable. No use trying to guess the vintage of anything more complex than a Napa Valley merlot.

"Nice to meet you," I said, shaking her hand. No nail polish, but neatly rounded fingernails and well-kept cuticles.

"You too," she said.

"You picked an incredible place to browse," I said, gesturing around the room. "Are you interested in buying, or are we just looking?"

I kept my tone even, because who knew? The only thing riskier to judge than age in LA was net worth. A beautiful twentysomething in short shorts had as good a likelihood of writing a check for a million bucks as anyone else.

"Oh, I don't know," she said vaguely. "A friend of mine had been looking forward to the auction. But she never made it."

I looked at her quizzically. "Are you bidding as her agent?"

"I wish. I wish." Tears sprang to her eyes, and she pulled a tissue out of a vinyl see-through tote that could have been either Kmart or Kate Spade. Amazing what designers could call chic.

Paige walked across the room, and I scurried to keep up with her long strides. She pointed to a classic Ming vase encased behind glass, the shaded blue flowers almost alive on the shiny porcelain.

"Don't you think that would have looked pretty on the Biedermeier table in Cassie Crawford's place? Or would the styles be too different to combine?"

I took a long moment to compose myself.

"I'm a fan of mixing epochs and styles," I said finally. "Biedermeier's straight lines gives it an unexpectedly modern feel. Oddly enough, the balance and harmony of Ming pieces does the same. Putting them together would create a very special synchronicity across centuries and continents."

"How interesting," she said. But I had the feeling she didn't really care much about Biedermeier, bling, or Ming.

"Is Cassie the friend who couldn't come?" I asked softly.

She nodded and dabbed at her eyes again. "You decorated beautifully for her. Exactly what she wanted."

"You saw the penthouse."

"The day before she died. She loved everything about it."

I nodded, starting to understand why she'd called. "So you heard about me from Cassie. I'm not really here to help you decorate, right?"

She smiled. "Well, you can if you want. But I've just felt so helpless. Someone has to solve her murder. You were there."

"And you're her friend. Maybe we can help each other."

She nodded. "Exactly what I was hoping."

Paige moved away from the vase and sat down on an ornate divan. I hesitated, but since the piece looked to be nineteenth-century French rather than fourteenth-century Chinese, I figured it had been put there for using, not selling. I sat down next to her and realized the seats had been positioned carefully so that we both directly faced an exquisite painting of Daoist immortals walking on water. According to the catalogue, the piece had a floor bid of five million.

"I didn't know Cassie had been at the penthouse the night before she died, but I'd guessed. Were you the only one with her?" I asked.

"Yes, just us," Paige said. "We didn't stay long. She had some papers she wanted to stash."

"In the library?" I ventured.

"Right." Paige let my deduction pass. "Cassie scampered up the ladder, and we joked that she could always have a future clearing gutters."

"Any idea what the papers were?"

She shook her head. "No. I thought maybe something about Roger. Information to protect herself if he turned cruel during the divorce."

"Had that been settled? That they'd divorce?"

"Not really. Cassie believed in happily ever after, but I told her she was in denial. She loved him. I don't know why, but she really did."

"She certainly wanted to impress him with the apartment."

"I don't think he had any intention of living there. He bought it for her. Smart, right? It looks better in front of a judge if you give the ex a place to live, even though it's not in the prenup. Three mil and he comes across as mister generous—and no judge will make him give up one of the houses he really cares about."

I nodded thoughtfully. "How do you and Cassie know each other?"

"We were friends since eighth grade," she said. "My dad was in the foreign service and we moved all the time—Chile, China, India, and Portugal. When we got to Orange County, the kids seemed very provincial, and I didn't try to make friends. But Cassie was nice to me and it stuck. I moved to Hong Kong in eleventh grade, but we stayed in touch."

"Did you go to college together?"

"No, I took a degree abroad. We connected back here."

"Close friends?"

"Very. And we kept getting closer. She didn't have a lot of people to talk to about her marriage. It was all too public. But we trusted each other. She knew I'd always be on her side."

I nodded, understanding. Paige and Cassie. Molly and me. In a wild, ever-changing world, the old bonds mattered. A friend should be more than someone you met on Facebook and sent a text message on her birthday. History had weight. Loyalty made a difference. Like the Ming vase, a real friend had irreplaceable worth.

"You must know the people in Cassie's life," I said. "Do you have a favorite suspect?"

Paige studied her fingernails for a moment. "I just think the police are missing something. Their perspective gets distorted when there's this much money involved."

"A billion can be distracting," I admitted.

"Cassie didn't care about being rich," Paige said. "Now that she's . . . gone, the press has turned her into the bimbo who got the billionaire. It's not fair."

"How would you describe her?"

For an answer, Paige turned to me and gave a little smile. "Let's start this way. What would you guess I do?"

I wisely hadn't tried to deduce her age or finances—now

I had to speculate about her career? Dancer or model seemed obvious. Maybe a producer or publicist. She had definite flair.

"Something in entertainment," I said, going for the obvious.

"I teach sixth grade at an inner-city school in LA," she said flatly.

I nodded, grateful that she'd ended the guessing game before I fully embarrassed myself. "It might have taken me awhile to come up with that," I admitted.

"Cassie and I stayed friends because we shared values," she said. "Being wealthy allowed her to be charitable, but she got annoyed at all the society women with their blatant displays and fancy balls."

I smiled. "I know the feeling. My husband always wants to know why he has to put on a tuxedo to make a donation."

"Cassie contributed in ways that people would never know."

I nodded again, not doubting her. But before we conferred sainthood on the deceased, I had a couple of questions.

"Did you know her friend Billy Mann?" I asked.

"I knew of him but never met him. They dated years ago and stayed good friends."

"I think they saw each other quite recently."

"Cassie didn't have an affair, if that's what you're suggesting," Paige said. "She didn't believe in them. Even for revenge."

I paused, taking it in. "You mean you think Roger dallied?"

"I do," she said evenly. "I think he dallied with your friend Molly. In fact, I don't have any doubt."

I turned away from her, and briefly focused on the painting centered on the opposite wall. Birds and plum blossoms fluttered around a kimono-clad woman who knelt sedately in the bottom left. I suddenly wanted to buy the painting and absorb its Zen vibes. Or maybe I just wanted to go join her in the seventeenth century. Though with my luck, her samurai husband would die under suspicious circumstances.

"Molly and Roger had a complex relationship," I said, echoing what my friend had once told me. "But not what you think. You really shouldn't make accusations."

Paige ran a finger across the smooth edge of her thumbnail.

"Cassie left her sunglasses in the penthouse."

"Pardon?"

"After we left that evening, she realized she'd forgotten her Chanel shades. She had to rush to a dinner, so I said I'd go back and get them for her. When I arrived, Molly and Roger were there."

"You saw them?"

"I came in with Cassie's keys, and I heard voices. So I tiptoed to the study and peeked in. Roger had his arm around a woman. I didn't even know who she was until Cassie died and I started reading all the rumors."

"Did they see you?"

"No. They had their heads down, giggling. I just tiptoed out again."

"Heads down, and if they didn't see you, they must have had their backs to you, is that right?" I asked.

"You sound like a prosecutor," she said. "I didn't know I was on the witness stand."

"Just trying to figure it all out," I replied calmly.

"You want to figure that it wasn't Molly. But it was. When I walked by her at Roger's party, I had no doubt. She wears Annick Goutal Passion perfume. Very distinctive. Same scent I'd noticed in the apartment."

"You smelled her?" I asked, baffled.

"I have a good nose," she said modestly.

I held out my wrist. "What am I wearing?"

She sniffed. "Easy. Jo Malone Wild Fig and Cassis. Also distinctive."

"Quite a talent," I said.

"I work nights at the fragrance counter at Bloomingdale's. Just don't get me started on Lovely versus Beautiful versus Happy. Can't do it."

Despite myself, I smiled. Paige was the real deal. Given her style, I'd unconsciously assumed that she topped off her teaching salary with a trust fund, not a job pushing perfume.

Then my smile faded. "You have no idea why they were at the penthouse," I said, getting back to her accusation. "Sitting in the study isn't exactly criminal behavior."

"So why all the secrecy? Roger had told Cassie he didn't want a key until they moved in."

"Then he made sure the police knew he didn't have a key," I added thoughtfully.

Our eyes met, and we exchanged a long glance. I wanted Paige to be wrong, but nothing about her suggested she was lying.

"So what's your theory?" I asked finally.

She strummed her fingers delicately against the divan. "Here's what I know. Three people were definitely in the penthouse the day before Cassie died: Roger, Molly, and me. Any one of us could have poisoned the tea. Here's the other thing I know. It wasn't me."

Chapter Thirteen

——— • ———

On Saturday night, Jimmy and I cuddled under a green blanket in the family room to watch *Shrek*. If kids have such short attention spans, how come they beg to sit through the same movie fifty times?

"We have all the sequels," I told Jimmy, looking hopefully at the lineup of unopened kids' DVDs on the shelf.

"The original," he said firmly.

Knowing the ritual, I turned down the sound so Jimmy could recite the funniest lines of dialogue. When we got to the final, rousing "I'm a Believer," Jimmy jumped up, danced around, and belted out the words. Very cute. Eventually, some movie studio would catch on and put out a karaoke DVD for six-year-olds. (And save a fortune on Eddie Murphy's fee.)

"Want a piggyback to your room?" I asked him when we turned off the movie.

"Yup!" He grinned and jumped on my back. I staggered slightly under the weight of his firm little body but let him wrap his legs around my waist. I dreaded the day that Jimmy would decide he'd become too grown up to be carried. On the other hand, my vertebrae would send a thank-you note.

I made it upstairs and plopped Jimmy on his bed. I'd recently redecorated his room, having been forced to replace the astronomy-themed wallpaper once Pluto was no longer a planet. Parents in this town competed to give their kids every educational edge, so normal kid décor (Spider-Man? cowboys?) was out of the question. I'd settled on a world-maps motif. I liked to think that if Jimmy got into Yale someday, he'd thank me for the bedspread that taught him how to spell Uzbekistan.

"Can I have a story, Mommy?" Jimmy asked.

"It's already late," I said, glancing at my watch. I suddenly felt exhausted.

"One chapter. *Please*." He reached over and handed me *James and the Giant Peach*, and I opened it to where we'd left off the previous night. For some reason, Roald Dahl's scariest scenes were more comforting to kids than milk and a Double Stuf Oreo. Sure enough, Jimmy fell asleep with a sweet smile on his face, lulled by the fantasy of the lonely orphan and his insect friends.

By the time I went to bed, my own fantasies involved creepier images than mutated bugs. I tossed and turned, spooked by Paige's vision of Molly and Roger buzzing around the penthouse. Admittedly, she'd seen them fully clothed in the library, not naked and necking. But my imagination provided the next scene. What was Molly hiding from me?

I flipped over and felt a little pool of perspiration forming between my breasts. I needed somebody to comfort me, but Dan had gone to a medical meeting in San Diego for the weekend to present a paper on a new technique for reattaching severed fingers. Right now, I was worried about severed friendship.

At 3 A.M., the phone rang. I leaped across the bed to answer it. Late-night calls came in regularly for Dan, and they rarely got my blood stirring anymore. But this time I felt my heart pounding. A hospital emergency when he wasn't home?

"Hello?" I said.

"Mom, I'm sorry to wake you up." Grant's voice sounded strained on the phone, soft and raspy.

"You didn't."

"Can you come pick me up?" he asked.

"Sure, where are you?"

"On campus. Tonight was the initiation into Delta ij, re-member?"

Of course I remembered. I hadn't liked the idea, but part of being a parent involves letting kids break free. He'd planned to sleep over Jake's afterward. Obviously, there had been a change in plan.

"Are you drunk?" I asked. We'd made a deal long ago that he'd never drive after drinking. If he got into a bad situation, he could call me any time of the night, no questions asked. Of course, I'd just asked a question.

"Not drunk, but it's a long story," he said. "I'm not up for driving home, and it's too late to go to Jake's."

"I'll come get you." Even as we talked, I quickly made my plan. I could dash out and be back home long before Jimmy woke up. Ashley was home in case anything happened. "Just stay where you are, honey. I'll be there."

He gave me an address, and twenty minutes later I pulled into the residential part of campus. Lights still shone in dorm-room windows, and I heard the sounds of late-night partying and drunken catcalls. Grant must have spotted me before I saw him, because he emerged from the shadows of a building and got into the Lexus.

"Let's go," he said.

I took off, feeling as if I were at the wheel of a getaway car, but not knowing why we needed to get away.

I took a few sideways glances at Grant who seemed pale and shaken. I didn't smell liquor on his breath, though maybe he'd been drinking vodka. He had red lacerations on his left arm and an angry welt swelling at his neck.

We drove for a few minutes without a word. Finally, Grant said softly, "Cone of silence, Mom, okay? What I tell you doesn't go any farther."

"Of course."

I waited.

"The night started out pretty typical," Grant said. "Three of us being initiated. A bunch of guys tied us to a tree and we had to figure out how to get free."

"How'd you do it?"

Grant shrugged. "They'd left a knife on the ground, just out of reach. I took off my shoe and kicked it over so it hit the handle at the right angle—and popped the knife up toward us."

"Very clever," I said.

"Delta ij's a secret society for physicists," Grant said. "Basic mechanics isn't much of a stretch."

"It's a stretch for me. I'm not used to dealing with geniuses."

Grant snorted. "Don't be too impressed. After that, we did the usual stupid games. Beer pong. Flip-cup. Professor Bohr had told them I'm too young, so not to make me drink. All cool."

"Thank goodness for that."

"Yeah, well this is where it gets strange," Grant said. "Did you know there's a whole system of tunnels under the campus?"

"I've heard stories."

"They're locked and off-limits, and you can get thrown out of school for being in them. But everyone does it."

I let the proverbial "Everyone does it" pass. Not the moment to be judgmental.

"We went into the tunnels and crept around for a while

with little flashlights," Grant continued. "Then Professor Bohr showed up and led us to this dark corner that had an open coffin. The first guy had to lie in it and tell about his weirdest sexual experience. The next guy the same. Then my turn. I lay down in the coffin"—he shuddered—"which was pretty creepy, by the way. He said I had to talk about death. Answer five questions."

I gripped the wheel. "What did he want to know?"

"Stuff about murder. Poisonings. Everything about Cassie Crawford and what you knew about her murder. Then he asked me if I thought Molly had killed her and she'd die for her sins."

Now I shuddered. "Any of the other guys say anything?"

"After a while, he told them all to leave, and he gave me a mug to drink from. He said something like 'Your cup of mead for Delta ij. Also known as Kirin tea.'"

"You drank?"

Grant nodded, miserably. "Being in Delta ij's a big deal. As far as hazing goes, it seemed pretty mild. I took a few gulps and Professor Bohr grabbed it back. Then he left. It was pitch-black in the tunnels, and I didn't know how to get out."

"You poor thing," I said.

"I eventually found my way," Grant said, embarrassed by my sympathy and trying to sound dismissive. "I even got back to my car. I probably shouldn't have called you."

"I'm glad you did," I said simply. He didn't have to explain himself. Fatigue. Fear. All good reasons not to drive.

Grant wrapped his arms around himself, as if he were suddenly cold. "If you want to know the truth," he said finally, "I felt sick. I threw up."

Involuntarily, I let the car swerve. My God, what had I gotten my son into?

"How do you feel now?" I asked, controlling my voice as best I could.

"I don't know. Better. I'm sure it was just anxiety," Grant said. He rocked back and forth in his seat. "Just anxiety," he repeated. "Nothing in the tea. But I got scared. Jeez, Mom, I got to tell you, Professor Bohr freaks me out."

When we got home, Grant slipped off to his room, and I plopped on my bed with a notepad and pencil. I made a list.

> Cassie: Drinks tea given to her by ???. Dies of arsenic poisoning.
> Grant: Drinks tea given to him by Hal Bohr. Gets sick.
> Me: Sips tea from Andy Daniels. Gets scared. (And pisses off husband.)

So much for tea being healthy. I wouldn't get near the stuff again unless the head of the FDA came back from Sri Lanka clutching pekoe leaves he'd picked himself. Back in A.D. 220, the famed physician Hua Tao said, "To drink *k'u t'u* constantly makes one think better." Sorry, pal. Looking at this list, I couldn't find anything sweet about bitter tea.

I got a couple of hours' rest, and when I woke up again Grant had slipped a note under my door saying that he felt fine and had gone off to play tennis. Nice that he could bounce back faster than an Andy Roddick serve. I paced for a while, and needing distraction, I headed to the greenhouse. I'd been ignoring my beautiful orchids, but now being in the sunny room with the brave little plants immediately made me feel calmer. I gave a light misting to the dainty flowers of a creamy white *Dendrobium* that seemed to have stretched upward in the sunlight. A fragile-looking *Cymbidium* on a long spindly stem had sprouted three broad-petaled pink flowers. I tenderly tied it to a support to keep it from sagging, but just looking at the beautiful blossoms made me smile. Like children, orchids turned out to be hardier than you expected.

My few rosebushes had bloomed full and fragrant. I'd just started repotting a Belle Amour rose plant when my ringing cell phone shattered my flower-induced tranquility. I pounced, worried that Grant might be in trouble again. But it was a woman's voice.

"Mrs. Fields? This is Elsa Franklin." My silence must have given me away, because she quickly added, "From the UCLA development office."

Oh, right. Cassie's onetime boss. Good thing I'd remembered, or I might have blurted that the only contribution I'd be making today was to a stress headache.

"Yes, of course. How are you?" I asked, unwittingly matching her patrician East Coast intonation.

Her manners must have curdled in the LA heat, because she immediately jumped to business. "I heard about Billy Mann's murder. We need to talk. Can we get together tonight?"

I demurred, since I'd already planned a special family dinner for the evening—take-out chicken sate and beef with ginger sauce, served on the handmade straw mats I'd picked up at the Vietnamese design store on 3rd Street. Unless it rained, we'd eat on the deck, under the silk-and-bamboo lotus-shaped lanterns imported from a small shop in Ho Chi Minh City. Once Americans bombed there; now we bought there.

"How about tomorrow?" I suggested.

"I'm leaving for Boston, and it can't wait," she said firmly. "There's a movie premiere at the Village Theater tonight at six P.M. I've invited a lot of donors, so I have to be there. Walk down the red carpet, and then we can sneak off during the film."

"Fine," I said resignedly. Maybe I could get home in time for sweet rice-cake dessert.

"Black tie, of course," she added, hanging up.

I clicked the phone shut. Black tie? I had to put on an evening gown to talk about Billy Mann? Maybe the yellow Nina Ricci.

Instead, I left the house in a pale green chiffon Valentino cocktail dress that was older than Ashley. Given how often I'd worn it, I figured the gown amortized per wearing better than a Gap T-shirt.

Down the street in front of the movie theater, a long row of limousines snaked slowly, dropping off actors, studio execs, and first-night hangers-on. The rest of the street had been cordoned off with red ropes, so I parked a few blocks away, probably the only person willing to arrive on foot. Klieg lights flared and the usual array of photographers lined the red carpet, but given that movies opened in LA as often as Starbucks stores, the excitement level was minimal. Still, I liked this theater, a 1930s Spanish-modern treasure that had been well restored over the years. The high tower and sweeping spire suggested a cathedral. And why not? On premiere nights, everyone came and prayed to the box-office gods.

I walked along Broxton Street, the thin straps on my Versace sandals cutting into my toes and the high heels threatening to end in a turned ankle. Male designers should be forced to do two laps around a track in any shoe they plan to sell. Or to include health insurance riders in the box.

A young man with very short hair, a black shirt, and too-tight black pants stopped me at the edge of the red carpet. I gave my name and he studied the clipboard in front of him.

"You're not here," he said officiously.

"Actually, I am here," I said. "I'm standing right in front of you."

"You're not on the list."

"Is that the A list or the B list? Sometimes I'm only on the C list."

"It's the *only* list," he said, missing the joke. "I can't let you through."

I shrugged. "No problem, I'll leave." I hadn't wanted to come, anyway. "Just please tell Elsa Franklin that I looked for her."

A clipboard-carrying colleague standing nearby overheard our exchange and quickly came over. She was about the same age as the first guy, but lacked the chip on her shoulder. "If Elsa Franklin invited her, she's probably a big donor," she whispered.

The young man clutched his list. "Money doesn't impress me," he said imperiously.

"In this town, that puts you on a list of one," I quipped.

His colleague laughed and tossed back her thick, long hair. "Great dress," she said smiling at me. "Whose is it?"

"Mine. Designed by Valentino."

She laughed and waved me ahead. "Valentino is a good enough admission ticket for me. Enjoy the show."

I walked quickly down the red carpet, darting by the photographers who had their lenses focused on Jessica Alba, decked out in a low-cut red gown that clung to her flawless body. A handsome stud with broad shoulders and sexy stubble kept his arm draped around her until one of the photographers shouted, "Hey, can we get Jessica alone?" He stepped back, abashed. I wanted to tell him not to feel bad. At least he'd been on the list.

I spotted Elsa standing ramrod straight near the entrance to the theater. Her long black-velvet skirt and high-necked blouse seemed more appropriate for a Connecticut Christmas than for a hot night in Hollywood. Several well-dressed couples had stopped to say hello to her, and, busy being gracious, she didn't notice me. As the crowd thinned, I gave a little wave, and Elsa quickly excused herself from the people around her and came over.

"Give me a few minutes and we'll go in together," she said in a conspiratorial tone.

I found a shady spot and watched Elsa curiously. Her calm, slightly above-it-all demeanor probably served her well as a fund-raiser, but when it came down to it, she might as well be a used-car salesman. Sure she had a worthy cause, but she measured her success by how much money people coughed up.

"I think my flock has been well-tended," she said, coming over to me as the last stragglers entered the theater.

"Tell me your connection here," I said.

"I do these events all the time," she said. "Movie premieres, backstage passes, boxes at Lakers games—just little bonuses for our best donors."

"As if they couldn't afford the tickets themselves," I said.

"It's not about money, it's about access. I arrange for Jessica Alba to come over, say hello, and pose for a couple of pictures. My hedge-fund director gets to brag to his buddies the next day that she seemed hot for him. The next donation is even easier to get."

"Celebrity sells," I agreed. I remembered Molly explaining why Roger wanted to invest in movies. Glamour greased the money wheels.

Elsa and I stepped inside the heavy doors of the theater, greeted by the welcome rush of cool air. Everyone else had taken their seats and the lobby stood virtually empty. I paused to look at the famous mural of the California gold rush stretching across the lobby wall. Probably more interesting than whatever was showing on the main screen.

"I can be quick," Elsa said, talking softly. "I wanted to share what happened after you visited me last time. I realized I should clear out Cassie's office and go through her files."

"Hadn't the police done that?" I asked, surprised.

"No. The police never came by or made any requests," she said.

Did the cops not know Cassie had worked for Elsa? I shouldn't be surprised. Unlike the handsome hunks on TV crime shows, real-life detectives in the LAPD got too busy to follow every lead. If they had a suspect in Molly, why waste a lot of time looking elsewhere?

"So what did you find in Cassie's files?" I asked.

"Mostly professional reports and memos about projects she had planned. But I came across an interesting note crumpled at the bottom of a drawer."

Elsa opened her small evening bag and took out a piece of paper folded into quarters.

"I called you because I needed someone else's opinion on what it means," she said, smoothing it out and handing it to me.

"Should I read it now?"

"Please."

I took a step forward, into slightly brighter light.

Hey Beautifull,

    Don't tell me how good life is. Mine sucks and your going to make it better. You owe me, dont forget. Owe me big. Pay up or that perfect life will be over. Is this a threat? Yeah, baby. But I'll get what I deserve from you, one way or another. Where there's a will theres a way.

                             A wet kiss from Billy

I read it through twice, and then a third time. Apart from the spelling mistakes, nothing jumped out at me except the obvious: Billy Mann threatening Cassie Crawford.

"Notice the date," Elsa said, pointing her finger at the bottom of the page. "Two weeks before she died."

"Any idea what he means when he says she owed him?"

"No, but he obviously wanted money. And from the first, he struck me as the ruthless, stop-at-nothing kind."

"Why?"

She looked at me oddly. "You met him. Tattooed motorcyclist with a shop in a bad neighborhood. Is that who you'd want for your daughter?"

"Maybe not, but it doesn't explain why he'd kill her."

"'Where there's a will there's a way,'" she quoted. "Perhaps she left him money."

"She can't leave him Roger's money."

Elsa looked frustrated. "Cassie had some money of her own. She'd told me about it when I first hired her, before she ever met Roger. Her father died in a car accident many years ago and she had an insurance trust. Her mother remarried a very wealthy man. Didn't you see them at her memorial service?"

I remembered seeing a couple not much older than me, their quiet dignity a contrast to Roger. The mother's anguish seemed so deep, palpable, and primal that I'd had to look away. Now it occurred to me that I'd come to think of Cassie as Roger's wife, Andy Daniels's fling, Elsa Franklin's employee, and Billy Mann's possible lover. I'd forgotten that she had also been someone's daughter. Maybe I didn't want to remember. The implications made me shudder.

"So you think she had her own money and wrote a will that left it to Billy, not Roger."

"It would make sense. Roger doesn't need any more funds. Billy obviously does."

I shook my head. "I don't know. Most women in their twenties wouldn't have a will. It's just not high in their minds that they might die."

Elsa looked away, focusing far off in the distance. "You can't compare Cassie to most women. She had a style all her own. Very determined and dogged. She liked to keep her life under control."

"And also her death," I suggested.

"Yes," Elsa echoed. "Also her death."

I looked back at the note, trying to hear Billy's voice in it.

"Are you going to give this to the police?" I asked.

She shrugged. "I'm not trying to make accusations. It's just something I found."

"But it could be evidence. Or at least lead the cops to make some connection between Cassie and Billy."

"I'd prefer not to get involved," she said primly. "It doesn't sit well with my position to be associated with something like this."

"Think about Cassie's parents," I said, discomfited that up until now, I hadn't done that myself. "Don't you think it would help them if the murder could be solved?"

"Then you keep the note," said Elsa. "Show it to Roger if you want. Give it to the police. I've kept a copy. Just try to keep me out of it."

The next day, I drove over to the county clerk's office, where Cassie Crawford's last will and testament would have been filed. A perky associate in Jack Rosenfeld's office, Rachel Royce, had already spent twenty minutes on the phone with me this morning, describing the ins and outs of probate, testators, bequests, legacies, and codicils. I didn't expect to remember any of it.

"I wonder if they've already had the reading of the will," I said when she'd finished.

"I can pretty much guarantee the answer is no," Rachel said cheerfully.

"Really? Too soon?"

"Too soon, too late—it just doesn't happen in real life. The attorney files the will and anybody who goes to the clerk's office can review it. Often, we also send copies to the heirs."

"That's it?"

"Totally," she said with a laugh. "Disappointing, right? All those great movie moments when the grieving family gathers and the tension builds. What would Hercule Poirot do without them? Or Perry Mason?"

"You don't think the county clerk's office will have enough drama?"

"A different kind, I'm afraid," she said, laughing again. "Anyway, good luck."

I got the address online, then drove over to the building on La Cienega that I'd seen so many times. I bounded in eagerly—then spent the morning bouncing from office to office, negotiating long lines, and listening to bored clerks announce that I was in the wrong place.

"But the woman over at death certificates told me to come here," I said, frustrated, at my fifth stop.

"She was wrong."

"It would be nice if someone here knew the correct information," I said, more testily than I'd intended. "All I'm looking for is the will of a Los Angeles resident who recently died."

"What day was it filed?"

"Don't know."

"Who filed it?"

"Don't know."

"Was it filed here or in one of our other locations?"

"Also don't know."

The clerk, a heavyset woman whose sleeveless shirt revealed stunning amounts of upper-arm flesh, offered a loud snort.

"Lady, you just said it'd be nice if someone here knew the correct information. It'd be nice if *you* knew some correct information, wouldn't it?"

"I've been waiting in line for hours," I said, tears of frustration popping into my eyes. "Can't you help me?"

"God helps those who help themselves," she said cryptically. Then, looking out to the line, she called, *"Next!"*

Chastened, I scuttled away. How was I supposed to untangle a murder when I couldn't even get untangled from a murderous bureaucracy?

Back in the parking lot, I took a deep breath, the smoggy Los Angeles air feeling surprisingly invigorating after the stultifying atmosphere inside. I pulled out my cell phone, which apparently hadn't gotten much reception in the maze I'd just escaped, and noticed two calls from Jack. I called his office back and he picked up immediately.

"Lacy, I called as soon as I got in. Rachel told me she spoke to you this morning. Something about wanting to read a will. What's up?"

I filled him in briefly on my conversation with Elsa, the threatening letter she'd shown me, and her speculation about Cassie's will.

"Interesting," he said. "Listen, I'll send one of my investigators to track down the will and get the information to you by tomorrow."

I gave a half turn and stared at the building where I'd just been. "I've been trying to get it all morning," I said finally.

"You're kidding," he said. Then he gave a little laugh. "Like to be self-sufficient, huh? I guess you can take the girl out of the Midwest, but you can't take the Midwest out of the girl."

"Not funny," I said.

"Sorry. Come by about three tomorrow."

Jack's office was on the twenty-eighth floor of one of the towering glass-and-steel buildings in Century City. When I got there the next day, I parked in the underground lot, then took the elevator directly to his floor. As one of the named partners in the firm, Jack had a corner office with the requisite wood paneling, shelves of law books, framed diplomas, and formal leather chairs. Sun poured in from windows that faced north and east and provided a panoramic view of the city. Behind his desk, Jack looked tanned and surprisingly relaxed.

"Been playing a lot of tennis?" I asked.

"Every morning," Jack admitted. "Though I should probably quit. Last week I played Ryan and he beat me six-one, six-one."

Since Jack's son Ryan was Grant's doubles partner, I smiled. "You should be proud."

"Proud? I'm a guy. I want my son to beat everyone in the world—except me."

"Not that you're competitive."

"Would you want a lawyer who liked to lose?"

I smiled. "Nope."

"Then let's score some points."

He hit an intercom and asked to see Rachel Royce. A moment later, a pretty young associate bounced into the office— porcelain skin, long, curly red hair, and a curvy body hidden under a lawyerly navy pantsuit.

"You must be Mrs. Fields," she said, offering a firm handshake despite her French-manicured fingernails. "Sorry if I sent you on a wild-goose chase yesterday."

"It was an experience," I said.

"Well, I have the information you need," she said, tapping a heavy file folder. "Remember I told you that the reading of the will happens only in movies and mystery novels? Turns out we can have one right here."

She sat down on a red leather sofa, which didn't seem to give an inch under her weight. Either the new leather was still stiff, or Rachel was too slim to make a dent.

"I have the complete document, but I'll just summarize the main points," Rachel said, all business as she pulled out a sheaf of papers. "The will was signed and witnessed a little over a year ago. The way the father's insurance trust was written, the money in Cassie's trust is transferred to her sister's trust. It's more complicated than that for tax reasons, but that's the basic outcome. Roger hadn't put any assets directly in her name. In terms of other gifts, she left a ten-thousand-dollar bequest to her alma mater, UCLA, for the general alumni fund. And fifty thousand dollars to William James Mann."

Rachel looked up. "Short reading and not much drama. But it's all I've got."

"Thank you, Rachel," Jack said.

Catching his dismissive tone, Rachel gathered her papers and put a summarizing memo on Jack's desk. "Let me know if there's anything more I can do," she said, before heading out.

The door closed, and in the silence that followed, Jack looked at me expectantly.

"Ten thousand to UCLA," I said finally. "Does that give Elsa Franklin a motive?"

Jack shook his head. "In this town? Come on, Lacy. Think about the benefit auction we went to last year. Someone bid fifty thousand to have coffee with Steven Spielberg. That's one expensive latte."

I laughed, remembering the evening. The real entertainment came from watching the town's alpha males compete to see who had the bigger checkbook. "Lunch with Tom Hanks went for something like forty thou, didn't it? He jumped up during the bidding to say Steven might have made *Jurassic Park,* but he'd personally make any kind of sandwich the winner wanted."

"He pretended to be furious that Steven took in more than he did."

"Pretended? Even Forrest Gump has an ego."

Jack smiled. "The point is that ten thou isn't very much in the general scheme of things."

"Cassie worked at the development office. It's possible she put in the provision so when she talked to potential donors about making bequests she could say, 'I believe in this so much I've done it myself.'"

Jack nodded. "I'll buy that. Pretty harmless. Which brings us to William James Mann."

"He obviously knew about Cassie's will, which is why he mentioned it in the note," I said slowly. "Somehow he parlayed that into a million-dollar diamond."

"A decent motive," Jack conceded.

"Better than Molly's, don't you think? Billy's looking like a pretty good suspect to me."

"A dead suspect, unfortunately. Interesting that the only two people who can really tell us what happened are both dead." He paused. "By the way, if Billy killed Cassie, who killed Billy?"

I groaned. "Do I have to solve everything today?"

"Better you than the police."

"Maybe that's what Roger concluded. Better him than the police," I said, an obvious scenario suddenly coming to me. "He figured out that Billy killed Cassie and couldn't wait for the courts to settle the score. So he got vengeance himself."

"Easier for a jury to understand if the same person killed both of them."

"You mean Roger?"

"Or his friendly bodyguard."

"Look, I can believe Roger setting his thug on the slime who killed his wife. One clean shot. Very elegant. He could justify it to himself. But his wife?" I hesitated. "No real motive. And so messy."

"Which is where Molly comes in." Jack rifled through a file on his desk. "My investigator says she has a gun license. And keeps a Smith and Wesson .38 Special revolver in her office."

"*Molly?*" I asked, stunned. We'd never talked about it, but I assumed that, like me, if my best friend supported the NRA she meant the National Restaurant Association. Her favorite Clint Eastwood movie was *The Bridges of Madison County*, not *Dirty Harry*. The news that she packed a pistol didn't make my day.

"Well, she works late in her office a lot, and she's all alone," I said, grasping for an explanation, "and she had a robbery about three years ago. Very scary."

Jack consulted his notes again. "From the police report, the only thing stolen was a T-shirt."

"That Brad Pitt wore for an audition," I explained.

"So an overzealous fan broke in three years ago. And last month Molly bought a gun."

Last month? What else didn't I know about my best friend? At this point, if he told me she turned into Xena the Warrior Princess at night I wouldn't be surprised.

I stood up. "Really, Jack, I don't understand this. Are your investigators looking for evidence for or against us?"

"Evidence is just evidence," Jack said, sounding more law-yerly than I generally liked.

"I don't know how we got onto Molly anyway. This meeting was about Billy's note and reading the will."

Jack leaned back in his big chair. "You got what you wanted. Always a little twist when you gather to read a will."

Chapter Fourteen

— • —

I suggested to Dan that we escape for the long weekend, just the two of us.

"But we never leave the kids," he reminded me.

"They're leaving us," I said. "Grant's going to his team's tennis tournament in San Diego. Ashley's whole class is building houses in Guadalajara. I suggested they help the homeless in Watts but got voted down. Jimmy got invited to a chalet at Big Bear Mountain. Carla Peters next door called because she's taking her Aidan and didn't want him in ski class alone."

"So *I* have to be alone instead?" Dan asked. His annoyance from the other day had disappeared. We hadn't discussed it—but marriage was like that.

"You're not alone. You have me," I said, putting my arms around him.

He kissed me and I moved closer, letting my body meld into his. He got the message. "If we'll have the house to ourselves, why don't we just enjoy it?" he whispered.

"Let's enjoy it right now." I slipped away to close the bedroom door, then sidled back to Dan, who hadn't moved from his spot a few feet from the bed.

"Have an affair with me," I said, sliding my hands under his shirt and feeling the firm muscles of his back.

"Can't," he said tugging at the top of my skirt. "I have a wife."

"I don't need to worry?" I asked as he pushed me backward toward the bed and we fell together onto the silk duvet.

"I still get excited around you, in case you can't tell," he said.

"Oh, I can tell. Too much to hide."

"I assume you're not complaining."

"I'm only complaining that you're still dressed," I said, giggling.

"We can fix that." He quickly stripped down, revealing his lean, tanned body. I looked at him admiringly and he came closer and began kissing my lips, my neck, then unfastening my top. "When did women's clothes get so complicated?" he asked, fumbling with an errant hook-and-eye.

"I'm glad you haven't been practicing on anyone else," I said.

He paused, then propped himself on his elbow next to me. "Okay, what's this about? What did I do wrong?"

I kissed him, not wanting to ruin the moment. "It's just what you said when I came to your office. Or didn't say. About flings being as common as brushing your teeth."

He sighed and ran his fingers lightly over my cheek. "I don't know what I said. All I could think was that someone had poisoned my wife. Call me crazy, but that upsets me. You had me worried."

"You had *me* worried," I admitted.

He kissed me tenderly, then again, his hand stroking my breasts. "What part of 'I love you and only you' don't you understand?" he asked.

"Mmm, you know what they say. Show, don't tell."

He rolled on top of me, putting his finger to his lips, and then to mine. "Okay, I won't tell," he whispered.

But for the next hour, he showed.

Our Friday-night flight to Phoenix went smoothly, except that my Stila lipstick got impounded at security.

"You can't carry this onboard," the guard announced, removing it from the clear plastic bag I'd sent through the X-ray machine, with my three-ounce containers of travel shampoo, conditioner, mouthwash, and Kiehl's body lotion.

"What's the problem?" I asked.

"It's not allowed onboard," he said, not exactly clearing things up.

The matte silver aluminum packaging resembled a bullet, but a government-approved TSA worker could probably tell the difference between a cartridge and a cosmetic.

"That was my favorite color," I said regretfully as the broad-shouldered guard tossed the lipstick into a box of impounded items—a discarded Poland Spring, two containers of Finesse shampoo, a tube of Vaseline, and a bottle of Tabasco sauce. (Could it mask the taste of airplane food?) It didn't make me feel any safer knowing none of those had made it on board.

"How come this one is okay?" I asked, pointing to a Clinique pinkberry lipstick that he'd left in the plastic bag.

He glanced at it. "Free gift with purchase," he said scornfully.

I tucked the X-rayed items back into my Longchamp bag and walked, bewildered, to the flight.

"Do you think security only confiscates things you paid for?" I asked Dan, as we settled into our coach seats.

He shrugged and opened the medical journal he'd brought along for the flight.

"Maybe it's part of TSA training," I continued. "Guards

learn how to recognize a bomb, a potential terrorist, and a Clinique gift with purchase."

"How would you identify that last one?" Dan asked. He put down his journal, willing to abandon the latest research on Restylane for this breakthrough report.

"Different color packaging," I said promptly. "The free gifts are pale green."

"Something I'd never learn reading *The Journal of Plastic Surgery,*" he said.

"Stick with me," I teased.

"I intend to," he said, reaching across the armrest and squeezing my knee.

Barely an hour later, we landed in Phoenix, rented a car, and drove to the Phoenician resort. In no time, we'd been whisked upstairs to a gracious, oversized room, and I felt myself unwind almost immediately. In the marble bathroom, I changed into the fluffy terry-cloth robe hanging on the door, turned on the waterfall faucet in the enormous bathtub, and sniffed the bottles lined up on the vanity from the resort's Centre for Well-Being. Hotels used to brag if they had room service. Now they all seemed to offer full-service spas with their own line of treatments. I tossed a generous handful of grapefruit-and-eucalyptus bath salts into the tub and closed my eyes as the scent filled the room.

"What's going on?" Dan asked, coming in.

"Aromatherapy," I said. "Ease the spirit and detoxify the body."

"If you need to relax, I have my own technique," he said, untying my terry. "It involves two naked bodies lounging in a tub."

"Mmmm . . . I'm willing to try that," I said. At home, Dan took an efficient four-minute shower every morning and would happily have turned our tub into adjunct storage for medical books. Thank goodness for vacations.

We got into the warm water and I lounged against Dan, my back to his chest. He gently massaged my shoulders, then let his hands slip forward to my breasts.

"Very romantic," I murmured, my eyes half closed. The steam from the water wafted around us and my own heat index began to rise, too. I twisted around to kiss him just as he hit a switch that made the Jacuzzi jets come alive.

"Yikes!" I yelped, buffeted by the power of the swirling water. Trying to right myself, I slipped and landed smack against Dan, our noses bumping. We both pulled back with quick howls of pain, then burst out laughing. He reached around to turn off the jets, somehow sending me splattering across the tub—which only made us both laugh harder.

"Yup, very romantic," Dan said, finally stilling the swirling water.

I wiped water from my eyes, still giggling. "Actually it's pretty dreamy that after all these years, we still have fun together," I said. "Of all the great feelings in the world, sharing a hoot with your husband has to be in the top five."

"And making love with my wife is in the top four," Dan said. He stood up and scooped me out of the water and into his arms.

"Careful!" I yelped, worried that he'd strain his back. But I managed to squelch any mood-wrecking remark, and Dan just grinned, lifted me higher, and carried me dripping wet into the bedroom. He put me down gently, then lay on top of me on the bed. We grabbed at each other eagerly.

Twenty minutes later, I decided that aromatherapy worked after all.

"I'm glad we still like making love," I murmured, once we both were sated and satisfied.

"I love making love," Dan said. "And I love you, as previously mentioned."

He pulled himself off me, and our wet (now with sweat)

bodies made a *thwuck* sound as we separated. We lay with our arms around each other, contented and calm. A few minutes passed, and finally I couldn't resist.

"What are you thinking about?" I asked.

"Nothing special," Dan said, as men always do. Then he added, "Though frankly, I'm wondering when you'll tell me what this weekend is really about."

"What do you mean?" I asked, my shoulders tensing.

"A weekend away. No questions about where we should go—you made reservations yourself. I noticed when we checked in that you've already signed me up for eighteen holes of golf tomorrow. Something's up. I know you."

"I just wanted to be with you," I said.

"You're not with me on the golf course."

Honesty won the day. "No, I thought I'd make a little visit to Cassie Crawford's parents. Hank and Lydia Taylor. They live in Scottsdale. About five miles from here."

Dan sighed. "Why didn't you mention this earlier?"

"Because you wouldn't have wanted to come."

"But now I'm here." He rolled onto his back.

"Don't be mad," I whispered, snuggling close.

"Of course I'm not mad." He stroked my hair gently. "I can worry, but I'll always encourage whatever you want to do, Lacy. You know that. You've done it for me since the day we met. It's the least I owe you."

"You don't owe me anything," I said, thinking what a good team Dan and I had always made. One thing I'd learned about the marriage game: If you wanted to have fun playing, you couldn't keep score.

"I'll always be on your side, but I wish you had a different hobby," Dan said. "I'm a lot happier when you're decorating than when you're detecting."

"Isn't that a tad patronizing?" I asked.

"Absolutely not. There's nothing patronizing about wanting to protect somebody you love. Even Gloria Steinem must know that."

"Probably," I admitted. "Remember when she dated that rich guy and said she liked being picked up in limousines and taken care of? Then she married some South African business-man. Don Bale, I think his name was. No, David. He died a few years ago, but officially Gloria Steinem is Christian Bale's stepmother! Isn't that cool?"

"Uh, Christian Bale?"

"The really cute actor who played Batman," I explained ea-gerly. "Oh, and he was in *The Prestige*, which I like a lot. We can watch the DVD when we get home. It's about two magicians in nineteenth-century London."

"Magicians in London," Dan repeated. He glanced over at me with an amused smile.

I laughed. "Sorry, sweetie. I guess I went from patronizing to *The Prestige* kind of fast."

"I like trying to keep up with you," Dan said, kissing my forehead. Then getting back to the main subject he added, "But the magic for me is going to be keeping you safe, and keeping the whole family out of danger while you try to solve your case."

"The family doesn't have anything to do with this," I said.

"Maybe more than you realize," Dan said mildly. "Ashley saw the police drag you away at a party. Not so terrible, maybe. But Grant's getting invited into that secret society because of you is something different."

"How do you know all this?" Dan had been busy at the hospital lately, and I hadn't bothered to fill him in on details. Or maybe I'd been avoiding the subject.

"The kids talk to me," he said, with just a hint of pride.

"Well, Ashley's story is true," I admitted "But I didn't have anything to do with Grant being asked into Delta ij."

"Think about it," Dan said. He kept his voice even, but I

could hear the hint of agitation. "Why would an exclusive college club open its doors to a high-school senior? It sounds to
me like the weird professor who's involved is using Grant, for
reasons we don't know. Maybe he's trying to send you a message. Or find out something about Cassie. I'm not sure. But I
hate to think that by the time I *am* sure, it's going to be too
late."

"Too late for what?"

"To save you. To save Grant. God knows, Lacy, somebody
involved here has already killed two people. You think he's
going to be stopped by some skinny little woman chasing him
down?"

I lay back against the thick pillows, my heart racing. I didn't
want to put my family in danger. Never would. But I also ob-
jected to Dan's frightening me this way. His warning seemed
too dramatic. I should ask him to take it back.

And if he hadn't called me "skinny," I probably would
have.

When I opened my eyes the next morning, Dan had already left
to start his eighteen holes. I lolled in the comfy bed for a few
minutes, but I couldn't exactly have a romantic morning solo.
I tossed on a T-shirt with khaki shorts and flip-flops and left
the room. Downstairs in the lobby, I wished I'd dressed better,
because a tall man in a well-cut suit nodded pleasantly and said,
"Good morning! Have a lovely day!" Since the resort seemed
well-staffed with doormen, receptionists, and concierges, I figured he must be the hotel's official greeter. Not a bad job. But
how did you explain it on a résumé?

Outside, I took a right past a raft of eager car attendants and
went up a few stairs to the cactus garden. Small signs described
each of them, and I strolled happily, studying the difference
between the tall branched saguaro and the flat broad-leaved
prickly pear. When I was at home, I loved the graceful fragility

of my hothouse orchids, but here the sturdy cactus made me smile. I liked the thought that they flaunted their prickly fronts in the face of predators and the hot dry desert air. How brave. Could I be as courageous under the onslaught of detectives, Dan, and death? Maybe I needed to grow a few more prickles.

I wandered to the end of the garden, then ambled back along another path and finally, deep in thought, headed up a steep incline. Suddenly, a golf cart came around a corner and began careening down the hill.

"Watch out!" I screamed.

But the vehicle was going too fast to stop. I tried to leap out of the way just as the cart whizzed by, but the front corner slammed into my hip, knocking me off my feet and onto the hard gravel.

"Ouch!" I yelped. Tiny pebbles pierced the bare skin on my legs, and my palms burned from the impact. At the bottom of the hill, the cart finally came to a stop. I tried to get back up, but my badly twisted ankle wouldn't support my weight. Two men got out of the cart, but they didn't seem in any rush to help me.

"You're on the golf course," one of them hollered.

"You hit me," I shouted back, my voice hoarse with tears.

"Path's for carts only," he snarled. "Didn't you see the sign?"

If there'd been a sign, I missed it. But given that I was now lying on the ground with blood dripping from my leg, wasn't that beside the point?

One of the men marched up the hill toward me, his head down, his arms swinging apelike from broad shoulders. In his black turtleneck and pants, he didn't look dressed for eighteen holes in the Arizona sun. He put his beefy hands under my arms and lifted me up.

"You better watch yourself," he said scowling.

Something about him seemed familiar.

"Do I know you?" I asked. Tentatively, I tried to put some weight on my right foot. It hurt, but the pain seemed bearable.

"Doubt it," he said. "But you might know my boss. Mr. Crawford."

"Roger," I blurted, shocked. No wonder the man seemed familiar. He had a different face than the last Crawford thug I'd met, but the same clothes, bearing, and style. Good that I had both feet under me or I would have fallen over again.

"You've got to learn to stay out of places you shouldn't be," he said glowering. "Dangerous."

I picked some bits of gravel out of my hand, scraping at my palm with my fingernail. "Why's Mr. Crawford so afraid of me?" I asked.

"He's not afraid of anything," the man in black said. "He just wants to protect his interests."

"So he sent you to knock me down?"

"Don't flatter yourself," the man said, walking away. "This time was an accident. Next one might not be."

I took a long shower, gently scrubbing the dirt out of my cuts, then fumbled through Dan's dopp kit, looking for a way to salve my wounds. I found his first-aid bag and rubbed on ointment, then covered the worst patches with sterile bandages. Not so bad. I put on crisp white pants and a slim-fitting Theory blouse in pale aqua. No way my ankle could handle heels, so I slipped on a pair of green flats. The color looked wrong with the blouse, so I changed to white sandals. I'd packed light—but fortunately, "light" had included four pairs of shoes for three days.

Back in the lobby again, a concierge gave me directions to the address I needed in Scottsdale.

"It's easy to find, but are you sure you wouldn't like me to call you a car service?" he asked.

"I think I can handle it."

"Whatever you think," he said politely.

In the car, I grimaced when I stepped on the gas, my ankle protesting at the pressure. I drove slowly, glancing in my rear-view mirror several times in case Roger had somebody following me. A red convertible—not a likely tail car—hung close behind me for a while. But the woman behind the wheel finally pulled into another lane and zoomed past.

I turned onto a street where the houses started getting larger and the hedges higher. Then the houses disappeared altogether, hidden inside gated communities. At a small sign for Eden Glen, I pulled up a long driveway, stopping at an elaborate gate that boasted curlicued ironwork sculptures of trees, snakes, apples, and people across the top. Maybe paradise had been more populated than I knew.

A guard made his way over to my car. "I'm here to see the Taylors," I told him. "They're expecting me."

"Mr. Taylor went out," he said.

"How about Mrs. Taylor?"

"She's at the house." He made no effort to move.

"Well, then, I'm here to see Mrs. Taylor."

"Hmm." He nodded slowly and went back to his booth. When had Americans become so obsessed with keeping people out? First the red carpet, now this. The guard made a call, then came back to my car and asked to see my license. He wrote down my plate number, checked my trunk, had me sign a form, and affixed a temporary sticker to my front window. I half expected him to demand a passport and visa and check that my vaccinations were in order.

"Take a left just down the road and the Taylors' will be the first house you come to on the right," the guard said. He reluctantly opened the gate, clearly uncomfortable letting in LA riffraff like me.

I drove in, and given the flowering gardens, the very green

trees, and the brightly blossoming plants, I could almost believe that I'd made it to Eden. But then I remembered what the Taylors had suffered. You couldn't find paradise in a place, after all.

The Taylor house was set so far back from the road that I almost missed it. But a perfectly green lawn caught my eye, and I made a quick turn into the long driveway, trying to figure out how big the water bills must be in Eden.

I got out of the car, taking in the sprawling stucco-and-glass fronted house. Some architect had no doubt enjoyed himself, creating several multileveled sections, curving walls, and a free-floating winding staircase in the center hall that was visible to the outside through the twelve-foot windows.

I rang the doorbell, but nobody answered. I rang again. A woman in a straw hat and a grass-stained and wrinkled version of my own outfit—white pants and a blue blouse—came around from a side garden. I vaguely recognized her from the memorial service. The grief lines around her eyes hadn't lessened and her lips seemed pinched. She'd looked thin in the black dress she wore to the service, but now her cheeks seemed gaunt and her pants hung off her hips. Maybe you couldn't be too rich, but at our age, you really could be too thin.

"Lacy Fields? I'm Lydia Taylor."

"A pleasure to meet you." I held out my hand, and she transferred a trowel from her right hand to her left so we could shake. Then she thought better of it, pulled her hand back, and wiped it against the pants.

"Actually, I'm too dirty to shake. I've been gardening."

"I'm sorry to interrupt," I said. "Is this a bad time?"

"It's always a bad time these days," she said. Tears sprung to her eyes, and she wiped at them with the back of her hand, leaving a muddy smudge across her cheek. I reached into my bag and handed her a tissue.

"Thanks," she said. She blew her nose. "I'm not always like

this. I've been trying very hard to stay positive for Hank. But some days are worse than others."

"My coming has probably made this one of those worse ones," I said apologetically.

She nodded. "Honestly, yes, but I wanted to meet you. I'm glad you called. You were the last person to talk to my daughter. I'm told she never regained consciousness after the EMTs arrived."

I swallowed hard, trying to get past the lump in my throat. The last person to talk to Cassie? I'd never thought of it that way. If, God forbid, our roles were reversed, what would I want Lydia Taylor to tell me?

"I don't think your daughter suffered," I said, putting my hand on her arm. We weren't friends, but we were both mothers. No greater bond necessary. "Everything happened within minutes. She couldn't have been frightened or even known what was happening."

"The police said you did CPR and tried to save her. Thank you for that."

"I wish I could have . . ."

"I know. We all wish."

Our eyes caught for a moment, and we both held them steady, motherly compassion passing between us. I still had my hand on her arm, and I gave it a small squeeze, then pulled back.

Finally, Lydia said, "Why don't we go to the back patio so we can sit and talk. Or would you rather be inside?"

"No, this is lovely. I'm not an air-conditioner person. Even in Scottsdale."

Lydia gave a small smile. "I'm with you. I might be the only person in Arizona who's always cold."

"You don't have a lot of fat to protect you," I said lightly.

Despite the ninety-degree heat, she folded her arms against her chest. It wasn't just the slim frame that had left her unprotected. When she heard her daughter had been murdered, her blood must have run cold. And how do you ever warm up again after that?

We walked around the property, past stylized gardens, an expansive free-form swimming pool, and an immaculate clay tennis court. The entire back of the house, facing the mountains, was glass, making it almost impossible to tell where inside met outside. I followed Lydia up a few stairs to a shaded retreat with three Italianate modern seating clusters; a cooking area with brick-walled grill, spit, and Viking stove; and a side ell with a glass dining table that could probably accommodate twenty. Calling it a patio seemed a stretch. I couldn't exactly picture sitting here and rocking in an L.L. Bean chair.

Lydia gestured for me to sit down, then opened a bamboo cabinet that turned out to be a well-disguised refrigerator.

"Water?" she asked.

"No thanks."

"You have to stay hydrated in the desert," she insisted. "I have Smart Water, Vitamin Water, Energy Water, and water collected from an underground spring in Patagonia and untouched by humans until you open the cap."

I laughed. "Anything is fine."

She handed me a bottle, then sat next to me.

"It's just beautiful here," I said, looking out to the mountains. "Have you lived here long?"

"I moved when Cassie was in college," Lydia said. "My first husband—Cassie's father—died when she was eight. I raised the girls myself."

"Not easy," I said, thinking of my own mother, who had struggled valiantly as a single parent. She worked all the time, and I rarely saw her sleep. Money had been short for us, though maybe not for Lydia.

"Hank and I had known each other for years, long before he became so . . ." She paused, letting the dirty word *wealthy* pass unsaid. "We got married when Cassie was sixteen. I tried to keep life as normal as possible. Once both girls got to college, I didn't feel guilty about moving. But maybe it was a mistake."

"Why?"

She gestured to the opulent surroundings. "The girls and I lived simply in California. When Cassie started getting involved with Roger, I didn't like it. Maybe Hank and I set the wrong example. But for me, it was never about the money."

"Was it for Cassie?"

Lydia shook her head. "She thought she loved Roger. We had a fight when I told her she really loved having a father figure. Roger was too old for her. He bossed her around, told her what to do. In some odd way, I think she associated that with what a father should be. Remember, she never really had one."

"Did they argue about money?"

"Not as far as I know. She'd always been frugal and self-sufficient. She signed a prenup."

"You know your own child," I said softly. "Did she seem happy with Roger?"

"I've thought about that a lot." Lydia looked down and brushed some dirt off her pants. "Her boyfriend before Roger didn't stack up as a mother's dream. But I liked him. Cassie always seemed happy around him."

"Billy Mann?" I asked.

She nodded, and another flash of pain darkened her face. So she already knew.

I took a deep breath.

"Your daughter left Billy some money, as you probably heard."

She nodded. "We'd discussed it. The lawyer who drafted the prenup insisted on a will, but he must have been surprised when Cassie decided she wouldn't leave everything to Roger."

Lydia gave a rough-edged laugh. "Roger doesn't need money and neither do we. Cassie cared about doing good with whatever she had."

"How did Billy figure in?"

"You don't know?" She glanced at me. "His younger brother is disabled. Ren, I think his name is. Wheelchair-bound. Billy's always been really good to him and Cassie loved that. Nothing better than a tattooed biker with a heart of gold."

How about a tattooed biker with a heart of gold and a twenty-carat yellow diamond?

"Did she give Billy any gifts"—I couldn't bring myself to say *while she was still alive* so I concluded, lamely—"before?"

Lydia didn't seem to notice. "Cassie and Roger gave him the boat where he lived."

And where he died. I shuddered, remembering the gory scene.

"Roger had owned the boat for years, paying for it to sit in drydock," Lydia continued. "He kept getting bigger ones and couldn't be bothered with selling his little starter. Cassie had the idea of giving it to Billy. He moved onto it and he brought his brother along all the time. Ren loved the freedom of being on the water."

"Roger didn't mind giving a gift to Cassie's old boyfriend?"

Lydia smiled. "I don't think he felt threatened, if that's what you mean."

But if Cassie had spent a night on the boat maybe he'd want revenge. In the form of a bullet through the back.

"Do you know anything about Cassie giving Billy a diamond?" I asked.

"No. Nothing. I can't imagine why she would." Lydia wrinkled her forehead—something not many could do in the age of Botox. Then, making sure I had the right impression, Lydia added, "My Cassie cared about people. She loved Roger—at least when she married him. She wanted to help Billy. Really, that's all."

I rubbed my temples, feeling my head starting to pound. Either desert dehydration had set in or all my detecting had depleted my neurons. If only that Smart Water could give me a few more IQ points.

I started to ask another question about the diamond, but Lydia sat back and tugged at the brim of her hat, shading her red-rimmed eyes. Talking about her lost child had left her drained. Off in the distance, the desert sun glanced off the craggy-faced mountains. The red rocks cast a rosy glow that seemed wrong for our mood. I thought of my last brush with Arizona landscape.

"It's so beautiful here," I said, looking off at the weathered peaks. "I know some people who've tried to reproduce the whole scene in LA. Something about creating energy fields with those red rocks."

Lydia gave a wan smile. "Does that mean you've encountered Andy Daniels?"

At hearing his name, my mouth dropped open. I made an effort to close it. "Yes. You know him?"

"His parents are old family friends of ours. They have a place in Sedona. Cassie used the connection to get her first job."

"Oh." A couple of cogs seemed to fall into place: how Cassie got the job at Genius Productions—and even more, why she would have left. The fact that Andy was an old family friend put his one-night romp in a different light. No wonder Andy had been mortified and Cassie had quit.

Lydia stood up and I realized the visit had ended. She walked with me back toward my car, but now the opulent home and spectacular setting didn't seem to matter. Could there be any greater proof that money couldn't buy happiness? My thoughts flashed to my own three children, and I felt an almost physical yearning to hug them. How much precious time did parents waste griping about their kids' missed curfews or loud music? Lydia had the painful perspective of knowing one should be grateful for every glorious (and not-so-glorious) moment together.

"I miss Cassie so much," Lydia said softly, staring off at her garden as we strolled. "She never really lived here, but the house seems empty without her. I just want to talk to her one more time. However inane it sounds, I'd trade everything I own just to have another day together."

"Not inane," I said fervently. "What mother wouldn't feel the same?"

"Thank you for understanding," Lydia said. Then she smiled wanly. "Unfortunately, nobody's offering me the trade."

"How is your other daughter doing?" I asked.

"It's hard to know. She has a good job. Friends. She lives in New York." Lydia shook her head. "People always say to me, 'At least you still have her.' True enough. But it's like losing both legs and being glad you still have your arms. You try."

I shuddered. The woman had lost her first husband, and then her daughter. Amazing she could still stand. Maybe we all possessed greater strength than we knew.

As if reading my thoughts, Lydia said, "The first loss was hard, but this has been devastating. Cassie looked just like her dad. When she'd smile, I'd see him. Now it's like losing him all over again. My beautiful daughter. My husband. Both their faces, gone forever."

I nodded dumbly. Any words of comfort seemed inadequate. Remind her of happy memories and the faces in photo albums? Convey how lucky she was to have Hank? At least in the midst of this deepest grief, she wasn't alone. Hank was no doubt a strong shoulder to lean on, but husbands weren't interchangeable, either.

"I'd like to ask you one more thing," Lydia said as we approached the Lexus. "I don't mean to be melodramatic, but did Cassie have any . . . final words?"

For a moment, I pictured Cassie on top of the ladder in the study, her arms spread wide. Like an angel, I'd thought. But a moment later she'd been on the floor bleeding. If only I could say what Lydia yearned to hear. That Cassie had murmured, *Tell my mother I love her.* Or that she'd whispered, *I've had a happy life.*

"She lost consciousness very quickly," I said. "She didn't have time for any messages."

"I know she fell from a ladder."

"I think she'd climbed up looking for something. The last thing I remember her saying was 'Delta.'" I paused, but Lydia's face didn't change. "Does that mean anything to you?"

She shook her head. "I'd like to think so," she said sadly. "But honestly it doesn't."

Chapter Fifteen

— • —

Delta.

I drove away, the word ringing in my head. Maybe it didn't mean anything to Cassie's mother, but it meant something to me.

Why hadn't I made the connection?

I sped a little too quickly up the elegant entryway to the Phoenician, swerving around some walkers out enjoying the sunny day. I left the car with the attendant and ran to our room—but Dan hadn't come back. His golf game must have ended by now, so I raced back through the hotel and out the back door, past one very well-tended field for croquet and another for lawn bowling. Slightly breathless, I got to a pool surrounded by lounge chairs. I didn't see Dan among the sunbathers sipping icy drinks, so I went across a bridge and down some stairs to another deck and pool.

Dan stood contemplating a shallow pond stocked with large, brightly colored koi. He still had on a golf shirt, but he'd changed to shorts and sandals.

"You had it right," I said, sidling up next to him.

He turned away from the fish and looked at me. "Hi, honey. Had what right?" he asked.

"Why Grant got asked to join Delta ij," I said, too wound up to bother with *hello.* "To me, our son is perfect, so any secret society should want him. But as you pointed out, he's a high schooler. Not a cool choice. Someone in the organization is trying to get information from him. Or from me."

Dan tapped his foot slowly. "What brought you around?"

"You, darling. I trust your instincts."

Dan gave a small smile. His concern hadn't melted on the back nine, but he seemed mollified now. Telling your husband he's right does that. I leaned my head briefly against his shoulder. In the pond just beneath us, more fish gathered, their mouths open, hoping for crumbs. Smart little critters. They knew that people standing above them meant food. Or at least it usually did. I wished I had something to throw them. Too bad they had to learn the human lesson that nothing in life was certain.

"Cassie's mother asked me if her daughter had any last words," I said. "I'm sure she hoped for something like, 'Tell my mom I love her.' Unfortunately, I didn't have anything like that to offer her."

"But you wanted to," Dan said sympathetically, knowing me well.

I nodded. "I doubt Cassie knew she'd die, or who knows what she might have said. But I suddenly had an image of her standing on the ladder and saying 'Delta.'" I paused for dramatic effect. "Delta," I repeated.

Dan didn't take the bait. "What did you think it meant at the time?" he asked.

"I didn't think about it," I said with a shrug. "I figured she'd started climbing out of sheer delirium. But the other day, her friend Paige told me they'd gone to the penthouse the night before so Cassie could stash some papers. Paige thought they had to do with the divorce. But maybe they were about Delta ij. So on the ladder, Cassie sent a final message after all."

Dan rubbed my shoulder, sensing my building tension.

"It's possible, but maybe 'Delta' meant something else. Weren't you in some Delta sorority?"

"Tri Delta," I reminded him.

"Which is where you met Molly, isn't it?" Dan asked. When I nodded, he said, "Maybe that's the connection."

"Cassie's been poisoned and she talks about her sorority? Why?"

"Maybe she thought a sorority sister had done the poisoning," he said mildly. "Molly. Tri Delta. Delta. It adds up."

I felt myself freeze. Delta? Molly? Could that really be what Cassie meant? No matter what I wanted to think, I had to look at the evidence. The night before Cassie died, Paige had seen Molly and Roger in the penthouse, arms around each other. Molly had never mentioned the visit. Deception by omission. What else might she have lied about?

I shook my head. No way I could let myself doubt my best friend.

"You never liked Molly," I said petulantly.

"She's your friend and she means a lot to you," Dan said. "But I'm just trying to be realistic."

Could you ever be realistic about the person who got you through the toughest times? Molly had won my loyalty forever when Ashley was born, but she'd shown her good heart long before. During my freshman year in college, my father—the abusive man my mother left when I turned two—died. Mom sounded almost relieved when she called to tell me, but the news hit me like a sledgehammer. I didn't remember him and never expected a reconciliation, but every little girl wants a daddy to take care of her, and now the finality hit me. I'd never have one. Molly had stayed up with me all night as I cried for what might have been. She held me tightly, never once questioning my pain. That night, I felt like she was the only person in the whole world who understood me.

You don't forget that.

"*You* were the one who made me think about Grant and Delta ij," I said to Dan now, feeling slightly confused. "Why are you twisting it now?"

"I'm not. I'm just trying to make sure we don't diagnose a zebra."

We'd been married long enough that I understood the reference. An old adage in medicine held that when you heard hooves, you should think horses, not zebras. In other words, a headache might be a brain tumor—but it was probably just a headache. Go for what was most likely.

"So Molly's your metaphoric horse?"

"You tell me," Dan said quietly.

"The first hooves you heard said Delta ij. I don't know how the group connects to Cassie, but we better find out. Especially if Grant's gotten involved."

Dan threw up an arm as if giving in, and at the gesture half a dozen fish leapt to the surface, their mouths open in wide Os. Misled again.

He turned away from the pond. "Since there's nothing we can do right now, we should just relax," he said, ever able to compartmentalize his emotions. "Should we change and take a dip?"

I shook my head. "I don't really feel like swimming."

"Get something to eat?"

"I'm not hungry, thanks."

He looked at me for a long moment, then put his arms around me. "Nothing's going to make my Lacy happy right now," he said, knowing me well.

"But I'm happy. Very happy." I gave my best fake grin.

"You're a lousy liar." He kissed me gently. "Do you want to leave?"

I sighed and leaned into him, burying my face in his chest. "Yes, I want to go home. I want to solve this case. But I dragged you to Phoenix, and you deserve a rest. It's not fair to get you back on a plane this afternoon."

"If you think you're on to something, you need to pursue it," he said simply. "I understand."

I felt a surge of gratitude. I couldn't carp anymore about Dan's being condescending. He loved me, and offered his support without strings.

"If you really don't mind . . ." I paused. "Listen, I will go back to LA, okay? But you stay here and have fun. Play more golf. Go to the spa and get a massage. Lie on a chaise and read journals."

"It's a deal," Dan said.

"You're sure you don't mind?"

"Of course not. But I'll wait on the massage. You're the only masseuse I want."

I got back to an empty house and almost immediately regretted having left Phoenix—and Dan. We could have hiked Camelback Mountain, had a romantic dinner, danced under the stars. Sure I needed to protect Grant, but he was at a tennis tournament in San Diego. The only immediate danger he faced was tendonitis.

Still, Grant would come home and head back to campus. Back to his secret society. My rational son would laugh at vague warnings to be careful. He needed facts—and so did I.

The connection to Delta ij seemed hazy at best, the evidence against Roger was a little clearer. What could be in the papers Cassie stashed in the study? Protection if Roger demanded a divorce, Paige had guessed. The secret he didn't want exposed. Could it be that instead of protecting her, the mystery papers had made him poison her?

But as she climbed the ladder, Cassie didn't say, "Roger." She said, "Delta."

I felt torn between my two possibilities. According to Grant, Professor Bohr had told the students in Delta ij that they might get asked questions about Cassie. Questions they couldn't answer.

I wondered if the answers lay on that shelf in the study.

I could call Detective Wilson and tell him what I knew. But I doubted he'd take any action. Even if he tried, what judge would issue a search warrant based on a single word? Wealth and status didn't mean Roger had the police in his pocket, but they made it pretty unlikely that Detective Wilson would want to rip up his penthouse on a hunch.

I went to the kitchen and turned on our shiny steel Italian espresso machine to make myself a double. Great investment. Just four hundred more espressos made at home instead of at Starbucks and the machine would pay for itself.

Small porcelain cup in hand, I went upstairs to my study. Twice I picked up the phone to call Molly then put it back down. Sure, I wanted to know what Roger and Molly were up to the night before Cassie died. But if I told her what Paige had said, she'd get defensive, and right now I just needed her help.

"Hi," I said when she picked up her cell phone. "Bad time or place?" In the wireless world, asking *How are you?* never made as much sense as asking *Where are you?*

"I'm at the gym," she said.

"Oh, then I won't bother you."

"Don't be silly. I'm lounging in the café, eating a croissant and reading a book on Pilates. I'd rather stretch my mind than my muscles."

Only Molly joined a gym because she liked the lunch. Her idea of exercise generally involved lifting the phone. "Any chance you actually bought sneakers?"

"Of course not. Chanel flats are as sporty as I get."

"Chanel, proud sponsor of the Paris Shopping Olympics."

"I'm going for the gold, babe," Molly said.

We both laughed. Apparently murder, mayhem, and mendacity couldn't ruin a good friendship.

"Anyway, I called for a reason," I said. I briefly filled her in on the stashed papers, Grant's secret society, and my "Delta" breakthrough.

"Interesting," Molly said when I finished. "I kind of hope your hunch is right. Sure would take the spotlight off me."

"And put it on Grant," I said softly.

"Oh God, I'm sorry," Molly blurted. "I wasn't thinking. It would be awful if he got caught up in this. What do we do?"

I liked that she'd made it *we,* rather than just me.

"I still have the key to the penthouse. I want to go over and see what's hidden on the bookshelf. Would you come with me?"

There was a long silence. "We can't do that," she said finally. "What if the police come? It doesn't matter if you have a key—it's got to be breaking and entering."

"I'm not planning on breaking anything. But I am worried about someone breaking my son's neck."

"You're being dramatic."

"Two people are dead. That's dramatic," I said, sounding a lot like Dan.

Molly didn't answer immediately. "Okay, here's an idea," she said finally. "How about I call Roger and tell him the story. He's on a business trip—London, Hong Kong, Moscow. A private plane makes the world very small. But he can get someone to let us in."

How could I tell her that I didn't want Roger to know? If he suspected the stashed papers involved him, they'd be gone by the time we got there.

"It's all too hypothetical to explain to a guy on a Gulfstream," I said, looking for an excuse. "Maybe you should give him another reason you need to get in."

"Like what?"

Oh, heck, how should I know? I was as lousy at lying as Pinocchio. "Tell him you can't find your gold Cartier Roadster watch. You think it must have fallen off when you were at the penthouse. You're in a panic because it's so pricy."

"Darling, my Cartier is a copy."

"Can't be. It's gorgeous."

"You think I'd spend twenty-five thousand dollars on a watch? No way. I got it for two hundred bucks at a little store-front near Hollywood and Vine. The one corner of America that's a mecca for all things fake—from tits to timepieces."

Despite myself, I laughed. "If it looked real to me, it looked real to him. Tell him you think you dropped it on the last visit. The night before Cassie died."

Ten minutes later, Molly called me back. "I reached Roger," she reported. "He said he'll buy me a new Roadster and have Cartier send it over."

"And?" I held my breath. Just how far had Molly's morals fallen?

"Tempting," she admitted. "But I told him the one I lost has sentimental value. I explained you have the key and could let me in. He didn't sound happy, but said to go ahead."

"Thanks, Molly." I let my breath out again. "When do you want to meet?"

"Tonight," she said. "Seven o'clock."

"Great. Let's meet in the lobby of Roger's building. I'll take you out to dinner afterward. A new Japanese restaurant opened with twenty kinds of eel on the menu."

"While we're eating slimy food, you can explain your slippery comment about where I was the night before Cassie died."

Since she'd let it pass a few minutes ago, I thought she'd missed the mention. But Molly didn't miss anything.

• • •

"So how did you know?" Molly called out to me, as soon as she came into the gleaming marble lobby of Roger's building.

A spiffily uniformed doorman had pushed open the front door for her, a smartly dressed lobby attendant escorted her in, and a concierge behind a desk smiled politely. Molly ignored all of them, striding across the lobby, her high heels clacking.

"Enough staff here," I said, getting up from the leather sling chair where I'd been waiting. "They should know what's going on."

"But they don't," Molly said. "Roger already complained to management about it. The garage elevator is unattended. No security cameras there."

She had a point. The main elevator from the parking garage came only as far as the lobby. Most guests would heed the small sign that said ALL VISITORS MUST BE ANNOUNCED and stop at the front desk. But what if they didn't? A modern sculpture with a plunging waterfall at its center stood behind the free-standing concierge desk and kept the two high-speed elevators hidden from view. Anybody who wanted to slip upstairs unde-tected could do it easily. The security system had more holes than a rock star's jeans.

"I've hardly ever been in the lobby," I admitted as we stepped into the elevator now. "There's a private penthouse lift from the garage that works with a pass card." I held up mine to show her. "I assume that's how you and Roger got in."

"So I'll ask again," Molly said, not confirming anything. "How did you know?"

"A friend of Cassie's saw you and Roger. She even identi-fied your perfume. Annick Goutal Passion."

Molly lifted a wrist to her nose and sniffed. "Is that a joke?"

"No. As good an ID as DNA in my book. Probably better than fingerprints. Roger and you were in the study, and eventually you'll tell me why. More important, he must have had a key to get in. Even though he made a big fuss the next day that he didn't."

We stepped off the elevator, and as I put my own key in the door, Molly grabbed my arm. "Are you sure you want to do this?" she asked.

I heard the edge of fear in her voice.

"What's wrong?"

"I don't know. You suspect Roger. What if you're right? He knows we're coming here tonight. I'm suddenly scared."

I hesitated, but then pushed the door open and patted her arm comfortingly. Whenever Jimmy got scared, we'd hum an old Simon and Garfunkel song together. It worked for him, and it usually made me feel braver, too. Now I tried it on Molly.

"*'Is there any danger?/No, no not really/Just lean on me,'*" I crooned softly.

She gave a small smile. "Okay, I'm leaning. What's the plan?"

"Let's play it safe," I whispered. "You stay here by the front door. I'll be quick. If anything happens, you can run out fast to get help."

Molly nodded and I offered a thumbs-up sign. Then, walking with more confidence than I felt (*"So I'll continue to continue to pretend/My life will never end . . ."* went the other Simon and Garfunkel tune in my head), I strode quickly into the study. I had only one place to focus: the bookshelf. Grabbing the library ladder, I rolled it to what seemed the right position. I had a strong visual image of where I'd been standing when Cassie scrambled up, and the angle of the ladder against the shelves. One advantage of being a decorator: Maybe I couldn't always remember names lately, and the dates of friends' birthdays blurred, but once I'd seen something, I never forgot it.

I climbed, just as Cassie had done, and got to the rung she'd reached. But I held on firmly, not wanting to repeat the end of the scene.

From where I stood, I could reach dozens of books. Where would Cassie have hidden something? I glanced at the titles. When I'd been in the midst of decorating for them, the Crawfords had sent over countless books, which I'd had an assistant arrange on the shelves. Most of them came from Roger—expensive, leather-bound volumes from a snotty English publisher, along with signed first editions of biography and philosophy books, purchased more for the show-off high price than for literary pleasure. But the section now in front of me seemed more Cassie's style: hardcovers she had probably read in college and that had excited her to new ways of thinking. Virginia Woolf butted against Ayn Rand and James Joyce, and all seemed well-thumbed. So did the save-the-world texts from Rachel Carson and Jane Addams. As her friend Paige had pointed out, I'd been unfair to pigeonhole Cassie as just another girl who married well.

I gripped the ladder tightly and scanned the titles again, looking for a clue. Some classic mysteries from Dorothy Sayers caught my eye. I pulled down *Gaudy Night* and flipped through it. A few underlined passages grabbed my attention, but they seemed more the mark of an eager reader than a secret message. No papers fluttered out. I put the book back and took down *Strong Poison*. How ironic would that be? This time I found a handwritten note tucked into the front. I opened it, heart pounding.

Happy 20th Birthday, Cassie! I love you always.

Love, Mom

I grimaced. Nice sentiment, but not the one I needed. I shoved the volume back into place. My plan suddenly seemed futile. Even assuming I'd put the ladder in exactly the right spot, I could spend all night flipping through the books within reach. If Cassie had just hidden a single page or two, I could easily miss it. Not knowing what I was looking for made this harder. Or maybe impossible.

My left hand slipped off the ladder, and I wiped my sweaty palm against my linen pants. Despite my efforts, my courage started draining, and I felt some of Molly's anxiety seeping in. *I'll continue to continue to pretend. . . .*

"Molly, is everything okay?" I called out.

I waited a beat but got no answer, and I realized she couldn't hear me. The penthouse was too big and the walls too thick. Cassie and Roger had picked an unusually well-built building. Right now, I would have preferred cheap Sheetrock that let voices carry.

Stepping down a rung, I looked despairingly at the neatly lined-up books in front of me. None jutted from the shelf to show it had been recently read. Maybe I should give up and call it a night, have dinner with Molly and look elsewhere for clues. Hesitating, I gave the shelves one final scan—and an ordinary-looking book with a brown binding caught my eye. Something about the size and shape of the volume seemed familiar. Then I noticed the title—*Words of Love*—and laughed out loud. The perfect title for a book you didn't want any man to open (or steal). I had the very same brown volume on my own shelf. Instead of pages, the fake binding had an empty center made for secret storage. Mine hid some of my best jewelry. (The fake Brillo box under the sink hid the rest.)

Certain that I'd found what I wanted, I grabbed the book and scuttled down the ladder. Safely on terra firma again, I opened the cover. Sure enough, the book was hollow. I lifted the velvet covering of an enclosed box and felt a wave of excitement as I pulled out a wad of papers.

I knew I should get back to Molly, but I couldn't resist a quick peek.

First came a worn newspaper clipping from the front page of the UCLA student newspaper *The Daily Bruin* reporting on the death of a junior named Derek Howe. A blurry photo showed a group of grieving students that included Cassie. From the date, I figured it must have been Cassie's freshman year at college. She had probably saved the page since then.

I quickly went on to the next item, a printout from a local newspaper in Connecticut. The story, from twelve years ago, detailed a house fire in a three-bedroom colonial that had killed a couple named Sandy and Jerry Baker. Their son, Nicholas, home from college on vacation, escaped unharmed. Neighbors expressed shock, and Sandy's sister, who had lived across the street, promised to do whatever she could for the devastated young man. She pooh-poohed reports that Nicholas could have started the conflagration.

I hesitated, trying to figure out how the two stories could be related. Two tragedies at opposite ends of the country, several years apart. A young man named Nicholas Baker orphaned. Another one, Derek Howe, dead. None of the people overlapped. But both reports had been important enough for Cassie to hide away.

Puzzled, I went on to the next page. This one seemed simpler: a document from the UCLA development office, where Cassie had worked. It described a discussion she had underway with Randall Scott, a Silicon Valley millionaire, to endow a chair in theoretical physics. The straightforward report had been submitted a few weeks earlier to Elsa Franklin.

Finally, I came to a yellow-lined page covered in small handwriting I assumed to be Cassie's. I couldn't take the time to read it now while Molly stood worrying and waiting. But maybe Cassie's notes explained how the other pieces fit together.

I tucked the pages into my Lulu Guinness pocketbook and raced out of the library. I'd grab Molly and we could head to the restaurant to discuss the papers that—possibly—had signed Cassie's death warrant.

"Molly, I'm set!" I called exuberantly as I rushed into the foyer.

The room stood empty. The front door remained open, just as I'd left it. But Molly hadn't stayed.

"Molly?" I called her name again, a little louder. No answer. I peered cautiously into the hallway. Nothing. She should have told me if she was leaving. I didn't feel like playing games.

Suddenly, a piece of metal jammed hard into my spine. I screamed, but a man's thickly callused hand clamped powerfully over my mouth.

"Shut up." A low, gravelly voice resonated in my ear. "Don't move or I'll shoot." I could feel my attacker's hot breath at the back of my neck.

Fight, I told myself.

I jerked back my head as hard as I could and tried to open my mouth enough to bite down on his flesh. But his viselike grip didn't ease. I twisted, trying to get away.

"Cut it out." He took the gun from my back and smacked the butt against my hip. Tears sprung to my eyes; I lifted my foot and stomped down, but my soft flats didn't make a dent in his metal-toed oxfords. Furious now, I swung my hip hard into his groin.

"Oww," he hollered. "Bitch!"

His gun clattered to the ground and I tried to take off. My legs churned, but like a character in an old Road Runner cartoon I didn't get anywhere, because he grabbed my arm. Not taking any chances, he looped his leg around both of mine, knocking me over. He fell on top of me, his knee in my chest and both hands at my throat.

"What do you want?" I gasped.

"What you just stole."

"I didn't steal anything."

"Give it to me, bitch."

Now he pointed the gun at my head, holding the cold metal against my temple. I started to hyperventilate, my breath coming too fast. I squeezed my eyes closed and tried to get under control. Whatever those papers contained, I wouldn't die for them. I had three children at home.

"In my Lulu Guinness," I said in a small voice. "Just papers. I didn't take anything you'd want."

Some of his weight came off me, but the gun stayed in place. "What's a frigging Lulu?" he asked. "That your lady friend?"

"My friend," I gasped. "Where's Molly? What's happened to her?"

"I told you to shut up," he said. "What'd you steal? Where's the Lulu?"

"My pocketbook."

He grabbed my black patent bag with one hand, unsnapped the clasp, and dumped the contents onto the floor, scattering keys, lipstick, Estée Lauder gold compact, wallet, cell phone, mini photo album, old receipts, pens, Advil, fabric swatches, a small notebook, and a spare pair of panty hose. My portable life.

"Papers," he said, his hands at my throat again.

"In the zippered compartment," I choked.

He found the papers, stuck them in his pocket, then picked up something from the scattered pile of items from my purse. With one swift move, he grabbed my arms and flipped me over so my face pressed painfully into the marble floor. He twisted my arms behind my back, then tied my arms and wrists so tightly I could hardly budge. It took me a moment to realize I'd been trussed with my own Donna Karan matte sheer neutrals panty hose.

"Get up," he said, dragging me to my feet. "Walk."

Putting one foot in front of the other seemed almost impossible. I staggered forward just a few steps and he yanked open the front hall closet.

"Molly!" I yelped.

She lay slouched on the closet floor, her Hermès scarf tied into her mouth as a gag and her arms held behind her by the rope belt she'd been wearing. An angry red lump swelled on her forehead. He shoved me into the closet with her, then wordlessly slammed the door. I heard the outside latch fall into place. Light seeped in from a crack, so at least we could see each other. Molly looked at me with wide, terrified eyes. I waited a beat before saying anything. Then, as I'd hoped, I heard the heavy front door of the penthouse open and close.

"He's gone," I whispered to Molly. "We'll be all right."

She moaned and rolled her head. I didn't want her fainting or passing out from sheer terror. *Continue to continue to pretend*, Simon and Garfunkel advised. Even fake courage could be contagious.

"Look at us," I said, trying to keep my tone light. "You're always so chic. You get bound with Hermès and I only get panty hose."

She seemed to perk up a little.

"What if I didn't have an extra pair of panty hose in my purse?" I continued. "Would he have let me go? Seems like our assailant wasn't too prepared."

Another moan from Molly, but this one sounded like she wanted to say something. Stopped by the gag, the word came out as a guttural grunt.

"Okay, he had a gun," I said, interpreting for her. "But he didn't shoot. We're alive."

Molly looked so miserable, she probably would have considered death a good option. I hadn't recognized our attacker, but something told me Roger had sent him. Another one of his entourage of thugs. Any fantasies Molly harbored about her rich guy as would-be husband had to be crumbling.

Molly made another garbled sound.

"Much as I'm enjoying this one-sided conversation, we

need to get out of here," I said. It made the most sense to get one of our hands free first. But I could tell Molly desperately needed to lose the gag.

I sidled around as best I could so we sat back-to-back. Then I pulled up onto my knees, getting my bound hands as close as possible to the knot in her scarf. I had thought I could just pull the whole thing down, but as soon as I tried I could tell that it had been tied too tightly.

"This is going to take a couple of minutes," I said. I ran my fingers over the knot. When Grant had first started hiking and camping, he'd walked around the house with a piece of rope, practicing his knot-making skills. Slip knots. Square knots. Granny knots. He had always tried to teach me how to do them. "It's the key to survival on a mountain," he'd explained earnestly. A closet wasn't exactly Kilimanjaro. But I still had to do this right.

I began picking at the gag, but nothing seemed to get loose. I manipulated the fabric as best I could, but facing backward and with my wrists bound, I couldn't make any headway. A few minutes later, I gave up in frustration. The silk wouldn't give.

"You should have worn a cheaper scarf," I said. "Polyester wouldn't be this difficult." I sat back down. "Let me try your hands."

My shoulders hurt from the odd position, and my upper arms had started to cramp. But the rope belt was easier to maneuver. The top half of the knot quickly gave way, and I felt a surge of triumph.

"Almost there," I promised her. I kept working at it, and persistence paid off. I got the material free and quickly unwound it from Molly's arms. She shook them, getting back her circulation, then quickly came behind me to release my bonds.

"I'm never wearing panty hose again," I said as she struggled. "From now on, it's bare legs and self-tanner."

Once she got me loose, I gave a huge sigh. I'd lost some

feeling in my fingers, so I began opening and shutting my fists to get the blood flowing again. My fingers started tingling—a good sign. Molly had started working on her gag, and now I came around to help. In a minute, we tossed the Hermès scarf to the ground.

"Thank god," said Molly. She rubbed the corners of her lips and opened her mouth tentatively, as if surprised to find she could talk again.

"You're okay," I said, giving her a quick hug.

But she wasn't. She touched the red welt on her forehead, then pushed at the door. "We're locked in. We're going to die," she said, her voice breaking.

"No, we're going to get out." I tried the door, knowing that every builder cut corners somewhere. "A closet doesn't have a very solid lock, just a simple latch. I could probably open it with a credit card. If I had one handy."

Molly buried her head in her hands and I saw her shoulders shaking. "I . . . I have to get out of here," she said, between sobs. "I c-c-can't stand this."

We'd already been here too long. If Molly couldn't hold herself together now, trying to jimmy the lock would just prolong the agony.

I looked around. Nothing in the closet except a few padded hangars I'd put in and the mandatory fire extinguisher the builder provided. Work with what you have, I figured. I lifted the heavy fire extinguisher from its holder on the back wall.

"Move out of the way," I said to Molly. She hesitated, then retreated to a corner.

"What are you doing?" she asked. At least the surprise had stopped her tears.

For an answer, I held the heavy metal canister from a rung on top and began swinging it back and forth, building momentum. Then I took a step forward and, with a huge grunt of effort, slammed it forward. The door trembled, but stood firm.

"Aim for the middle," Molly suggested, suddenly part of the plan. "The spot where the folding doors come together might be vulnerable."

"Okay." Panting from the exertion, I started swinging the fire extinguisher again. My arm felt like rubber, but I didn't care.

"Do it!" Molly shouted.

This time I released the handle, throwing the canister with all the force I could muster. I fell back from the rebound and landed hard on my butt. Which gave me the perfect seat to watch the door splinter open.

"Free!" said Molly, as I scrambled to stand up. "You're Wonder Woman."

She started to rush out, but I grabbed her hand. "I don't want to fall into another trap," I said.

"You think he's still outside? Waiting for us?" Molly asked.

I thought for a moment. "I don't think he really wanted to hurt us. He just had to give himself enough time to get away."

I stepped cautiously out of the closet, then crept to the quiet front hall. Molly followed. The contents of my purse still sat scattered on the floor, and I scooped them back into the black patent bag. Even my wallet had been left behind. I opened it. The credit cards were untouched—as was the cash.

"Let's get out of here," I said, no longer worried.

"Should we call the police?" Molly asked.

"What do we tell them? Our story's not exactly going to hold up under questioning. We came to the penthouse to look for a Cartier Roadster you hadn't really lost."

"But maybe Roger told someone about the watch. This thief heard about the story and followed us to steal it," Molly said.

"He didn't even take my wallet," I said. "Only sixty bucks in cash, but a normal thief wouldn't let it go. You have to figure our attacker got just what he wanted. If he'd come for a twenty-five-thousand-dollar watch, he wouldn't rush out with some worthless papers instead."

"You think they're worthless?" Molly asked.

I waited a beat before answering. "Honestly, to somebody, they're probably priceless."

Chapter Sixteen

—— • ——

M olly felt too unhinged to go home alone, so I brought her to my house and opened a bottle of wine. She needed something to calm her down. For dinner we ate Triscuits directly from the box and hunks of blue cheese and Jarlsberg from the fridge. Grown-up comfort food. I suggested she spend the night.

"Lots of empty bedrooms tonight," I said, sweeping away some crumbs.

"You told me the kids are away. Where's Dan?" Molly asked.

I gave her an abridged version of our brief fling in Phoenix: Dan's initial reluctance about my detecting, then his unconditional encouragement.

"You're lucky," Molly said. "You and Dan may not be perfect, but it sure looks that way to the rest of us. You have everything that matters. You even look good together. Like Ken and Barbie."

"I thought Barbie dumped Ken for some new surfer dude," I said, remembering a headline about Mattel's big switch.

"The surfer turned out to be the doll version of New Coke," Molly said. "So Ken came back. Stick with what works."

"I'm sticking, I'm sticking," I said. I took a sip of wine and then refilled Molly's glass. "Dan's first theory was that Cassie's murder may be connected to Delta ij. Grant's secret society." I didn't mention that Dan's second theory, espoused in Phoenix, tied the murder to Molly. "From what I glimpsed of Cassie's hidden papers tonight, I think he may be right."

"The papers weren't about Roger?" Molly asked, surprised.

"No." I filled her in on what I'd seen.

Molly seemed unimpressed. "An old newspaper clipping. An office report on a potential donor. And a diary. How does that add up to murder?"

"I don't know," I said. "But given that I've just had a gun in my face and seen my best friend gagged with her own Hermès scarf, I'm taking it seriously."

Molly nodded. "I guess I should call Roger to tell him what happened. It's his penthouse."

And maybe his hitman, I thought.

I shrugged. "Whatever you think."

"I hate to admit that I lied about what we were looking for."

I took a deep breath. "Molly, don't you think Roger already knows?"

From the shocked expression on her face, I realized she hadn't thought that at all. I didn't mind that love was blind. But it shouldn't also be stupid.

Molly left early the next morning, and I went to my computer to Google Derek Howe, the student who'd died. An hour later I sat back, amazed as ever by how much you could find out on the Internet. All those vast databases collecting information. I always warned Ashley that the funny pictures she posted online could be seen by friends, relatives, and strangers. You didn't need a dusty library to dig up the past anymore—just a couple of mouse clicks.

Following a few links, I learned that Derek Howe had been found dead in the front hallway of the physics building his junior year at UCLA. He'd been an honors student, science genius, and all-around star. The cause of death in a healthy, athletic twenty-year-old wasn't immediately obvious. The coroner settled on cardiac arrhythmia. The department head concluded that Derek had been leaving an all-nighter at his research lab, since the body was found at 5 A.M. by a security guard coming to work. Derek's grieving parents had set up a foundation in his name.

A tragedy, no question about it. But as I reread the pages I'd printed, nothing jumped out at me. I went down to the kitchen, looking for some diversion. *Why had Cassie kept a clipping about Derek's death?* I wondered as I washed some fresh strawberries, removed the stems, and put them on a plate. *How did Derek connect to Randall Scott?* I asked myself as I took a ripe cantaloupe and began slicing. I'd looked up Randall Scott, too. He had founded a high-tech company during the first Silicon Valley boom, then sold it for enough millions that he would never have to work again. Three years later, he had another idea and began putting in twenty-hour days all over again just for the fun of it. The new company went public, doubling Randall's net worth. He'd just announced his third start-up. "Nothing makes me happier than long nights eating donuts and working with my fellow geeks," he'd said in one interview.

"Hi, Mom!"

Startled, I looked up from the cutting board as Grant sauntered into the kitchen and dropped his tennis bag.

"Hi, honey," I said, bringing myself back to the moment. "How was the meet?"

"Pretty good. Ryan and I made it to the finals in doubles, then lost in a tiebreaker in the fifth set. Bummer."

He didn't seem too upset, so I said, "Sounds like you did great."

He took a strawberry from the plate, then looked at the cantaloupe. "Is this fruit for me or Jimmy?"

"Whoever wants."

"Then why is it all cut in little shapes?"

I looked down. Deep in thought about murder and millionaires, I'd cut the melon into tiny geometric pieces.

"I guess my mind was elsewhere," I said, slightly embarrassed.

"Anything I can help with?" he asked. Before I could answer, he popped a piece of cantaloupe in his mouth. "Juicy," he said, catching a dribble before it hit his chin. Then, going for another bite, he added, "But the circles and squares taste the same, just so you know."

I took a piece myself and chewed slowly. "Mmm, try a triangle," I joked. "Tastes like chicken."

Grant laughed and slid onto a stool at the counter. "So what's up?" he asked, turning serious. "What got you busy thinking?"

"Derek Howe," I said.

Grant nodded, recognizing the name. "I've heard about him. The kid who died on campus a few years ago, right?"

"Right." I looked up surprised. "What have you heard?"

"Not a lot. Some guys in Delta ij lit a candle for him the night of the initiation."

I put down the paring knife and stared at my son.

"So Derek Howe was in Delta ij?"

"Nobody publishes lists, but yeah."

"Did he die during the initiation? Is that why they lit the candle?" I asked. It wouldn't be the first hazing scandal on a college campus.

Grant shook his head. "Nope. He'd been in Delta ij since he was a freshman, and he died his junior year."

"Okay, but his junior year, would he have taken part in the initiation somehow?"

"You're asking me stuff I don't know," Grant said. He picked up an oversize strawberry and took a bite. "We did it in secret groups. You only see the people you're with. Anyway, I think he died after being in his lab all night or something like that."

Don't get Grant involved, I told myself. But then another voice argued back *He already* is *involved.*

"Could you find out one thing for me?" I asked, remembering the date on the newspaper article. "Not a big deal. Just the date of the Delta ij initiation the year Derek Howe died."

"February 13," Grant said, without missing a beat.

My knife clattered to the floor and Grant reached down to pick it up. "Apparently, having initiation on the thirteenth was a Delta ij tradition for years," he continued amiably. "I guess Professor Bohr changed it a few years ago. I don't know why."

Changed it because it happened to be the same day on which Derek Howe had died? Professor Bohr. I had to talk to him again. I took a deep breath.

"So tell me more about your tennis meet," I said to Grant, ready to change the subject now. "Hit any hundred-mile-an-hour serves?"

By late afternoon, Dan had come home, bearing turquoise-and-silver earrings for me from an artsy store in Scottsdale.

"They're pretty, but I wasn't sure if they were 'you,'" he said as I put them on.

I smiled. "I love them. And what's 'me' isn't that clear-cut."

"I know that. And I'm glad." He stroked my arm. "A lot of guys complain that marriage is dull or their wives have gotten predictable. Definitely not my complaint."

"You probably have others."

"Not many. You're worth it."

"You are too," I said, kissing him.

"The weekend turned awfully boring after you left," Dan said. "And you?"

Not boring. "I missed you," I said honestly. "Grant's home, and Ashley and Jimmy should be back tonight. We'll all have dinner together."

"What are you doing until then?"

"Making sure you don't find me dull and predictable," I teased.

"Give me a hint."

Oh, dear. How much could I push Dan's good nature—not to mention his goodwill? Maybe this time I'd leave out a few details.

"Just going to Santa Monica," I said. "You know, where the farmers' market is. Want to come?"

"No thanks. You can buy baby beets without me." He smiled. "Have fun."

I slinked out of the house, feeling like a heel. The farmers' market *was* in Santa Monica, but I didn't actually plan to go there. I hadn't perjured myself, but I felt a little guilty parsing my words so carefully. Dan wasn't a Ninth Circuit judge. But I couldn't bring myself to admit I had e-mailed Hal Bohr to ask if we could meet tomorrow in his office. Hal had replied immediately, suggesting we meet today, at a skateboarding park near the Santa Monica pier.

I drove to the address Hal had given me. The park wouldn't make it into any LA travel guides, since it turned out to be little more than a street corner where some teenage boys had set up ramps. But when I pulled up, I saw Hal Bohr, in flowered orange shorts, flying up one of the sloped boards, twisting once in the air, and landing gracefully on the other side.

"Nice!" I said clapping, as I got out of my car.

He turned around and grinned, then, clutching his board,

pretended to bow. He fit right in with the teenagers around him—somewhat awkward, trying too hard to be cool. As in his office, social niceties seemed to escape him. Instead of coming over to say hello, he moved over to a low stone wall that had been rigged for more tricks. Taking off from a short downhill, he soared into the air again, went across the wall, spun around, and came down, this time with a clumsy thud. He tripped over the board but managed to stay standing.

"Chopped, dude!" called one of the young men holding his own neon-colored board.

Hal got on his skateboard and zigzagged across the pavement in my direction. Just when I thought he'd crash into me, he jumped backward so the board flipped into the air. He caught it and held it above his head like a trophy.

"The intrepid Lacy Fields comes to see me again," he said. "Can I teach you how to kick flip? Do an ollie?"

"No thanks."

"Really, it's easy-peasy. Just follows the laws of physics. A body in motion stays in motion. What goes up must come down. All very fundamental. First-year Newtonian principles."

"I want to talk to you about Derek Howe," I said, knowing Hal could go off on tangents forever. "He died the night of a Delta ij initiation." I'd promised Grant not to discuss his own initiation—and I wouldn't.

"Coincidence. Or co-ink-ee-dink, as some like to say. Tragic, tragic. Hard-working boy. I'd been busy with the ceremony that night and he stayed in the lab. I needed some results for the morning."

"You mean he worked in *your* lab?"

"I put his name on the breakthrough paper I published," Hal said defensively. "In fact, I listed all three of my research assistants. Of course, I got first author. And full credit as the genius. Because I am."

A thought occurred to me. "Could it really have been Derek's breakthrough?" I asked softly.

If I'd hit a chord, it wasn't obvious. Hal threw back his head and laughed raucously. "My undergraduate assistants crunch numbers. Crunch data. Crunch my M&Ms. If one of them turned out an original theory, I'd eat my kaleidoscope. Never happens."

I knew enough about college campuses not to be fooled by the ivory towers. Academics could be as cutthroat and competitive as CEOs. But even with that, killing a student to take credit for his work sounded far-fetched.

"Let's talk about Cassie Crawford," I said, ready to explore a different direction. "Why did she care so much about Derek?"

"I don't think she cared soooo much. She cared a little." He held thumb and forefinger an inch apart. "It was her freshman year, and he took her out on a couple of dates. Then he died."

Cassie and Derek had dated? Interesting information. But I didn't need to let on that it seemed important. "Hal, I really meant why Cassie cared recently. Last time we spoke, you said she'd been asking you a lot of questions about Derek."

Hal looked around, then pointed in the direction of the giant Ferris wheel at Santa Monica pier.

"How much do you like riding that Ferris wheel?" he asked.

"Never been on it," I admitted.

"Unacceptable." He put down the skateboard and grabbed my hand. "We're going right now."

"Actually, we're not." I shook my hand free. "I don't like heights."

"That's why you need to go," he said. "Gives some perspective. Go way up high and everything below seems so small. You wonder why you'd fretted so much. Like fussing about ants."

"Another time," I demurred.

With a demonic half smile on his face, he turned to me and whispered, "Worried we'll get to the top and I'll throw you off?"

"It never occurred to me," I said.

"Well, Lacy Fields, maybe it should occur to you. You worry about the wrong things. And people like that end up dead."

We had a rousing family dinner, with everyone sitting on the deck and competing to tell their best stories from the weekend. Take-out food served on bright-colored plastic plates didn't exactly qualify me for the Martha Stewart Medal, but I'd go for camaraderie over cuisine any day. In the glow of the candles, I looked at my children and knew all over again that I'd do anything in the world to keep them safe. I didn't really understand Hal Bohr's agenda—or his final threat to me. Now I wished I'd issued a threat in return. *You want to know who ends up dead, Professor? Anyone who threatens my children.*

The next morning, I got the kids off to school, then called Paige to say I needed to talk urgently.

"I'm going for a power walk in the mountains when I finish teaching," she said. "I have an early day. You can join me."

I peeked out the window at the gray, drizzly sky. Anybody who bragged about LA sunshine had never been here in the winter.

"Interested in meeting me for a pedicure first?" I asked. "I know a great place run by a registered nurse. Very sterile. My treat."

"No thanks. Seems silly to have someone else polish your toes when you can do it yourself."

"As long as you can still reach them," I joked. But she took me seriously.

"Oh. I didn't mean to insult you. Maybe you should do yoga."

"Never tried," I admitted.

"Then let's meet at the Yoshi Bikram yoga studio. I'll switch and do the power walk tomorrow. I can be flexible."

I'd bet she could be flexible. I pictured her long legs tucked behind her ears. Well, at least we'd be sitting. Lesser of two evils. "What time?" I asked resignedly.

When I arrived, early that afternoon, Paige had already changed into pale blue spandex shorts and matching top that left a wide expanse of tanned, toned midriff exposed. I hastily threw on my gray sweats.

"You may be uncomfortable in that," she said, eyeing my outfit as we walked to the studio. As soon as she pushed open the door, I staggered back.

"Why's it so hot in here?" I asked.

"Bikram's done in a warm room to help the muscles relax and encourage an energy flow."

"More like a sweat flow," I said, wiping my brow. "What's the temperature in here?"

"About one hundred thirty degrees."

I clutched my chest. "I think you die at one hundred seven. The brain fries or something. Jimmy had to go to the ER once for a fever of one hundred five."

"That's different," she said. She calmly settled on to a mat, folded her lithe legs so her heels rested on her thighs, and waved to me to join her. "I'll show you a few positions before the yogi gets here. Classic lotus. Very simple."

I sat down and stuck my legs straight in front of me. I had a better way to spend a few minutes.

"Paige, I need your help. You and Cassie were close friends. Did she ever talk about a guy named Derek Howe? She might have dated him for a while back in college."

"I don't know the name," she said, her back straight and her hands resting gracefully on her knees. She closed her eyes, a peaceful expression crossing her face.

"He died," I said urgently. "The papers Cassie hid in the

library that night with you weren't about Roger—one was about him."

Paige's eyes shot open. I'd clearly blown her yoga bliss. "Oh, you mean Doogie. Sure. She hadn't talked about him in years, but he came up recently. Something about his death had her worried. It started because a rich guy wanted to donate an endowed chair for the physics department. I forget who."

"Randall Scott," I said.

She unwrapped one lissome leg from lotus position and tucked it behind her. "Right. It would have been the Randall Scott Chair in Theoretical Physics. Cassie figured the first person to get it would be a young professor named Hal Bohr. Something about that worried her."

"She didn't like Bohr?" I asked. I felt my heart pounding harder and clenched my fists. Better if I didn't faint from the heat before she answered.

Paige moved her willowy limbs again. "King Pigeon position," she said. "Want to try it? Your muscles should be warm by now."

I crossed my legs Indian-style. "Bohr," I repeated.

She nodded, her long, supple neck glistening. "Roger had introduced Cassie to Randall, so she worried about any whiff of scandal. Nothing could go wrong. If I remember, she'd dug up some connection between Bohr and Doogie that she didn't like. She decided to discuss it with her boss, Elsa."

"Did she ever do that?"

"I don't know," said Paige, stretching her nimble torso backward. She stayed there a moment, then pulled herself back up. "We spent most of our time talking about Roger."

Worry about the wrong things and you end up dead.

"Cassie planned for every eventuality with Roger," Paige said, back on her favorite subject. "She even talked about cashing out some jewelry so she'd have her own money if he left. She didn't want to be desperate during a divorce."

My brain had turned soggy from the heat. I dropped my head to my knees.

"Nice stretching!" Paige said encouragingly.

Cashing out jewelry. Selling a necklace at Christie's. Billy with a million-dollar diamond. "Do you know how she planned to sell?"

"Secretly. Roger couldn't know, in case he *didn't* plan to leave." Paige rolled her eyes, obviously disliking deception. "I think she asked someone to do it for her. Not me. I'm not good at conniving."

"How about Billy Mann?"

"Could be. Cassie trusted him. The biker with a heart of gold, she called him." Paige slowly rolled her shoulders forward and backward, loosening her upper body. Then she looked up at me. "Are you okay? Do you want to stretch some more before Yogi Yoshi arrives?"

I staggered to my feet, seeing black spots in front of my eyes.

"I think I'm stretched about as far as I can go," I said.

Just then, the door opened and a yogi dressed in white minced in on pale bare feet.

"Ah, good afternoon, ladies," he said.

I gave a loud, wheezing cough and tried to get past him. He looked at me and raised his thin eyebrows. I had sweat pouring down my face, hair stuck to my forehead, and a hand clutching the door so I didn't fall over. "I like my studio filled with tranquility," he said in a high reedy voice. "I'm not feeling that now. We clearly need to seek harmony."

"I'm with you on that," I gasped. "Harmony and tranquility. I could use them. But I know a better place to look."

Without changing out of my sweats, I drove over to Jack Rosenfeld's office. From the look the receptionist gave me, I might as well have come in wearing sackcloth and ashes.

"He's on a conference call and can't be disturbed," she told me when I asked for Jack.

"I swear I'm a client," I said, repeating my name. "I was in the other day. Better dressed."

"He's on a long conference call. With London."

"It's the middle of the night there."

"Then Hong Kong."

I sighed. "Is Rachel Royce available?"

She turned her back to make a call and seemed surprised when she hung up. "Ms. Royce said you can come right back," she reported.

I gave her the haughtiest glance I could muster, then scurried down the long hall. As an associate in the firm, Rachel had a less impressive office than Jack's, but the large window still offered a decent view. Three vases of flowers at various stages of wilting suggested grateful clients, amorous admirers, or both.

"Hi, Lacy," she said, bouncing up with her bright smile. Apparently nobody had told her that associates at law firms were overworked and miserable. "Would you like to sit down?"

"My sweats are kind of sweaty," I admitted, brushing a hand across my backside.

"Don't worry." But she gestured to a hard-backed chair instead of the upholstered couch.

"Are you working with Jack on this crazy case I'm involved in?" I asked, perching on the edge of the chair.

She nodded. "Yes, but Jack's the senior partner. I'm not really supposed to have direct client contact."

"Well, he's busy. Plus he thinks Molly's a reasonable suspect."

"She has motive," Rachel conceded. "And then there's the fact that you were at the scene of two crimes."

I hadn't really thought of it that way.

"I found out why Billy Mann had the necklace," I blurted.

"Cassie gave it to him to sell for her. She didn't want Roger to know."

Rachel rolled a green Cross pen through her fingers. "She'd authorized the sale at auction?"

"I don't know if they had a notarized signature," I said. "But she asked him to do it. Aboveboard. Maybe he didn't look like it, but Billy was a reliable friend. Nothing more to it than that."

"How about what you told Detective Wilson?" Rachel asked, her eyes twinkling and her lips twitching to keep from smiling. "About Billy Mann being every woman's fantasy."

"You heard about that?"

"It's been the most forwarded e-mail in the office."

I laughed. "It got me out of the interrogation room. And possibly gave Mrs. Wilson a couple of interesting nights."

Rachel grinned. "I wish I'd met the guy."

"You would have liked him. Billy took care of people. He'd always been there for his disabled brother, and he was there for Cassie when she needed him. I'm convinced now they weren't doing anything illicit."

"Looks can be deceiving," Rachel agreed, glancing at one of the vases of flowers. I wondered what slick stud had sent them—and then turned out to be a creep.

"Billy wasn't what he seemed. I sensed that the first time I met him. It's why I went on his motorbike."

Rachel looked at me dubiously. Maybe she didn't know that part of the story—or maybe I'd given myself more credit than I deserved.

"Anyway, his parading me in that yellow dress made sense, too. Instead of protecting himself, he'd been preserving Cassie's reputation."

Now Rachel was completely lost. But she made a note to herself, and I knew she'd figure it out later.

"So you think Cassie and Billy were friends. She handed him the diamond to sell."

"Right."

Rachel tapped her pen against the desk. "At the risk of sounding like Jack, that's all very well, but it doesn't mean he didn't kill her. If Cassie gave him the diamond surreptitiously, he had every reason to want her dead so he could keep the money."

"It's not who he was," I said, frustrated. "We have to think differently. Molly Archer Casting is famous for casting against type. Let's try it. Forget Billy and Roger. Forget me and Molly. Something else had Cassie's attention just before she died. A professor of physics named Hal Bohr."

"Really?" Rachel laughed. "Wasn't there a famous physicist Niels Bohr? I remember that from high school, but don't ask me anything more about him."

"Different guy." I paused. "Anyway, are you ready for a long story?"

Rachel smiled. "Not too long. I charge by the hour, you know. But I'm much cheaper than Jack."

"And less judgmental, I hope. Especially when I tell you that I tried to take some papers from Cassie's apartment the other day. Somebody attacked me on the way out and grabbed them. Then he tied my hands and locked me in a closet."

Rachel blinked a few times. "For real?" she asked.

I nodded.

Rachel groaned. "Lacy, you know Jack has to hear this." She got up. "Come on with me."

We hurried down a hall and around a corner.

"Conference call over?" I asked, as we walked into Jack's office.

He nodded. "And lunch was just beginning. Late lunch. Very late lunch." He looked longingly at a pretty plate of lobster salad waiting on his round conference table. Another nice thing about being a partner at a fancy firm—an in-house chef.

"You can eat," I said.

"And Lacy can tell you about her escapade the other night," said Rachel.

Jack crossed to the conference table. "Is the story going to make me lose my appetite?" he asked.

I shook my head and launched into the relevant details. When I got to the part about the secret compartment in the book, Jack looked impressed. As I outlined the documents I'd seen, Rachel took furious notes. But once I began to describe the man with the gun dragging me to a closet, Jack put down his fork.

"Does Dan know about this?" he asked when I'd finished.

"No. And with attorney-client privilege, I assume he never will."

Jack pushed away his plate. "Lacy, you've definitely given us something new to pursue. But I'm glad you've spent some time with Rachel because you see how competent she is. As you realized with the will, it works a lot better if we do the investigating."

"Are you going to give any of this to the police?" I asked. "Maybe not my part in it. But just enough to get them on the right trail?"

Jack and Rachel exchanged a glance. "There's not a lot of real evidence here," Jack said finally. "Cassie could have hidden papers for reasons that had nothing to do with her death."

"But after she'd been poisoned, she got on the ladder to get them," I said. "As if she somehow knew."

"That may sound a little, um . . . mystical to someone like Detective Wilson," Rachel said.

"We'll do what we think is best," Jack said appeasingly.

I stood up and tugged at the drawstring of my sweatpants. With all this anxiety, I'd lost some weight. Though maybe the cabbage diet would have been easier.

"I'll do what I think is best, too," I said, done for the day with my condescending legal counsel. "But just so you know, my new goal is harmony and tranquility."

Chapter Seventeen

—— • ——

"Somebody must know!" I screamed.

At 4 A.M., I bolted upright in bed, my silk Natori nightgown clinging to my sweaty back and the sheet tangled around my legs. I'd thrown one pillow to the floor and had another clutched against my chest.

Dan turned over in bed and put a hand on my knee. "You okay?" he asked groggily.

"I guess so." I held the pillow tighter, trying to calm down.

"You must have had a nightmare."

"Mmm," I said, my mind still foggy. "Sorry I woke you."

"No problem. Let's go back to sleep." A moment later, Dan had done just that. After all those years as an intern and resident, working twenty-four-hour shifts in hospitals, he could return to REM sleep after any interruption.

But not me. I lay back and tried to recall the images from my nightmare. I'd been running down a dark tunnel that had no exit. Leering skeletons dangled from the ceiling, laughing at me. Cassie suddenly appeared and held out her arms, begging me to help. But as I got near, she morphed into a two-headed creature and gave a blood-curdling scream as another skeleton swayed between us.

Now I shuddered and reached down to retrieve the goose-down pillow. I tucked it under my head and straightened out the sheets around me. None of the horrors had happened, I reminded myself. Only the sweat was real.

I closed my eyes, but the vision of a morphing Cassie wouldn't go away. Back when she'd asked me to decorate her penthouse, I figured I had a handle on just who she was. I could sum her up simply: pretty girl who married the rich older guy. But the more I learned, the more complicated she seemed. Wasn't that true with all of us? Peel back one layer and find another.

So the nightmare had a kernel of truth. My subconscious had changed the complex Cassie into a morphing form. And the inscrutable people from her past became the dangerously dangling bags of bones. Skeletons of death. Skeletons in the closet. Thank you, Dr. Freud.

Conundrum solved, I could get back to sleep.

Only I didn't. I lay staring at the ceiling, my eyes wide open. Too bad I hadn't gone to medical school. I didn't want to be a doctor, but I wouldn't mind sleeping like one.

As the first whispers of dawn crept around the curtains, I gave up any thoughts of sleep and tiptoed into my study. Might as well catch up on my e-mail. As usual, my inbox was crammed with shopping offers. My spam filter kept out most of the Viagra scams, but every vendor in America seemed to have something to sell me. I mindlessly followed some links and got engrossed by the sale at J. Crew. Pretty polo shirts on sale, two for forty-five dollars. Great colors. I picked bright sherbet and strawberry ice—both sounded yummy—and pressed PURCHASE. Oh gosh, snookered again. Did I really need more tops? Not a surprise that the Internet economy was growing. So was insomnia.

Exhausted, I leaned back in my chair and stared out the window, letting my thoughts circle back to Cassie. What had I screamed as I woke up? *Somebody must know.* Well, true enough. Maybe I should listen to my unconscious for once. Freshman year in college, away from home and upset by Derek's death, Cassie must have shared her fears with a friend. Paige had been far away, but girls typically needed a soul mate. I thought of Ashley, whose friendships waxed and waned over the years, but who always found a current BF—best friend—to share secret thoughts.

At 7:30, I picked up the phone and dialed Lydia Taylor.

"It's Lacy Fields. I hope I'm not waking you up," I said when she answered.

"Not at all. I don't sleep much lately." Her voice sounded weary, but not from the hour.

"Listen, I just wondered if you knew Cassie's freshman-year roommate."

If it seemed an abrupt question for before breakfast, she didn't balk. Nothing could be shocking to her anymore.

"She had two roommates," Lydia said evenly, "but she only stayed close to one of them. Judi Murphy. Lovely girl. She flew in for the memorial service. And she's called me several times. It helps so much to hear from Cassie's friends."

I could imagine what a call like that would mean. A young voice, a connection to her daughter.

"Maybe Judi knows something about an incident from freshman year." I hesitated. "I could call her. But she might be more comfortable talking to you."

"I'd be delighted," Lydia said quickly. She seemed grateful for something to do, a way to fill the morning that didn't involve sad thoughts.

"It's pretty vague," I admitted. "But here's the outline. Cassie dated a guy named Derek Howe in her freshman year. Doogie, the kids might have called him. He died unexpectedly from a cardiac arrhythmia."

Lydia waited. "You want to know more about his death?" she asked.

"Or his life. He did physics research with a professor named Hal Bohr. And he'd been a member of a secret society called Delta ij."

"Delta," Lydia said immediately, her voice breaking. She hadn't forgotten Cassie's last word. How could she?

We hung up and I went back to the bedroom. Dan had gotten out of bed, and I knocked gently on the closed bathroom door.

"Can I come in?"

"Sure." He swung open the door, and I smiled at the sight of my handsome husband, a navy Polo towel wrapped around his waist, his face covered in thickly lathered shaving cream.

"You look good this way," I said. I leaned in to kiss him and giggled as I came away with a white mustache. I wiped my face. "Smell good, too," I said.

"Art of Shaving. Sandalwood," Dan said. "You bought it for me."

"Then I have very good taste. In shaving cream and men."

He finished lathering with the boar-bristle shaving brush, then picked up the ivory-handled razor I'd also bought him. Definitely better than the disposable Bic and can of Colgate he used to use.

I sat down on the Carrara marble bench behind the flowered ceramic vessel sink. I'd redecorated the bathroom a couple of years ago, and it had turned into the best room in the house. As good a place as any to have a conversation.

"Honey, how likely is it that a healthy college kid would die from a cardiac arrhythmia?" I asked, looking at Dan in the mirror as he shaved.

"Not likely, but it happens," he said. He didn't ask why I wanted to know. "You hear about it with athletes from time to time. A football player collapses during a practice and dies for no obvious reason. The autopsy shows a thickening of the heart wall. Or only one vessel supplying the heart instead of three. Some kind of heart defect that had gone undetected, probably since birth."

I nodded. "So it's a physical finding after death?"

"Not always. Often it's a diagnosis of exclusion. The heart stopped, so something must have been wrong with the heart. More specifically, the heart started beating so fast that it couldn't refill between beats. No blood gets pumped to the brain or body, and death is pretty rapid."

Dan finished shaving the right side of his face, then switched the razor to his left hand to continue. As always, I felt a little thrill at watching my perfectly ambidextrous husband. Maybe he had a few flaws, but he had no weak side. Literally.

"Is there a way you could kill someone and make it *look* like he'd died of an arrhythmia?"

Dan's razor-holding hand stopped in the middle of a downstroke. Oops. I hoped he hadn't cut himself. Maybe I should have waited until the splashing-on-aftershave portion of the ritual to ask.

But he quickly recovered. "Have I mentioned that I'm a doctor? I don't usually try to figure out how to kill people."

"Well, if you can save them, you can kill them," I said cheerfully. "It's just the inverse, right? Simple math. Like the numerator and denominator."

Despite himself, Dan laughed. He turned around and looked at me affectionately. "You're the smartest woman I know, but you're completely clueless about math, aren't you."

"Guilty as charged." I grinned. "Grant definitely didn't get his science talent from me. I'm not sure I'm even the real mother."

"He got his good nature from somebody. That would be you."

We smiled at each other. I had the feeling we'd finally gotten over our minor blip. Somehow, both of us remembered again the endearing little things that had made us fall in love.

Dan turned back to the mirror. "I don't know how you'd mimic an arrhythmia," Dan said. "But you can cause one. The most obvious way would be with a shot of potassium."

Interesting, but I didn't want to show too much excitement. Oh, heck, why not? "Would the potassium be evident in an autopsy? I mean, could you ever prove it?"

Dan shook his head. "No. It would just get absorbed into the body. The blood chemistry changes pretty dramatically after death. The cells break down and potassium is released. You couldn't tell what had been there before."

An excellent way to kill someone. Easy and undetectable.

"So you could put some extra potassium into the potato salad and nobody would be the wiser?" I asked.

"Not that simple. You'd have to inject it." Finished shaving, Dan cupped water into his hands and rinsed off the last traces of lather. "But an injection site would be pretty easy to miss."

"You always know everything," I said.

Dan dried his face with the fluffy towel. "I'm better at killing people than I realized," he joked. "Don't let anybody at the hospital know, okay?" He leaned over and kissed me gently on the lips. No shaving cream this time—just affection.

Lydia called me back at noon, her voice more energetic now. "I reached Judi," she said. "She's an associate at an advertising agency in Chicago, but she left a client meeting to talk to me." She sounded surprised—her life was so diminished she could hardly believe anyone would cut short a pitch to take her call.

"Did she know what you were talking about?" I asked.

"More or less. She'd heard of Delta ij, but didn't know anything about it. Apparently, it's one of those big-deal mysteries on campus, like Skull and Bones at Yale. A lot of myths, but nobody ever admits to being a member. Part of the mystique."

"How about Derek?" I asked.

"They liked each other," Lydia reported. "Derek spent a lot of late hours in his lab, and Cassie would come by with oatmeal cookies or Reese's peanut butter cups."

"Probably the healthiest food he ate," I joked.

"I loved that Judi remembered it," Lydia said softly. Now she had another image to hold on to: her sweet daughter bearing sweets. I heard her voice fill briefly with emotion, then she cleared her throat. "Anyway, they ran into a problem with that professor you mentioned, Hal Bohr."

I hazarded a guess. "Allergic to peanuts?" I ventured. "Didn't want any more Reese's in his lab?"

Lydia gave a little laugh. "No, he liked having Cassie come by. She started bringing him little treats, too. Only he took it wrong." She took a deep breath. "According to Judi, the professor got—well, obsessed with Cassie. Asked her out a few times. Followed her home when she left the lab. One Saturday night, he showed up at their dorm room. When Judi told him Cassie and Derek had gone to a party, he started screaming that he had a date with her and she'd promised not to see Derek anymore."

"All fantasy?" I asked.

"A hundred percent. According to Judi, Cassie tried not to be cruel but made her position very clear. Not interested."

"Made even more awkward because her boyfriend worked in his lab."

"I guess."

"Did she report Hal to anyone?" I asked.

"Cassie thought it would just make him worse. She thought he was crazy. Judi talked to one of the deans, who took it very seriously. But then Derek died, and Professor Bohr was away the next semester. When he came back in Cassie's sophomore year, it all seemed to have blown over."

We both fell silent. Not the report I'd expected.

"I hope that's helpful," Lydia said finally.

"Definitely," I said firmly. Though right now, I didn't have a clue what it might mean.

As soon as we hung up, I went online and Googled Hal Bohr. I got to his personal home page, which then linked to various physics journals. Several reprinted his papers and praised his brilliant research. One offered an analysis of his apparently famous twenty-page mathematical proof. Oh, great. Anything in English?

I tried Wikipedia, which was somewhat more understandable. "Despite the coincidence of name and fame, Hal Bohr isn't related to Niels Bohr, who won the Nobel Prize in 1922," the entry concluded. "But they will forever be linked as two of the world's most eminent physicists." I paused for a moment, wondering who had submitted the information. Anybody could have written it. Maybe Hal himself.

Curious, I went to the entry on Niels Bohr and scanned through the discussion of his great contributions. *The electron's orbital angular momentum is quantized as* $L = n\hbar$. Hmm. Who knew. Maybe I could drop that in conversation with Grant sometime and impress him.

I kept reading. Actually, old Niels sounded pretty interesting. Cared about truth and philosophy. Said clever things like "Never talk faster than you think." Escaped from Denmark during World War II and eventually came to Los Alamos to advise on the atomic bomb. While there, used the pseudonym Nicholas Baker.

I suddenly gasped.

Nicholas Baker?

The name reverberated from the clipping in Cassie's secret cache. I didn't have it in hand anymore, but every word I'd read had been burned in my brain. A married couple named Sandy and Jerry Baker had died in a Connecticut fire. They'd left behind a son named Nicholas.

I got up and walked around the room, trying to get some perspective. How many Nicholas Bakers would there be in America? Hundreds? At least. Thousands? Maybe. Millions? No way. I shook my head, wishing I had a better grasp on math. On the other hand, it didn't really matter. One way or another, "Nicholas Baker" was a common enough name that I couldn't draw conclusions.

Oh, for heaven's sake, of course I could.

I went into the kitchen and took a Greek yogurt from the refrigerator. Zero percent fat, but it would help me think. I sat down at the table and slowly stirred my spoon around in the creamy mixture. Almost as good as ice cream. Well, not really, but the Greeks definitely had a corner on the yummy-yogurt market.

Okay, Nicholas Baker.

Cassie must have had a reason to keep the article about the Connecticut fire with her important papers. The tragedy had occurred about a dozen years ago, which meant the orphaned Nicholas would be about the same age now as Hal Bohr. It wouldn't be far-fetched to imagine the young scientist Nicholas Baker changing his name to Bohr. A reverse-name-change joke that only he would get, and a way of removing himself from the horror that had happened at home.

I finished the yogurt, proud of my eighty-calorie lunch. Feeling virtuous, I opened the freezer and took a spoonful of Edy's Chocolate Peanut Butter Cup time-limited special ice cream. One spoonful couldn't hurt. Mmm, excellent. Maybe one more spoonful. And since I might never find the flavor again, a third.

I managed to stop myself before I'd eaten the entire container—but not by much. I closed the freezer and went back to my study.

Let's say my guess was right and Nicholas Baker and Professor Hal Bohr were one and the same. So what? Nothing illegal about changing your name. The slightly crazy, self-absorbed Nicholas/Hal would have liked launching his career with the famous scientist's name. It didn't make him a murderer.

I glanced at my watch, eager for a distraction. Jimmy should be home soon, and I'd drive him to his swimming lesson, then find someplace special to take him for his after-swimming snack. (Not ice cream, I thought guiltily.) An afternoon with my son might clear my head.

Only Jimmy didn't come home.

I watched for him out the window for a while, then wandered outside into the cool but sunny day and mindlessly picked some weeds in the garden. I checked the time again. School ended early today, and our neighbor Carla Peters had carpool duty. She never ran late.

Finally, I looked down the street and saw Carla walking toward me, her new puppy, a labradoodle (the chic cross between a Labrador and a poodle), running frantically around on its leash.

"Lucky you!" Carla said, giving a cheerful wave when she saw me. "So now it turns out you officially have two genius children!"

"What? What are you doing home?" I looked at her, confused.

"Trying to teach this pup that the proper place to poo isn't on my needlepoint carpet," she said. She crouched next to him and patted him on the head. "Don't let those puppy-dog eyes fool you. He's a monster."

At the moment, I couldn't work up any polite interest in animal etiquette. "Where's Jimmy?" I asked anxiously. "I thought you picked him up. He's not here."

"I know." She stood up slowly. "That's what I meant about another genius child. Jimmy went off to some special after-school program at UCLA, didn't he?"

I tried to quiet my pounding heart. "I don't know anything about it."

Carla took a sharp breath and twisted the leash around her fingers. "The woman who picked him up had a note from you."

"I didn't write it," I said softly.

"She'd given it to Ms. Berkeley," Carla said, quickly transferring any fault to the first-grade teacher.

"Did you see the woman? Or her car?"

Carla shook her head. "Jimmy had already left with her. Ms. Berkeley seemed really proud that Jimmy had been invited to this gifted program. I planned to ask you about it. See if Aidan could get in."

The puppy nipped at my ankle, then raced around in a circle, twisting its leash into a hopeless tangle around my leg. These designer dogs promised the best traits of both breeds, but this one seemed to be the worst. Like when the mogul marries the model—and the kids end up with his looks and her brains.

"Carla, you have to track down Ms. Berkeley and find out what else she knows," I said urgently. "What the woman looked like. Anything. I'm going to drive over to UCLA."

"My God," Carla said. The color had drained from her face. She tried to untangle the leash, ducking around my legs as agitated as the puppy. "Don't panic yet. I'm sure there's an explanation. Maybe it's something Grant set up."

"Maybe," I said. Though not with a forged note from me. Grant wouldn't do that.

I grabbed my bag and got in my car, racing down the driveway and swerving a little too fast onto the street. I careened through Pacific Palisades, trying to pick the fastest route to Westwood. I turned onto Sunset, then decided to gamble on the thruway. My lucky day—for traffic, at least. No backups. Maybe I should take it as a sign that everything would be all right.

I zoomed into the left lane. Carla could be right about a

reasonable explanation. Maybe Dan had written the note and the teacher had just made a mistake. Grateful that the Lexus had a voice-activated Bluetooth, I called Dan's office, but the nurse said Dan had just begun a complicated facial surgery and wouldn't be reachable for a few hours.

"I can page him for you if it's an emergency," she said.

"Not yet," I said. I wanted to be a little clearer before I dragged Dan, scalpel in hand, away from the operating room. "Have him call me when he can."

I tried the next number on my speed dial, but Grant didn't answer his cell phone. I left another message for him to call me.

Speeding up, I darted around a cruising convertible, then pushed hard on the gas to pass a Porsche doing eighty. I felt the car veer and gripped the wheel. *Slow down,* I told myself. I watched the odometer slip back to sixty-five and tried to get my head into some more rational mode. It could all be a misunderstanding. No big deal. Some special program Grant knew about for Jimmy and discussed with Dan. I'd been distracted and they hadn't bothered me.

Or else it was a very smart ploy.

Jimmy's school issued a five-page memo each year called "Safety First." Teachers went to a two-day "safe students" seminar. Children and teachers were all wise to the dangers of abductions, kidnapping. . . . God, I didn't even want to think about it.

But nothing would make a teacher drop her defenses faster than telling her she had the smartest kid in the school. Ms. Berkeley had been proud. Carla wanted her son taken next.

Taken. I shuddered. Who would have taken Jimmy—and why?

Dan and I lived nicely, but anyone looking for major ransom wouldn't pick a doctor's child. Too much big media money in LA—and right here in Pacific Palisades—to even think of us. Jimmy had gone to a birthday party in a house that had a bowling alley and miniature-golf course in the basement, plus a fifty-seat movie theater in a separate wing.

My cell phone rang, and as soon as I said hello, I heard Carla's voice.

"I spoke to Ms. Berkeley," she said. "You don't have to worry. The woman who picked up Jimmy was completely legitimate. Had a UCLA ID. Left information about the program. Her name's Sandy Baker."

Sandy Baker, the woman who died in the fire.

I swerved, barely missing an eighteen-wheeler barreling along next to me. The truck driver shook his head, then for some reason gave me a thumbs-up sign. I slowed down and got into the lane behind him. Again, Sandy Baker was a common enough name, but I couldn't keep believing in coincidence.

"Any description of her?" I asked, my voice shaky.

"Ms. Berkelely said she looked like an academic. Plainly dressed but with a nice scarf. Gray hair pulled back in a bun. Tall and patrician."

Exactly how I would have described Elsa Franklin.

I hung up and took the exit for Westwood, caroming through the street and onto the campus. I abandoned the car in an illegal spot, but didn't care. I raced over to the development office. Kate, the assistant, sat at the front desk

"You're Lacy Fields, aren't you?" she asked when I rushed in, panting slightly.

"Yes. Good memory."

"Not really. Elsa said you might come by."

I looked around frantically. "Does she have a little boy with her?"

"Pardon?"

"A boy named Jimmy. My son."

Kate shrugged. "I doubt it. Elsa's not really a kid person."

Not believing her, I swung around in the direction of Elsa's office. *"Jimmy!"* I called, cupping my hands on either side of my mouth to make a megaphone.

"Nobody's back there," Kate said.

"I need to talk to Elsa," I persisted, starting toward the back.

"She's not here."

I stopped and looked at Kate. "Where is she?"

"I don't know. But she left this for you." She handed me a sealed envelope. Hands shaking, I ripped it open and took out an embossed Crane's card, the classy kind people once used for thank-you notes. But this had a single sentence: *Go to the front entrance of the physics building.* Then a phone number, written neatly in the middle of the page.

I left the office and dialed the number.

"Elsa Franklin?" I asked.

"Are you at the physics building?"

"No."

The phone went dead.

I found the building, and dialed again.

"I'm here," I said.

"Good. Don't talk to anyone. Don't call anyone. Stay on the phone and do exactly what I tell you."

"Why should I?"

She paused, just briefly. "You're here. So you know why."

Chapter Eighteen

——— • ———

E lsa's instructions were direct. Turn right. Turn left. Go straight. I followed the walkways and went by the music building. The gentle sounds of a violin drifted from an open window. Whoever scored the soundtrack of my life needed to add oboe and drums.

"Are you still there?" Elsa asked, her tone curt and controlled.

"Yes. Just passing a courtyard. A big landscaped lawn."

"Dickson Court. Keep going and turn right at the bridge."

"I don't see a bridge," I said anxiously.

She snorted. "It's what we call it around here. Not exactly the Golden Gate. More like a road."

Not a time to quibble over nouns. I turned on to the road.

"After the truck goes by, cross the street and head toward Murphy Hall," she said.

A Verizon truck rumbled by. I suddenly realized Elsa could see me and was watching my every move. Maybe that meant Jimmy was nearby. I spun around, hoping against hope that I'd spot my baby.

Elsa, catching my abrupt move, misinterpreted.

"Don't try to attract attention," she said. "Play this straight or you'll never . . ." She paused, too smart to make a threat over the phone.

"Is Jimmy with you?" I asked, more breathless than I intended.

"You're almost at a building," she said, ignoring me. "Go in the small entrance directly ahead."

I did as told, then followed her instructions across a corridor, down a staircase, and through a metal door—which slammed loudly behind me. In the dim light, I tried to figure out where I could be. Low ceilings, hanging wires, an insistent humming sound. *The tunnels*, I suddenly realized. The mythical underground—which turned out to be real. Where Grant had been for the Delta ij initiation.

"Good work," someone hissed.

I gasped, realizing that the voice came from behind me and not through the phone. I started to turn, but suddenly a rope was wrapped around my neck, choking me. Instinctively, I clawed at it, trying to breathe, but the noose only got tighter.

"Don't," I gagged. "I'll do whatever you want. I just want my son."

"Then move."

The rope loosened slightly and I managed to swallow—just as the cold, hard end of a gun jabbed into my back.

"You don't have to shoot me," I said, calmer than I would have expected.

"Don't tell me what to do. This is your own fault."

"I'm only here to get Jimmy."

"Why would you think I had him?"

I didn't answer, but I didn't have to. She already knew.

"You passed the test," she said. "Or, from your point of view, failed. The name Sandy Baker meant something to you, and you showed up. If you hadn't, Jimmy could have just gone home."

"Don't hurt him," I whispered. "Do whatever you want to me, but don't hurt Jimmy."

"How heroic." She gave a nasty chuckle. "I'm sure Jimmy won't mind when his mother's dead."

I had a noose at my neck and a gun in my back, but an impulse to fight. Instead, I staggered forward. We could be headed toward Jimmy. I pictured him alone and terrified right now, left in a dark corner. Whatever happened, I had to get to him.

"Tell me what you know," she said, yanking at the rope.

"You're Sandy Baker's sister," I said softly. "I figured it out this afternoon. She must have asked you to take care of Nicholas, right? Just before she died in the fire."

I heard her take a deep breath. A loud hissing sounded from one of the pipes in the tunnel, accented by the clicking of my heels against the cement floor. Elsa stepped silently in soft-soled shoes that would allow her to run. Or kill.

"The firemen had carried Sandy to the front lawn," she said finally, her voice hoarse. "Horribly burned. Unrecognizable. When I arrived, she had a moment of lucidity. I made a promise. She loved her son."

"Even though he'd started the fire?"

"Nobody ever proved that. Sandy had no idea. Nicholas's illness had just started. It happens at that age, sometimes."

"Schizophrenia?" I hazarded. "Or was he just delusional? Bipolar?"

"The diagnoses are never clear," she said. "Nicholas has a brilliant mind. Mental illness seems to go with being a math genius. As if the brain wiring that makes someone extraordinary means he can't live normally, too."

The mad genius theory? Is that what she'd told herself? Like John Nash in *A Beautiful Mind*. But I wondered if any actual medical research supported the connection. Dan would know. But I could only ask if I ever saw him again. Tears sprang to my eyes. I had to hug my husband and children again; it was all I really wanted. But pleading with Elsa wouldn't help. Instead, I had to keep talking until we got to Jimmy. And then figure out how to escape.

"So let's see," I said conversationally, as if chatting about the weather. "Nicholas Baker moved out here and changed his name to Hal Bohr. You followed. Why didn't you want anybody to know you're related?"

"I liked keeping an eye on him from a distance," she said. "He didn't always know who I was, anyway. All the medication and treatments wiped out some of his memory. He thinks of me as Elsa Franklin, not Auntie. It's better that way."

"But the delusions got dangerous. He imagined that Cassie Crawford was in love with him, so he killed her boyfriend, Derek, to get her back."

"And got away with it," she said proudly.

My hands felt clammy and my knees trembled as I made myself move forward. The glow from Elsa's flashlight illuminated a wide circle, several feet in front of me, and I finally dared to glance around and try to get my bearings. Students had obviously cavorted through here often, spray-painting Greek letters—the names of fraternities—on various girders. The underground graffiti suggested good-natured mischief. Nothing like what Hal Bohr had done to Derek.

Or could have done to Grant. I shuddered, thinking of my older son down here in the dark during his initiation to Delta ij, lying in a casket when the famous professor Hal Bohr told him to. Years earlier, Derek had no doubt done the same. But that time, the great physicist had closed the lid. Derek still wouldn't have sensed danger. Just part of the ritual. Professor Bohr wouldn't let anything happen.

"Let me guess," I said more to myself than to Elsa. "After Derek passed out in the casket, Hal gave him the shot of potassium that stopped his heart. Then it was easy enough to drag him upstairs to the physics building. Nobody would suspect murder."

"A horrible tragedy," Elsa agreed. "If anybody got suspicious about the death happening the same night as the initiation, there would have been one of those typical investigations into hazing and secret societies. But even that never happened."

"So Hal was safe. You whisked him away for a semester and got him more treatment. How did Cassie figure it out?"

"By being too good at her job," Elsa growled. "Once she'd convinced Randall Scott to make a huge donation, I insisted we accept it, no further discussion. But something about Delta ij nagged at her. She didn't want any scandal tarnishing her precious donors, so she went to talk to Hal. Seeing her brought back all Hal's old . . . confusion. Forget Delta ij—he thought he'd impress her by telling her the truth."

"All or nothing," I said suddenly.

"What?"

"All or nothing. That's what Grant told me Delta ij means. You had everything working just right—Hal hailed as a genius, big donations coming in, your own identity safe. But one wrong word and it could all come tumbling down. All or nothing. You had to kill Cassie."

"For my sister," Elsa said. "Hal didn't have a parent to protect him. I knew what Sandy would want. I listened to her."

Is that how people passed time in heaven? Ordering murders?

"You're more loyal than any mother could be," I said. But that wasn't quite true. I'd kill Elsa right now to get Jimmy back. Without a moment's hesitation.

For Elsa, the details must have been easy. She told Cassie they needed to talk privately and got invited to the penthouse. Hal had probably already told her about the family connection, and she'd researched it further. The conversation scared Cassie enough that she hid the papers that night in the library. But not before Elsa had slipped the bottles of Kirin tea into the refrigerator. Elsa had worked with her long enough to know what she liked. Simple, untraceable, and not a bit messy.

"We got into a bit of a tiff the night before she died," Elsa said, as if correcting my thoughts. "I told her that turning down Randall Scott was just throwing away money. For emphasis, I tossed a quarter across the room. Cracked the corner on some fancy frame."

"The Rothko," I said, breathing heavily.

"Whatever. Everything seemed fine until you showed up at my door," Elsa said irritably. "You'd been with Cassie when she died. I didn't know what she might have said, but you took the bait to investigate Billy Mann."

"He'd always been Cassie's confidant. Once you realized they'd gotten close again, he had to die, too."

"The second time's easier," Elsa said with a chuckle. "I can't wait to see how easy it is the third time."

A wave of heat flushed through my body as I envisioned the gunshot wound at the top of Billy's tattoo—no doubt made with the very weapon that was now jabbed into my back. I had to think of something else. My mind made the obvious leaps.

"The letter you showed me that night on the red carpet. From Billy to Cassie. You wrote it yourself, right?"

"Of course I wrote it," Elsa said, pleased with herself. "Spelling mistakes and all. And you fell for it. Have to admit that it threw you off track for a while."

"I admit," I said.

She laughed and I joined in, my terror briefly converted to a high-pitched giggle.

But our odd connection, forged in the dark, was about to end.

"We're here," Elsa said suddenly.

She shoved me hard around a corner, and the ray of her

light briefly caught the edge of a heavy wooden structure. Then she flicked off the beam, and in the sudden darkness something struck the back of my head with such force that I fell over, crumpling from the shock. I thought I'd been shot but then realized she'd hit me with the butt of the gun.

I got to my feet, flailing, but Elsa came at me with her full strength, smacking the gun into my jaw. I staggered back, blood gushing from my chin. She dove for my legs, lifting me off the ground and upending me so that I plunged into a shallow hole.

The casket.

I fought to sit up, but she'd grabbed the rope that still hung loosely around my neck and pulled hard.

"Awwggh!" I screamed, feeling the air rushing from me.

"Don't worry, I won't kill you," she snarled. "You get to kill yourself. Choose your own method of death, Lacy Fields." She slipped the end of the rope through a loop in the casket top and pulled. "I recommend suffocation, but since you're not the holding-still type, there's a decision. If you get the lid up, the rope pulls and strangles you. Very clever, hmm? I like to think that Nicholas got some of his genius from me."

With a sickening *whoosh,* the lid of the casket slammed shut. Plunged into utter blackness, I felt a dank, oppressive heat searing into me. The acrid smells of mold and blood and fear filled my nostrils, but the oxygen seemed to have been ripped from my lungs and I could hardly breathe. From the outside of my death trap, I heard a latch snap and a bolt slide into place.

Then silence. Utter, absolute silence. Except for the sounds of my heart, pounding so loudly that the thumping reverberated in my ears.

Wait a minute, I thought. *She said we were going to see Jimmy.*

That I'd been tricked seemed worse than death. That I'd never hold Jimmy again, intolerable. My sudden, gasping sobs echoed in the closed chamber. Tears streaked down and clogged my throat. I coughed, choking on my own grief.

I closed my eyes, trying to regain some semblance of control. My hands had been wedged against the sides of the casket, but without too much effort, I pulled them free. Elbows pressed close to my body, I stretched my arms, touching the top without much effort. I couldn't get much leverage, but the little push I managed yielded no results. Not a surprise. The latch and bolt I'd heard had probably sealed the casket—and my fate.

No, I couldn't let myself believe that.

I brought my hands to my neck and felt the rope that circled it. Running my fingers along it, I touched the loop that the rope ran through, but then couldn't reach any farther. For Elsa's choking plan to work, the rope needed a third anchor point. Had she secured it outside the casket? If so, the rope might be propping the casket open just enough to let me breathe for a while.

But I couldn't count on it.

I had to do something. Without any other plan, I resolved to get the cord off my neck. I didn't have much room to move, but I lifted my head an inch or two and tugged the noose upward. Too tight. I tucked my chin and twisted my head slightly, like I did when taking off the Donna Karan sweater with the too-narrow funnel neckline. But no luck. If only the rope had that one percent Lycra that made everything fit better.

I put my head back and stared into the darkness. My body had been pouring out so much fight-or-flight adrenaline that I felt exhausted. Since right now I could neither fight nor flee, maybe I should take a nap. Not have to think. At least preserve my strength.

Then I gritted my teeth. Preserve my strength for what? So I could die rested? Warren Zevon had it right: I'll sleep when I'm dead. I wasn't dead yet.

A rope could be cut, but I didn't happen to have scissors in my pocket. So what did I have? A metal watch band might do the trick, but I happened to be wearing my Jaeger-LeCoultre with the satin strap. Very chic, but too soft to hack through Jell-O. I felt the other wrist and, despite myself, smiled. As always, I had on the diamond tennis bracelet that Dan had given me for my last birthday. Weren't diamonds the strongest mineral on earth? If they could engrave glass, they could also sever a tough twine.

I carefully unlatched the bracelet, and holding an end in each hand I held it against the taut rope segment that ran from my neck to the loop. I started sawing, half expecting the cord to shred like the string cheese I put in Jimmy's lunch. But after long minutes of trying, I'd barely sliced off a few fibers.

Well, so what? This wasn't much different than going to the gym and working out with weights. One set of reps, followed by a brief rest, then another set. Stick with the program and you saw results.

I went at it again. Fifty pulls back and forth. Rest. Fifty pulls. Rest. Fifty pulls. Rest. Fifty . . .

Snap!

The last strands gave way and I touched the now-severed end of the rope. I'd done it! I felt a surge of triumph. I couldn't wait to tell Dan how his birthday gift had saved me.

And then, just as quickly, the elation sapped from my veins. Tell Dan? How did I plan to do that? The desperate reality hit me, made worse by the brief fantasy of freedom.

"Help!" I screamed. "Somebody help!"

I'd never been claustrophobic before, but the tight space suddenly seemed intolerable. I pounded my fists furiously against the top of the casket and kicked my legs as frantically as a toddler having a tantrum. My knee smashed into the wood and a stinging pain coursed through my leg, but I just flailed more frenetically.

"I have to get out! Get me out!" I screamed to some unknown—and nonexistent—savior. Hysterical, I smashed my foot incessantly up against the coffin wall, willing the pointy toe of my pump to drill through the wood and let me escape. Saved by Dolce & Gabbana? But almost immediately, the shoe crumpled—boucle silk being no match for mahogany.

"Ouch!" I yelled, as my big toe suffered the impact. "Ouch! Help me! I can't stand it!" A distant part of my brain heard the out-of-control panic but didn't have a clue how to control it.

"I'm going to die here! This isn't fair!" I hollered. Then, howling and hollering, I roared, "This isn't fair! Someone save me!"

What greater dread could there be? I'd been buried alive. Inside a coffin, buried alive. The grimmest nightmare of every slasher flick. *Saw IV* could be a Disney Channel promo next to this.

"Get me out! I don't deserve to die this way!" I screamed. Then I upped the volume, almost blowing out my own ears. *"Get me out of here!!"*

Nothing could be worse than this horror. Nothing, nothing, nothing!

At least it's you, not Jimmy.

The thought of my baby was like a glass of cold water dumped on my madness. I abruptly stopped flailing, and my screams echoed off into silence. Whatever misery I felt, I had one job: to get back to my three children. I couldn't abandon them. I had to find Jimmy. I had to protect Grant and Ashley.

I lay very still, assessing the damage. My throat hurt from the screaming and my knuckles stung from being grated against the walls. Sweat dripped down my forehead and my blouse clumped against my damp back. But my emotions were back in check.

Which meant I could think—and make a plan. At home, I lived by making lists; I could do the same right now, organizing the options in my head.

First possibility: A white knight would come to rescue me. I'd always been lucky in life—from marrying Dan to finding my favorite Fendi for half price on eBay. Why not assume I'd be blessed now? Frat boys would choose tonight to scamper through the tunnels with mischief in mind and spray paint in hand. I'd yell, they'd save me, end of story.

Nice tale, but even King Arthur couldn't find me down here. The tunnels wound endlessly under the campus, and the coffin sat hidden far off in a corner where nobody would be likely to prowl. Muffled by the thick wood of the coffin, my screams for help would travel just a few feet. Even if the heroes of my fictional frat heard yelping, they'd attribute it to ghosts (or rats) in the tunnel—and rush to get out.

As my mother used to say, You have to make your own luck.

Second possibility: Find a way to signal for help. If we could send messages to Mars these days, I should be able to tell someone where I was. But my pocketbook had long since disappeared, whisked out of sight forever by Elsa. I didn't have a cell phone or a BlackBerry or even a whistle. I scrounged in my pocket, as if I might unexpectedly find one of those devices that locate skiers buried under thirty-foot avalanches. Instead, I came up with one embarrassingly scruffy used Kleenex. Something else Mother said: Carry a pressed handkerchief. If only she'd added, and bring an emergency flare.

Any other possibilities? When there's nothing left, you have to do something. I rummaged around until I felt the tennis bracelet that had dropped at my side. If it worked once, couldn't it work again? This time, instead of ripping through a rope, I had to cut a big enough hole in the side of the casket that I could slip through. It might take some time—but I didn't exactly have a bus to catch. I sucked in my stomach, to convince myself that the hole didn't have to be so big. Then I pinched a few of the diamonds on the bracelet between thumb and forefinger and, with jaw set, began scraping at the wood. And scraping and scraping. And scraping.

In the pitch dark, I had no sense of how much time passed, but the narrow bracelet didn't seem up to this task. My fingers got swollen and sore. My nails cracked and began breaking. I touched the hard wooden panel on which I'd been working and felt only the slightest indentation in the area. I had to stay positive. Keep going. *An hour and you'll be out*, my best cheerleader voice insisted.

I started scraping at the wood again. Quantifying the passing time might give me some perspective, or at least a moderate sense of control. Easy enough. *One one-thousand, two one-thousand, three one-thousand*. When I reached *sixty one-thousand* I said "One minute" out loud—then started the chant again.

One one-thousand . . .

Rub, scrape, count.

"Two minutes."

Ouch. I stuck the sorest finger in my mouth and licked off the blood. No time to feel sorry for myself. Keep going. I wouldn't get discouraged.

"Ten minutes."

One one-thousand . . .

Nothing existed anymore except my little ritual.

"Forty minutes."

I pictured myself shimmying through the hole. Pictured Dan kissing me and the children hugging me.

"Fifty-nine minutes."

I took a deep breath and allowed myself to stop long enough to assess my progress. I tentatively touched the wood again. Tears popped into my eyes. The definition of futility. Almost an hour, and I'd made only the smallest ridge. After so many years exposed to heat and vapor underground, shouldn't the wood have softened just the teensiest bit? Apparently, a coffin ready to carry its occupant into eternity didn't surrender to a steam pipe.

I lay very still, crossing my hands over my chest. The classic movie pose for a corpse. I brought my hands back to my side. No sense prepping for my own funeral.

The make-a-hole strategy had been reasonable enough. It just hadn't worked. Time to reconsider. Everyone always talked about thinking outside the box. I had to think—and get myself out of this box.

Okay, I'd just pretend this was one of those "Ask Marilyn" logic problems I read every week in *Parade*. Maybe Marilyn was in the *Guinness World Records* book for having the world's highest IQ, but I'd been number three in my class in Rural Oaks High School. Or maybe number four.

Problem: Lacy is trapped in a locked casket.

Wait a minute. A coffin didn't usually have a lock. I'd been to enough funerals to know that after the lid came down, nobody worried that the corpse could climb out.

But I'd heard Elsa throw the bolt. Just to be sure, I gathered all my strength and heaved upward against the lid. Nothing. I pushed again. No movement. It was locked tight.

I assumed that no funeral parlor had a sideline in locked caskets, so Hal had probably made the creepy alteration before he brought down Derek. A simple enough fix for someone moderately skilled with tools. I'd watched my handy husband Dan do plenty of projects at home like this. All he'd have to do was drill two holes in the right spots, slide in the screws, then fit the lock across them.

I ran my aching hand up and down the edge of the coffin where lid and bottom met. Nothing but smooth wood. But who could really tell? My fingers seemed to have lost all feeling during their hour-long assault on the wood. I tried again with the palm of my hand, slowly covering every inch.

And got stabbed by the sharp edge of a screw.

Perfect! Never had a cut felt so good. I focused all my attention on that thin screw. An eighth of an inch from the end, pressed against the wood, were two small metal pieces, spread from the screw like tiny wings. My heart beat a little harder, but I tried not to get excited. I could be wrong, but my best guess said it was a toggle bolt. I used them all the time (or had the contractor use them) when hanging a heavy picture on a Sheetrock wall. Like when I hung the Rothko in Roger Crawford's study. The wings lay flat against the screw until you pushed it through, and then they spread out to grip either side of the hole. They worked perfectly when trying to secure something to a hollow space—which Sheetrock happened to be.

And what could be more hollow than the inside of a coffin?

I knew my sore fingers couldn't budge the screw. I needed traction. I grabbed the edge of my blouse, but it was too short to reach. I tugged at the buttons, then squirmed around until I could get it off. See, I really was lucky. I happened to be wearing a linen Calvin Klein. A silk blouse would have been too slippery.

Whispering a little prayer, I wrapped a corner of the blouse around the screw and turned. It took a few tries, but finally the metal gave. I pushed hard—and sure enough, the wings retracted and went through the hole. I heard something clank on the outside of the coffin.

Half done.

Heart in my mouth, I found the second screw and repeated the process. Turn the screw, push. Nothing happened. Push again, harder. Nothing.

In my excitement, I'd angled the screw sideways instead of straight ahead. I took a deep breath and carefully tried again. As if by magic, the wings pulled back and went forward. The other side of the lock had been freed. I pushed again, and this time the screws and toggle bolt gave way fully—and the lock they held in place clattered noisily to the ground.

Thrilled, I clapped my hands together. Bravo! I deserved a round of applause. But I didn't want to get too exhilarated yet.

Almost afraid to try, I reached up one more time and gave a firm shove to the coffin lid.

Which groaned and squeaked—and lifted.

I did a half sit-up and kept raising the top.

Just like that, I was free.

Chapter Nineteen

—— • ——

Cautiously, I swung my legs over the sides of the coffin. My legs felt stiff and sore and my arms ached, but I didn't seem to have any permanent damage. I pulled my blouse back on, kicked off my broken shoes, and stepped onto the hard ground. I hesitated for a moment, listening. But Elsa would have left long ago, confident she'd finished her job. And determined to protect Hal rather than make him an accomplice, she wouldn't have shared her plan.

I took a few shaky steps. After escaping the coffin, I felt oddly calm, confident that I could find my way out of the tunnels. I stubbed my toe, hit a few dead ends, and bumped into wire-strewn walls—but eventually I turned the knob on a door that opened.

A moment later, I emerged into the cool night air.

The campus still seemed lively, and, finally able to look at my watch, I saw it was just after 9 P.M. I'd been trapped for hours—though it felt like days.

I had no car keys, no phone, no money. A student hurried

past me in the opposite direction, and I reached out to stop him.

"Excuse me, could I bother you for a moment?"

He looked at me, then shied back. "Are you okay, ma'am?" Unwittingly, he touched his hand to his neck, and I realized I still had on the noose necklace.

"Oh, this." I untied the ends I'd so painstakingly cut and let the rope drop to the ground. Looking down, I realized that in the pitch dark, I'd fastened my blouse like a madwoman. Buttoning it now to get everything lined up wouldn't make me seem any saner.

"Should I call the campus police for you?" he asked.

I shook my head. Not the campus police—they would just warn Elsa. Not the Westwood police, either. I'd track down McSweeney and Wilson. But first things first.

"Listen, do you think I could borrow your phone to call my husband?"

He handed it to me, and shakily I dialed. Dan must be frantic with worry. Jimmy gone. His wife gone. I imagined the police had been mobilized and Dan would be out desperately combing the neighborhood. Poor man. Whatever I'd just been through, his night must have been equally filled with panic.

"Hello?" Dan said, picking up his cell phone on the first ring.

"Dan . . ." My voice broke. An hour ago, I didn't think I'd ever hear my husband's voice again.

"Hi, babe. How are you?" he asked. He sounded unexpectedly cheerful. I could hear a mariachi band in the background.

"I'm . . . fine," I said. His question had been generic, without any edge of concern.

"Want to join us at South of the Border? Tacos are better than usual. I'm here with our three fabulous children."

Dan's Mexican night with the kids. I'd forgotten. He must have figured that was why I hadn't come home.

"Jimmy's with you?" I croaked, hardly able to speak.

"He's one of our three children," Dan laughed.

"Ashley? Grant?"

"Bingo. You got the other two." He turned from the phone. "Hey, kids, Mom remembers all your names," he teased. I heard giggles.

"Did Jimmy . . ." I hardly knew what to ask.

"Jimmy had fun on campus this afternoon," Dan said helpfully. "Great that you arranged it. Grant brought him home. We had a little confusion because you hadn't mentioned anything, but it all worked out."

"I'm so glad," I whispered, clutching the phone in disbelief. "Oh my God, I'm so glad. Thank you, honey, I love you. I really do."

"I love you, too," Dan said. Then picking up something in my treacly tone, he asked, "Are you okay, Lacy?"

"Fine," I said, meaning it now. "Just perfect."

"Good. See you later. Sorry about taking the kids out to dinner so late. I got held up at the hospital."

"Give them all a hug for me. And a big kiss. Tell them I love them more than anything in the world. I miss them terribly."

"You haven't been gone that long," Dan said jovially.

I hung up. I shook my head, admiring Elsa's carefully plotted plan. She'd brought Jimmy to campus as a decoy to get to me. Nothing would have connected her to my disappearance. Even if someone at Jimmy's school later recognized her, she had a signed note from me. I'd be too dead to deny it.

"Can I have my phone back?" asked the student, who'd already been nicer than necessary to the crazy woman.

"One more?" I pleaded.

He nodded glumly.

I made the call.

• • •

The cab dropped me off in front of the Beverly Hills Hotel and I asked the driver to wait. I walked through the gracious lobby. Despite the warm night, the fireplace glowed, and couples sipping expensive scotch snuggled on the deep sofas while a string trio filled the high-ceilinged room with soft music. I'd rebuttoned my blouse, but the wrinkled linen couldn't hide the small tears from the sharp screws. My legs were black and blue from my kicking, and though I'd removed the noose, a rope burn had left angry red welts on my neck. With shoes long since discarded, I limped across the floor barefoot, wiping my still-bloody fingers on my skirt.

"Good evening, ma'am." At the entrance to the Polo Lounge, the maître d' smiled cordially. I might have been Julia Roberts arriving in Chanel. "May I help you this evening?"

I immediately felt warmed. Easy to be a snob when you spent all day with Hollywood glitterati eating forty-dollar Kobe burgers. Much harder to be a gentleman toward someone who obviously didn't belong.

"I'm looking for Roger Crawford."

His face changed very subtly. Okay, I did belong. "Let me take you to the table," he said affably.

We walked through the beautiful room, with its peachy pink walls and deep carpet, then out into the foliage-filled garden, where twinkling lights added their own luster to a star-filled sky. (Not to mention star-filled tables. Was that Scarlett Johannsson?) Walking quickly, the maître d' led me to a table in a quiet enclave, where Molly and Roger sat, their heads close, deep in conversation, with a bottle of Dom Perignon propped in an ice bucket. The maître d' must have nodded to a waiter, because another chair and full place setting instantly appeared.

"Are you okay?" Molly asked anxiously as soon as she saw me. "You said on the phone it was urgent. I'm glad you came. Sit down. You look . . ."

"I look awful and I don't care," I said, ending that conversation. I sat down on the edge of the chair and leaned across to Roger. "You can call off your thugs. It's over. Elsa Franklin killed Cassie. Detective Wilson and McSweeney are on their way."

"What?" asked Molly. "Who's that?"

Instead of answering, I stayed focused on Roger. "You wouldn't have figured it out, I don't think. Elsa's sister died in the fire you read about. The son changed his name to Hal Bohr. He killed a student Cassie knew. . . ."

"Named Derek Howe," Roger interrupted, obviously following along. He'd studied the articles from Cassie's cache, too.

"Elsa has been protecting him. Once Cassie uncovered the truth, Elsa killed her. I have a lot more details, but that's enough for now."

A waiter discreetly came by and slipped me a menu, and my stomach immediately growled. How long since I'd eaten?

"The McCarthy salad," I said without even glancing down. The signature dish came laden with bacon, eggs, and cheese, but I felt bulletproof tonight. The cholesterol wouldn't kill me. As for calories, having spent hours facing death in a casket, I refused to fret about the size of my thighs.

"I'll bring it right away," the waiter said, disappearing.

Molly took a sip of champagne, then strummed her fingers on the table. "Could we back up? I have no idea what anybody's talking about. Could one of you tell me?"

I exchanged a look with Roger.

"Tell her," Roger said with a sigh.

I grabbed a roll from the bread basket and took a big bite.

"Remember those papers Cassie hid in the library? Roger has them now. The thief who grabbed them was one of his thugs."

"Not 'thug,' bodyguard," Roger amended.

Molly looked puzzled. "You mean the guy who tied me

up and threw me in the closet?" Suddenly understanding, she opened her eyes wide and said to Roger, "*You* sent him?"

"He'd been watching the place for me," Roger said. "When you told me Lacy was coming over, I got worried. He had a strict order that nothing was to be taken out. He didn't know that you were"—Roger paused, then concluded mildly—"that you were you."

I reached for the butter and slathered a knifeful on the bread. "Now my turn for a question," I said. "To be blunt— what's up with you two?"

Roger smiled and touched Molly's arm lightly. "Now that we have an answer on Cassie's killer, it's clear we've picked the right moment. Molly and I will be partners. If not for life, for a very long time." He looked at her. "Yes?"

"Yes," she said happily.

I felt my heart sink. Could my best friend be so stupid? Marry a guy who didn't expect it to last for life?

Molly must have caught my pained expression, because she giggled. "*Business* partners," she said.

Oh. Well, that was better.

"Molly knows this business better than anyone," Roger said. "I'd been wanting her with me for a long time, but Cassie's death made the whole thing—confusing."

"Hard to work with someone you think might be a killer," I said.

"I never doubted Roger," Molly said loyally.

"And I didn't suspect Molly," Roger added quickly.

Not quite true on either side, but I'd let them get away with it. This was Hollywood, after all.

"We'd talked about a deal, but I insisted Molly keep it quiet," Roger said. "You know what this business is like. A rumor starts and everything changes."

"But now we're officially launching Archer-Crawford Productions," Molly said delightedly. "You can read all about it in *Variety* tomorrow."

"If Molly hadn't insisted on having her name first, we could have announced it last week," Roger said, laughing.

"Just so you know, Lacy," Molly said, looking at me with a smile, "it's always been business, not romance."

"Molly made that clear early," Roger said. "She's right. I'm not the best person to be married to. Looking back, I wish I'd made Cassie happier."

The waiter brought my heaping salad, and I immediately dug in. "Well, congratulations on the new business," I said, swallowing the first delicious bite. "And Roger, I even understand what happened after Cassie died. You tried to scare me away because you like to stay in control. You didn't know what I'd find." I took another bite. "I get it. I do. But one thing I haven't figured out. Why were you two at the penthouse together the night before Cassie died?"

Their eyes locked for a moment.

"Honestly?" Molly asked.

"Honestly," I insisted.

"Molly wanted to see how the decorating had come out," Roger said. "Make sure I'd be happy with it."

I looked at my best friend. "But *I'd* decorated. You were checking up on me?"

"I felt responsible," Molly said. "The next day, I begged Roger not to let on that we'd been there. I didn't want you to be insulted."

"I *am* insulted," I admitted.

"Don't be." Roger poured some champagne into my glass. "I'm grateful for everything you've done, Lacy. You're a good person. You helped Cassie when she needed it. Now you've helped me. You've solved a murder. I'm glad I couldn't scare you away." He lifted his glass. "To you."

I took a sip of the champagne—very tasty—and stood up. "Thank you," I said.

"Is there anything at all I can do for you?" Roger asked. "Make it clear how indebted I am?"

"Yup," I said. I put out my hand. "Do you have a hundred bucks I could borrow? I have a cab waiting outside to take me home and I don't have a dime."

Roger laughed and took out his wallet. "I could do even better than a hundred, if you'd like."

"Nope, I think that's plenty." I grinned. "As long as I can kiss my husband and kids good night, I'm rich enough."

Acknowledgments

I'm very grateful to have Jane Gelfman and Trish Lande Grader at my side and on my side. Jane is an intrepid agent, and Trish a terrific editor who always makes my books better. I appreciate their insights and warm encouragement. My thanks to the whole team at Touchstone including Trish Todd, Mark Gompertz, Marcia Burch, and Ellen Silberman. In writing this book, I've turned for advice to many people, including Hollywood reporter Jeanne Wolf, art dealer Margot Stein, and jewelry designer Leslie Berman. They are the best in their fields—and a lot of fun, too. Thanks also to Susan Fine for friendship worth writing about; to my partner on other books, Lynn Schnurnberger; and to my mom, Libby Kaplan.

At *Parade,* I really do have a job to kill for, with great colleagues and the best bosses in America. I'm enormously thankful to the indomitable Walter Anderson for being my adviser, hero, and endless source of inspiration; and to Randy Siegel for his smarts, good humor, and warm spirit. Both of them combine business savvy and huge creative talent, and their support and friendship make me happy every day.

My amazing sons, Zachary and Matthew, are funny, clever, and quick. I admire their sharp minds and generous souls. They're as good as it gets and I couldn't be prouder. Many of their bright comments and good ideas found a way into this book, and they even managed to teach me the basics of physics. Finally, my husband, Ron: He is my great supporter and love, and after all these years, he can still make me laugh. How lucky am I.

A Job To Kill For

For Discussion

1. What makes Lacy a good detective? How do her roles as interior designer, wife, mother, and friend help her solve the case?

2. The victim dies and the most important clue, "delta," is dropped all in the first few pages. Were you instantly engrossed in *A Job to Kill For,* or did you need to get acquainted with the characters first? At what point in the mystery was the book hardest for you to put down?

3. What do you think was Lacy's primary motivation for solving Cassie's murder? Do you think she was afraid of being labeled a suspect because she was the last to see Cassie alive? Or was she more concerned with protecting her loved ones?

4. What do Lacy's relationship and interactions with the detectives say about her character? How do you think she decides whether or not to trust them? Does Detective McSweeney's gender seem to play a part in how Lacy relates to her?

5. How does the glitzy Hollywood setting of the novel play in to your understanding of the characters and the story? Does the mention of brand-name clothing, expensive jewelry, and celebrities help you relate to the characters or make them seem unreal?

6. "But nothing matched having one person who understood your deepest soul—and did everything to protect it" (page 74). Discuss Lacy's relationship with Molly. Though they met in college they went on to lead very different lives, but remain as close as sisters. What do you think works as the glue that holds their relationship together? Do you think that Lacy ever becomes suspicious of Molly? Do you have friends to whom you would be unconditionally loyal?

7. The key to any good mystery story is lots and lots of red herrings. It seems that everyone Lacy comes into contact with is a possible suspect. Of whom were you most suspicious before the killer was found? Even after the killer was found, did anyone else remain suspect? What still seemed questionable by the end of the book?

8. Discuss your feelings about Lacy's three kids. How do you think they most help Lacy in her investigation? What do you think of her response when they are used to manipulate her? Would you do the same? If you read *Looks to Die For,* how have the children changed since the first book?

9. Several characters in the story tell Lacy that "everyone cheats." In turn, she wonders if her husband Dan is completely faithful. "Maybe my detecting skills would be better used at home" (page 150). Do you think Dan gives Lacy reason to doubt him? Or is she naturally suspicious of anyone and everyone since she's so wrapped up in the murder investigation? If you read the first Lacy Fields mystery, *Looks to Die For,* what was your first impression of Dan?

10. Accessories just may be a girl's best friend in Hollywood, but in Lacy's case they are plot points. What were some of your favorite accessories-centric moments? How did Lacy and Molly's accessories work against them? How did they help Lacy get out of a dangerous situation?

11. Do you have high hopes for Molly and Roger's business venture? What have we learned about each of them that suggests that Archer-Crawford Productions will be successful? What have we learned that may cause trouble in the business?

Enhance Your Book Club

1. The Lacy Fields mysteries would make great movies. Which actors would you like to see in the starring role? What part/role would you like to play?
2. Let Lacy's sleuthing get you in the mood for your own murder mystery party. Find out how to host one at your book club: www.host-party.com.
3. Learn more about the energy vortexes in Sedona that Andy Daniels uses: www.lovesedona.com/01.htm.
4. Need a hiding place to stash secret papers like Cassie? Learn how to make the hollowed-out book she uses: www.wikihow.com/Make-a-Hollow-Book